To Cara —,

Hope you enjoy the story,

Best Wishes,

Paul J Mila

12/24/08

FIREWORKS

Terrorists have planned an explosive July 4th for New York. Can two divers and a dolphin foil their deadly plot?

A Novel

Paul J. Mila

authorHOUSE®

AuthorHouse™
1663 Liberty Drive, Suite 200
Bloomington, IN 47403
www.authorhouse.com
Phone: 1-800-839-8640

First published by AuthorHouse 10/10/2008

ISBN: 978-1-4389-0068-1 (sc)
ISBN: 978-1-4389-0069-8 (hc)

Printed in the United States of America
Bloomington, Indiana

This book is printed on acid-free paper.

Front cover photo copyright credit: © Steve Bloom / stevebloom.com

DEDICATION

This book is dedicated to my friend, Nicholas "Nick" Fittipaldi
July 5th, 1944 – January 10th, 2007

Nick's "dash" was a lifetime filled with love, generosity and fun.
The Cozumel people loved Nick. He was a good friend to all who
knew him.

Paul and Nick at the Havana Club, Cozumel Mexico.

Paul with a rum & coke, Nick with his trademark Cuban cigar.

ACKNOWLEDGMENTS

A heartfelt *"Thank You,"* to the following friends and family, who generously devoted their time, reading, editing and correcting early versions of the manuscript. Each person provided a unique perspective and contribution, which improved the story.

Sid Burgreen, Carol Catalano, Fred Chiappetta,
James Colligan, Alison Dennis, Steven DeWolfe,
Robert Donato, Erv Francis, Robert Greco, Kathy
Heinz, Judith Hemenway, Marilyn Holland, Martha
Katz, Steve Katz, Richard London, Carol Mila,
Laura Mitton, Brian Paradine, Adrienne Rein,
Karen Sunde, Joseph Troiano, Richard Wilkins

"Thank You," to the following individuals who granted permission to use their names in the story: "Cozumel Kelly" (Kelly Mattheis), Jaime Rameriz, Gavin Scott, Martha Katz. We could not locate Osama bin Laden to obtain his permission. But if he would like to inform the U.S. Government of his whereabouts, we will gladly send him a release form.

Technical advisors on police procedures: Michael Monahan, Police Officer, NYPD, Retired. Author of BARRACUDA. Richard Wilkins, Detective 3rd Grade, NYPD, Retired.

Copyeditor: Alexandra Petri

Remaining errors and shortcomings in the book are exclusively the author's fault.

Front cover photo copyright credit: © Steve Bloom / stevebloom.com

Chapter 1
Pakistan, Near the Afghanistan Border

May 12th

Tony Delgado never heard the incoming automatic weapons fire until his world exploded around him. *Crack, phitt,* the first round whistled past his ear. *Tat-tat-tat - phitt, zing, zing,* a staccato burst, another close miss, two ricochets. Bullet-blasted rocks stung his cheek. Tony wiped blood from his face and feared he might not celebrate his twenty-eighth birthday. "Shit!" he exclaimed, grabbing his M16 and floppy camouflage hat, containing his most treasured possession.

"Haul ass, buddy!" Tony's internal survival voice screamed at him. He leaped from his rocky outpost, and attempted to outrun his fate.

Six thousand miles away at CIA headquarters in Langley, Virginia, Agent John Gillen sat inside a darkened, console-lit room, viewing Pakistan's mountainous terrain from two thousand feet above like a hunting hawk seeking prey. Using GPS coordinates Delgado had transmitted, he searched for his target: a band of enemy fighters, whom Delgado had identified as a high-value target, sitting outside a cave. Gillen skillfully maneuvered an unmanned Predator

1

drone using a joystick, not unlike one his children use to play their video games. Gillen mulled over his absurd situation. Earlier that morning, as his neighbors left their driveways going to work on the Hill in D.C., or at the high-tech companies dominating northern Virginia's suburban corporate parks, Gillen drove off to war. He thought, *Forget about the supermarket shopping list Jean stuffed in your pocket, and focus on your mission!*

"Got it!" Gillen exclaimed, finally spotting the Al Qaeda encampment on the tiny aircraft's real-time video system. His brow furrowed and his heart raced as he concentrated, lining up the Predator for the kill.

"Okay, shoot when ready," a voice said behind him. Biting his lip, Gillen pressed the button releasing one of the drone's two Hellfire missiles. He grimaced, watching the group suddenly dash inside the cave, led by a white robed figure, noticeably taller than the rest. "Damn!" exclaimed senior agent Stephen Andrews, looking over Gillen's shoulder. "What the hell spooked them?" he asked, rhetorically. Seconds later they watched the cave disappear, obliterated in a violent smoky explosion. Gillen circled the drone for a second shot, but when the smoke cleared no human targets appeared within the rocky rubble at the cave entrance. Telemetry data indicated the drone's fuel supply was low, so he guided the small craft toward its secret Afghanistan base. "Nice try," said Andrews, patting Gillen's back as he left the room. "I'll tell the boss what happened."

"Thanks, Steve," sighed Gillen, frustrated. He took a deep breath, leaned back in his chair and loosened his tie. Salty perspiration stung his blue eyes, and he wiped his brow. He stared at the blank monitor. *I hope Tony gets out alive*, he prayed. Several minutes later he pulled out his wife's shopping list and read her orders.

Tony heard the Hellfire missile's booming explosion as he scrambled for his life, hoping his impending death would not be in vain. But he did not realize the shots, which had nearly killed him, had also alerted the targeted group, and they had scrambled safely into their cave. *Tat-tat-tat-tat. Pfitt-pfitt-zing-zing.* More automatic small-arms fire whistled past his head. Some ricocheted, spraying deadly lead. He spun, fired a burst toward his pursuers and then ran toward a rock outcropping, which promised temporary safety. Pausing to catch his breath, sucking hot dusty air, Tony reflected how his promising mission had turned deadly so quickly.

The previous night under cover of darkness, U.S. Navy SEAL Tony Delgado, his partner and another two-man SEAL team, all on loan to the CIA, had secretly dropped into Pakistan's remote mountains after a short helicopter ride from Afghanistan. Local tribal chiefs seeking a huge reward had informed U.S. Intelligence that the world's most infamous terrorist was holed-up in a near-by cave, but American ground forces were prohibited from the area. The SEALS' covert assignment was clear: Locate the target and relay the coordinates to CIA Headquarters. A deadly Predator drone would be dispatched from a secret base in Afghanistan. Flying high and silently, the small airborne robot would relay real-time video via satellite to Langley, where the decision to shoot would be made. After the SEALS had completed their mission, helicopters would retrieve them at night. No U.S. ground troop involvement would ever be proven nor admitted.

One team had been successfully dropped into its designated search area. The helicopter had taken off and twenty minutes later descended toward the second target area. Tony and his partner rappelled twenty feet from the low-hovering craft. Tony landed first and then heard a sickening, wet *snap* as his partner's foot landed on a loose rock, breaking his ankle. Tony carefully removed his partner's boot and stared, momentarily dumbfounded, at the shiny white bone shard glistening in the moonlight, protruding through his partner's bloody sock. The injured soldier was hoisted aboard the copter, but Tony elected continuing his mission alone. He traveled through the night carrying his M16, observation gear and communications equipment.

At dawn, Tony spotted thin, wispy smoke rising behind a mountainous ridge. He circled the ridge and found a depression surrounded by boulders and sparse bushes, about two hundred yards from the smoke source, a small cooking fire at a cave entrance. It was an ideal observation spot, protected and near the target. Tony was so close he could smell meat cooking on a spit. *Probably lamb*, he surmised. He went about his business methodically with minimum effort. Using binoculars coated to minimize reflection and glare, he scanned the location and saw several men engaged in animated conversation. Then, he deployed a small antenna and established a satellite communication link to his Afghanistan base and to Langley. Next, he assembled a parabolic microphone similar to equipment television networks use during basketball games to pick up a bouncing ball's thumping sound. But this military unit incorporated highly advanced micro-technology, so it was only a foot in diameter and much more sensitive than commercial microphones. He aimed it toward the men and, using ear buds, confirmed the mike was picking up their conversation. Tony listened for several moments, just long enough to realize they were speaking a language he did not understand. Then he attached the mike to the antenna, transmitting via the satellite uplink to CIA headquarters, where agents would translate and analyze the conversation. One man stood, catching Tony's attention: tall and slender, he estimated about six-four, wearing a white flowing robe. Focusing his binoculars, Tony realized he had struck pay dirt: He had located the world's most wanted terrorist! He glanced at his M-16 and thought about taking the shot. Then Tony shook his head. *Wish I had a 50 cal sniper rifle.* He took a deep breath and sighed, *oh well, orders are orders. Just report back.* Tony contacted his base, provided an assessment of his onsite observations and read the cave site's GPS coordinates. His superiors quickly dispatched the drone, and ordered Tony to wait and observe.

As the mountain sun rose, blistering heat reflected off rocky terrain. Distant images shimmered, distorted, like objects viewed on a sun-baked highway. Tony removed his hat, wiped his brow and looked at the photograph recently received from home, taped inside his hat. It was a picture of his 24-year-old wife, Betty, 3-year-old son, Anthony Junior, and 7-month-old daughter, Jennifer, whom he had not yet met in person. Tony sipped water from his canteen, looked at the photograph and smiled. He imagined holding Jennifer in his arms for the first time, when he would return home in three weeks and also celebrate his birthday.

Trained in evasion tactics and concealment, Tony had waited, camouflaged, as unmoving as the rocks surrounding him. For almost an hour he remained very still, knowing the killer drone was coming, waiting for the explosion signaling his mission was successfully completed. Too still. Vultures circling the area noticed his unmoving form. To their instinct and experience he resembled death, and food. One, then two, four, then six large-winged birds circled his position. Armed Taliban sentries stationed in the hills guarding the encampment noticed the buzzards circling, languidly, high above some object of interest. Bored and curious, the men investigated. Approaching within a hundred yards of Tony's position they still did not notice him.

Seeking relief from the stifling heat Tony shifted position, removing his CIA-issued Dragonskin body armor vest. "There!" one soldier exclaimed, pointing toward Tony. They realized they had trapped a lone soldier, possibly American, spying on the Al Qaeda encampment. Before the group's leader could communicate his strategy for capturing the spy alive, the youngest Taliban soldier opened fire. The deadly chase was on.

Chapter 2
Cozumel, Mexico

May 12ᵗʰ

The Dorado II cut through Cozumel's sapphire blue water, heading south toward a deep reef called Punta Sur. Manuel, the boat captain, looked over his shoulder and smiled at Terry and Joe Manetta, co-owners of DiveWithTerry. "The Dorado II is much faster than the old Dorado," he remarked, as the wind tussled his thick, short hair, no longer jet-black but flecked with gray.

"Sure is, Manuel," replied Joe. Turning to Terry, his wife of nine years, Joe said, "Buying this new boat was a smart move, Ter."

"Well, since we've grown the business I thought we needed something a little bigger, and the extra speed really helps," she said, giving her husband an affectionate squeeze and a peck on the lips.

"Mommy's kissing Daddy, Mommy's kissing Daddy," teased their 8-year-old daughter, Jacqueline, who preferred being called Jackie.

"Ugh! Mush!" chimed in Peter, her twin brother, as the six dive customers aboard laughed.

"Evidently the paying customers think you two are quite an entertaining comedy team," said their mother, laughing. "But don't get too used to it. You're only on this ride because your sitter cancelled, and I need dad's help as a second dive master today."

"Hey, we like the personal service of two dive masters for only six divers," commented Elise, one of Terry's regular customers.

"Well, normally either Joe or I would take out a small group like this. But the Devil's Throat is challenging, and I like having a second dive master when I tackle it. Especially when I have customers who haven't dived it before."

"Is it dangerous?" asked Tom, Elise's boyfriend.

"Well, not exactly dangerous, but you're in an overhead environment without direct surface access. And visibility can be limited, especially if divers kick up the sand. Under those conditions an anxiety-prone diver may experience a panic attack. That would cause a serious problem. So, a second dive master helps. Once we're down we can split into two groups. If some don't feel comfortable entering the tunnels, one dive master can guide them around the outside while the other takes the rest through the tunnel system and the Devil's Throat."

"I wouldn't be scared to swim into the Devil's Throat!" exclaimed Peter.

"You'd be chicken," taunted Jackie.

"Would not!"

"Would so! Besides I'm older than you, Peter. The doctor told me. By two minutes."

"So what?" he replied, defensively

"Hey kids, let's cool it," demanded Joe, in a tone stronger than he intended.

His first wife and two children were killed in an auto accident on Long Island, east of New York City, thirteen years ago. He felt lucky having a second chance raising a family. He had missed the sibling rivalry and byplay, and actually enjoyed playing referee.

"You two can't be certified divers for another two years anyway, so just enjoy snorkeling for now."

"This'll be a long day for them, Joe," said Terry. "Two dives and a long surface interval in between. I'm afraid they'll get bored and distract Manuel while he's following our bubbles."

"Yeah, well maybe . . ."

"Uncle Jaime, Uncle Jaime!" exclaimed Peter, pointing toward a small white boat sporting a blue canopy, providing shade for passengers. They turned and saw their good friend, 54-year-old Jaime Ramirez, piloting his 25-foot glass-bottom boat, the *Jolly Mon*, with several tourists aboard.

"Hola Peter, hola Jackie," Jaime waved cheerfully, smiling his salesman's smile. Blue polarized wraparound sunglasses hid his friendly, relaxed eyes. A white, broad-brimmed hat protected his pate from the intense Caribbean sun. "How about coming snorkeling with us?"

"Dad, Mom, could we? Please?" Jackie pleaded.

"That would solve the boredom problem," Joe said to Terry. "Where are you going, Jaime?"

"Not far. Just to French Reef. We'll snorkel near shore."

"Thanks for your offer. Pull alongside and we'll discharge our extra passengers," Terry said.

Jaime maneuvered the *Jolly Mon* next to the *Dorado II,* and Joe handed him two gear bags containing the children's snorkel equipment while Jackie and Peter stepped nimbly across to Jaime's boat.

"I'll bring them back later this afternoon," said Jaime.

"Great! When you come, stay for dinner," said Terry, waving as the boats parted.

"Gracias! See you later. Adios," exclaimed Jaime as Peter and Jackie, grinning broadly, waved to their parents.

"Relative or family friend?" asked Elise.

"Jaime's a great friend. Might as well be family," explained Joe. "A real character, too. Came from Puerto Vallarta to sell real estate in Cozumel. We met him accidentally. We were looking for a larger house and he found us one. Jaime made a fortune selling beachfront condos, mostly to Americans seeking their Caribbean dream. Now he lives a laid-back life, taking tourists to the nearby reefs in his glass-bottom boat."

"Hey, I could handle that life," said Elise, wistfully, smiling at Tom.

"Well, I think Jackie and Peter will be occupied," said Terry, watching the children settle aboard the *Jolly Mon*. "Manuel. Let's head for Punta Sur and the Devil's Throat."

Chapter 3
Pakistan

May 12th

Tony caught his breath and scrambled for his life across open ground, desperately seeking shelter. His mind raced, but he could not devise a plan other than putting distance between him and his pursuers. But this inhospitable, unforgiving terrain of jagged mountains, caves, steep valleys, sand and scrub-brush was the Taliban fighters' home. They knew the rugged landscape, the shortcuts and hiding places. Tony realized they were closing in. He noticed a protected area fifty yards away, sheltered on three sides by large boulders. There, he thought he could make a stand and hold off his attackers until dark, when the helicopter would track his GPS signal and pluck him to safety. Okay, get your ass behind those rocks! his inner voice ordered. He turned, fired another short burst and then made a break, zigzagging like a fullback hell-bent toward his objective. Tony's slim, lanky six-foot-three frame quickly ate up the yards.

Bullets stitched the ground behind his heels. He was close, only one hundred feet to safety. Fifty feet. Now, only twenty feet. So close! But his pursuers were too near and had too much firepower to keep missing their prey. *Tat-tat-tat.* Three AK47 slugs ripped into Tony's back, shredding his lungs and heart. He fell face down, spread eagle on the hard rocky ground. His floppy camouflage hat landed several inches in front of his face. The last thing on earth Tony's large brown eyes saw was his family's photograph, taped inside. Smiling at him, sitting on the front porch steps of their modest New Mexico home, were his beautiful wife, Betty, Anthony Junior, and Jennifer, the baby daughter he would never hold. He focused his eyes on their faces as long as he could. His family blurred through his tears, and then dimmed. Finally, their images faded into blackness.

The Taliban sentries carefully approached and saw the M16's muzzle protruding beneath Tony's body. They hesitated, not sure if he was dead or alive. But the trigger-happy young soldier noticed Tony's open eyes and fired another quick burst into his back. "Jahl! (Impulsive!)," the leader exclaimed, scolding the young soldier, ripping the weapon from his hands. "He was probably American. If he were still alive I would have interrogated him and learned how they found us. Then you could have killed him later."

The youngster bowed his head, realizing his mistake. He spoke a slightly different Arabic dialect, but he clearly understood his leader's displeasure. "Ana asif" (I am sorry), he said softly. The senior officer pushed him aside and threw his rifle at his feet. Then the officer knelt by Tony's body and tore his blood-soaked camouflage fatigues, searching for dog tags or other identification, to show the world they had killed a United States soldier. "Nothing," he spat, disgusted, wiping his bloody hands on Tony's pants leg. His spirits improved briefly when he spotted Tony's GPS transmitter, but then turned to anger when he realized his soldier's bullet had shattered the device.

"If this still worked we could have lured his rescuers into a trap, perhaps even destroying a helicopter and killing more Americans," he said, through gritted teeth. The group shook their heads, glancing disapprovingly at the young, undisciplined soldier.

Another soldier said, "When we were chasing the American I heard a big explosion near the camp. We should get back."

"Yes, we'll return now," agreed the Taliban leader. The young soldier picked up Tony's hat, looked inside and ripped out the photograph.

11

"Look. The infidel's whore and his offspring. What respectable married woman would let herself be photographed like this, showing her long hair?" He tore the photograph, tossing the pieces into the hot wind. They floated to the ground near Tony's corpse. Rivulets of Tony's blood soon covered the torn smiling faces.

The senior Taliban leader addressed the young soldier. "Well, my hotheaded son of Allah, you have the privilege of carrying the American's body to camp." The shamed youngster knew it would be a long, difficult hike but did not object. He realized it was better to comply silently. He hoisted Tony's body over his shoulder in a fireman's carry. Staggering under dead weight, he followed his Taliban team. After several minutes the leader glanced over his shoulder and saw the young soldier lagging far behind, stumbling as he tired. He beckoned one of his men. "Go back and help him," he ordered. The two soldiers tied ropes around Tony's boots and dragged his body along the dusty, rocky ground as they caught up to the rest of the band.

The soldiers marched toward camp taking a shortcut through a nearby pass. They were so focused on learning what happened after the explosion they neglected to inspect the area where they had first spotted Tony. Reaching camp they found the group moving boulders aside, nervously glancing skyward. Their leader emerged from the cave. The senior Taliban soldier recognized him and approached. "Assala'amu alaikum (Peace be upon you), Osama," he said, respectfully.

"Walaikam assala'am (And unto you also peace)," Osama Bin Laden replied.

"I am concerned for your safety. Perhaps you should leave. The Americans may come. But first, look at the present I've brought you," the officer said, grinning, as he motioned the young soldier to step forward. He staggered and dumped the SEAL's body in front of their leader. It landed face up, with a heavy, dusty thump.

Bin Laden looked at Tony's bloodied face, noting his sad expression, his sightless eyes. He briefly wondered what his final thoughts had been before death's black curtain descended, erasing his consciousness. Then he smiled. "Thank you for your fine gift.

I'm sure . . ." Before he could finish, a voice spoke from within the cave's dark recess.

"Wait, Osama! Before you continue I must do something." A short, wiry, thirty-ish young man stepped forward into the sunlight. His piercing coal-black eyes struck some as intense and dedicated, others thought mad. He was Bin Laden's trusted Saudi assistant, a veteran of numerous deadly terrorist attacks, the volatile Ahmed Mohammed. He rolled Tony's body over, unsheathed a long knife with a razor-sharp serrated blade. Then, he grabbed Tony's short dark hair, pulled his head back and sliced his throat. After several viciously deft strokes he triumphantly raised the severed head. The men applauded and laughed. He tucked the bloody head under his arm and picked up a tent pole. Looking around, he spotted a crack in the rocks several yards away. He worked the tent pole into the crack until it was firmly set, and then pushed loose rocks against it forming a mound at the base providing additional support. He held Tony's head between his hands. Tony's dead eyes stared back at him. Then, raising the head, he jammed it into the pole. A mixture of blood and brains trickled down the pole, pooling in an oozy gray-red mass at the base. The Al Qaeda men hooted and howled as Ahmed stepped back, hands on hips, admiring his handiwork, like an insane Michelangelo assessing a new creation. "When the Americans arrive they'll see how we treat infidels who desecrate our holy land. And if they don't come, the jackals and vultures will enjoy a feast."

"Well said, Ahmed. This cave was a fine place, but we'll find another with help from our many loyal friends. We'll leave tonight at dark. But first I want you to present your plan." Bin Laden dismissed the sentries. "Please resume your guard duties. We will generously reward your excellent work today."

Smiling, the senior Taliban commander left the Al Qaeda members to their meeting. "Goodbye my brothers. Allah Ackbar!" (God is great!) he exclaimed, as he led his men back into the mountains.

Bin Laden turned and addressed the group. "Prepare yourselves for good news, loyal friends. Our brother Ahmed Mohammed has spent the past year planning an attack against our greatest enemy.

Ahmed, please share your wonderful plan." The men formed a circle near the cave entrance.

Ahmed stepped into the middle of the circle. He began speaking quietly, then louder as he gesticulated wildly. His voice rose to a piercing crescendo as, arms spread, he reached his grand finale. ". . . so, in less than two months the United States, Islam's sworn enemy, will celebrate its national birthday, its Independence Day. These sinners feast like filthy swine, drink all day, and at night gather with their whores to watch skyrockets exploding. We will give the Great Satan a birthday it will never forget and help our Palestinian brothers achieve independence from American Zionist tyranny and oppression. We will humiliate the Americans and their British allies, kill thousands of infidels and cripple America's economy."

The terrorist band stood and cheered Ahmed's rousing diatribe, shooting AK 47s into the cloudless, hazy blue sky. Ahmed presided over an animated question and answer session, never realizing the parabolic microphone diligently set up by the late Tony Delgado was transmitting their meeting live, back to CIA headquarters in Langley, Virginia. A senior intelligence agent specializing in foreign languages monitored the transmission, recording it for further analysis. His brow knitted as he concentrated, simultaneously listening and translating. Several Al Qaeda men were sitting just inside the cave entrance, so the transmission was spotty. Random static interrupted snippets of garbled conversation. But the agent heard enough. He pulled off his headset and called across to an adjoining cubicle. "Hey Jeff, you better call the boss. Quick! He'll want to hear this."

Chapter 4
Cozumel

May 12th

Joe watched Terry checking out the equipment as the Dorado II approached the dive site, Punta Sur. He admired the graceful way she moved, no wasted motion, always under control. He appreciated her taut, athletic figure even more than when he first met her. *Even after having two kids, she still looks great*, Joe smiled to himself. *Man, I am one lucky guy.* He thought Terry always looked beautiful, whether she wore her long auburn hair down or tied it in a bun for diving. He noticed Terry was unusually quiet. He knew she was fiddling with the tanks, weights and regulators just to keep occupied. None of the dive customers noticed her demeanor change, but Joe did. And he knew why.

Ten years ago a local drug lord named Oscar had almost murdered Terry when she was diving the Devil's Throat. He had ordered Terry killed when she accidentally stumbled onto his drug smuggling scheme, using a shipwreck to transfer cocaine molded to appear as coral. Oscar's accomplice, a deckhand hired by Terry, had switched her scuba tank for one contaminated with carbon monoxide. Terry had passed out during the dive and only quick thinking by another diver saved her from drowning. Unfortunately, the rescue diver's quick ascent landed both Terry and him in the hospital with

15

decompression sickness, known as "the bends." Consequently, Terry usually avoided this dive unless her customers specifically requested it. Joe Manetta, then an NYPD detective conducting an international drug smuggling investigation, had interviewed Terry in the hospital. She agreed to help Joe in his investigation, which required teaching him to dive. And one evening, over a candle-lit dinner at a local restaurant named *Pancho's Backyard,* they fell in love.

The Devil's Throat had become easier to navigate after hurricane Wilma had re-sculpted some of its more thrilling features, such as dark, twisting tunnels. But many divers still considered it a rite of passage, one of Cozumel's most interesting dives. "We are here," announced Manuel.

"Okay, let's suit up. Here's the dive plan," said Terry. "We'll descend to 85 feet relatively quickly, in order to save air and minutes of no-decompression time. If everyone is comfortable at the bottom, follow me into the cave. Joe will trail behind to assist anyone having a problem. If you don't feel like penetrating the cave system Joe will take you around the outside, and we'll meet you when we exit. The rest will follow me through a dark, descending, twisting tunnel until we reach the formation called The Devil's Throat, where the tunnel is not much wider than your shoulders. Visibility is only several feet because divers ahead usually stir up sand, so remain calm. The piece-de-resistance is that you must ascend several feet over a mound, then invert yourself head-down to pass under the low ceiling and exit the cave at 125 feet. All the while, keep moving so you don't spend more time than your dive computer or decompression tables allow at this depth. Otherwise you'll have to perform a decompression stop before surfacing, and you might not have sufficient air remaining to do so. After exiting the cave we'll immediately, but slowly, ascend to 100 feet, then 90, then 80. Ascending buys more decompression time on your computer so we'll continue the dive, gradually ascending as we fin along. After a three-minute safety stop at 15 feet we'll surface and wait for the boat to pick us up. Any questions?"

Joe watched the divers for signs of anxiety or nervousness, the possible precursor to a panic attack. He saw none. He watched Terry's sharp green eyes make contact with each diver's eyes, also looking for the same indications. He noticed her eyes soften, confirming his own analysis. Terry nodded and jumped in. She descended several feet to check the current and confirm that Manuel had parked the boat in the correct location for a swift descent to the cave. She surfaced after several seconds. "Current's okay, and we're good to go."

Joe said, "Okay, step to the rear platform and jump in one at a time using a giant stride entry." The divers splashed in and assembled as a group at the surface. When everyone confirmed they were ready he said, "Let's go down."

The eight divers pressed the deflate button on their BC's and descended as if on a slow elevator, equalizing their ears every few feet to prevent the increasing water pressure from rupturing their eardrums. At the bottom Terry swam toward the cave. She pointed to the entrance and then to each diver, flashing the "OK" sign with her fingers. When each responded affirmatively she led the group into the cave.

Joe entered last and checked his dive computer. The readout indicated 85 feet, and displayed the number "19", the minutes they could safely remain at this depth without a required decompression stop. In the dark cave he turned his flashlight on and said a prayer: *Energizer Bunny, don't fail me now!* Going deeper he checked his computer and noticed the minutes of safe time were decreasing faster than actual elapsed time because they were descending: 90 feet, 11 minutes; 30 seconds later, 100 feet, 9 minutes. The cave widened momentarily and Terry stopped, shining her flashlight on an oddly shaped yellow tube sponge, growing on the cave wall. Joe glanced at his computer: 105 feet, 8 minutes left. He thought, *Keep moving, Terry!* Soon the tunnel narrowed, and his shoulders rubbed against the walls. His tank bumped the ceiling. He knew the metallic scraping sound unsettled some divers, but none were having difficulty. The divers ahead kicked up some sand. Even with the flashlight it was dark; visibility so hazy Joe could not see the fins of the diver less than three feet ahead. He checked his dive computer. The readout displayed 120 feet, 4 minutes. Coming to the mound he went up and over, then inverted, head down. One hundred-twenty-five feet, only 3 minutes before running out of no-decompression time.

Finally they saw a dim light ahead and then exited the cave. The divers looked up and saw a bright light. It was the glorious Caribbean sun shining through the surface, not the light of a near death experience. A familiar sight when glancing up from the bottom, these divers will never take it for granted again. They ascended as planned, to 100 feet, then 90, then 80. Joe's computer indicated 15 minutes of no-deco time remained. They continued the dive, slowly ascending. At 70 feet a silvery glint caught Terry's eyes. It was a large barracuda, she estimated five feet long, hovering under a ledge. *He's probably hoping an easy meal swims past,* she thought, pointing him out. Several divers gave the fearsome looking fish a wide berth, but Bill swam closer with his camera. Just as he pressed the shutter the barracuda rewarded him with a toothy grin. *Smile, you're on candid camera,* Bill said to himself. Spooked by the flash, the barracuda swam away seeking a new hiding place. After a three-minute safety stop at fifteen feet they surfaced. Bobbing in the water waiting for Manuel to retrieve them Elise exclaimed to her boyfriend, "Wasn't that a great dive, Tom?"

"Wow, what do we do for an encore?" he shouted to Terry. He noticed she wasn't wearing her dive computer. "Hey, what happened to your computer?" he asked.

"The battery died this morning, and I didn't have a spare."

"We had only about two minutes of no deco time left. How'd you cut it so close without a computer?"

"Experience," Terry replied, with a wink and a smile. Back aboard the *Dorado II*, the group exchanged observations and impressions about their experience.

"Pretty impressive dive," said Bob Jamison to his buddy, Bill.

"Yeah," agreed Bill. "We're used to diving the kelp forests off Santa Barbara. That can get a bit spooky and dark. But you always know the open surface is above you. I think I got a nice shot of the 'cuda. He was a big ol' boy!"

"That confinement was freaking me out," commented Ginny Daley to her dive buddy, Meg Ritter.

"Me too, Ginny," replied Meg, turning to Bill and Bob. "We're from St. Louis. Ginny and I usually dive in old mine quarries. It's cold water diving, not much to see. But at least you can pop up to the surface whenever you want. I was getting nervous. I enjoyed the dive, but I was sure happy to see the sun above us."

"Well, you all did fine," commented Terry. "And you can add a new skill to your dive resumes. We're heading to Paradise Beach for our surface interval. The bottom is soft sand, no rocks, so Manuel will beach the boat and you can hop off, use the banos, have a light snack, or visit Coco."

"Who's Coco?" asked Ginny.

"The resident crocodile," replied Terry.

"Crocs? Here in Cozumel?" asked Bill Webber.

"Yep. The island's interior is peppered with fresh-water lagoons. Well, let me correct that. They're actually brackish, part salt water, part fresh. The water looks like tea. At various points they're connected to the sea and the crocs move in and out to hunt, usually at night. We've seen them while diving but very rarely. Mostly they hang out in the lagoon. There's plenty of fish, birds, crabs and other yummies to sustain them. Coco suns himself next to the beach club's parking lot. You can take a walk and say hello if you like."

"Looks like the morning dive boat crowd beat us here," said Joe as the *Dorado II* approached the concrete pier extending from Paradise Beach. Boats from Dive Palancar, Sand Dollar, and Papa Hogs were already moored, so Manuel expertly guided the *Dorado* up to the sandy beach. Terry lowered a small ladder from the boat, and everyone waded ashore.

"Shuffle through the water," Terry advised, leaning over the ladder. "You don't want to disturb a yellow stingray sleeping in the sand. Their stingers are really painful!" Meg looked down and noticed a large school of Bermuda chubs swimming around her toes.

"Hey, stop nibbling! I just did my toenails last night!"

"I guess they like the bright red color you used," laughed Bill, as Meg scampered to shore. They noticed the stone and brick remains of several houses, destroyed to their foundations.

"What are those?" asked Ginny.

"They're homes Hurricane Gilbert destroyed in 1988," replied Terry.

"Wow! Must have been some big storm," she said, walking past. They used the restrooms, bought snacks and went to visit Coco. Standing alongside a wavy chain link fence Ginny called, "Coco, Coco, here Coco."

Meg looked at the brown water. "Yep. Terry's right. Looks like Lipton. Oh look, there's a fish. Oop's, he's gone. Can't see a damn thing in this water. Where's that croc?"

"Uh, you might want to move your foot away from the fence," whispered Bob.

"What? Oh my God!" exclaimed Meg as she looked down then jumped back. "He's right here!"

At the base of the fence what they thought was a log blinked its eyes and moved. "Oh my," said Ginny. Then looking around the lagoon's edge, she observed, "Look at all the crab legs, claws, other parts. I guess Coco's well fed."

"He's a pretty good size. What do you think, about seven feet?" Asked Bob.

"Yeah, at least," agreed Bill.

After several minutes, Coco slipped into the lagoon with nary a ripple. "Guess he wants to cool off," said Ginny. Checking her watch, she said, "Hey, we better return to the boat. We've been here over a half hour. I think Terry said we'd be staying about 45 minutes."

Terry, Joe and Manuel enjoyed a quiet rest aboard the slowly rocking *Dorado*. She heard Manuel snoring, drowning out the more pleasing sound of small waves lapping at the *Dorado's* hull. Shaking him, she recognized a small boat approaching, throwing up a big wake. She waved and the captain cut his engines, then veered toward the pier. "Back so soon?" Terry shouted to Jaime aboard the *Jolly Mon*.

"Si, Terry. Some guests must return to their cruise ship in an hour. By the time I return to the marina and they catch taxis into town and then a water taxi to their ship, they'll just make it."

"Well, why not drop off your little stowaways now? They can snorkel with us on our second dive. We'll be doing a shallow dive on Delilah. But the dinner invitation is still on, okay?"

"Sure thing," Jaime said as Peter and Jackie hopped onto the pier. They waved goodbye to Jaime, ran along the beach and then swam through the shallow water to the Dorado.

"Mom, Dad, we saw Notchka and her daughter," exclaimed Jackie, climbing aboard.

"And some new dolphins, too," added Peter.

"That's great! Tell us all about your dolphin encounter at dinner," said Terry. "For now, get yourselves settled. We'll shove off as soon as our divers return."

Chapter 5
CIA Headquarters, Langley Virginia

May 12th

O kay, what was so important that you beeped me in my staff meeting?" boomed Deputy Director of Intelligence, Thomas Walsh. At 61, Walsh had accrued enough government service to retire on a comfortable pension. Many new agents regarded him superficially as a desk-bound Cold War warrior, but as a young agent he had run his share of dangerous covert ops in global hot spots, many behind the former Iron Curtain. Officially, four KGB adversaries did not survive their confrontations with CIA Agent Walsh. His own unofficial body count was six, but he never pressed the point. Walsh had considered retirement in the boring aftermath of the Soviet Union's demise, but the rising threat of radical Islamic terrorism re-kindled his patriotic fire to protect his country. Although his silver hair was thinning, he still projected a "take no prisoners" attitude, and his rock-hard six-foot-four frame commanded a ton of respect.

"Sir, we picked up important intel from our ground contact in Pakistan. Looks like a major Al Qaeda operation could be going down soon," replied his new assistant, 31-year-old Jeff Becker, recently promoted and eager to impress his new boss.

"Soon? How soon, Jeff?"

"Well, we don't really know that yet, sir."

"Did you make direct contact with your ground contact? Did you speak to him?" Jeff Becker felt his armpits dampen under his boss' rapid-fire interrogation.

"No sir, you see . . ."

"Damn it, Jeff, I wish before you call me out of a meeting you'd verify . . ."

"Excuse me sir, but our ground contact is dead. He lost his life sending us this information."

The DDI's hard gray eyes softened. He blinked, drew a deep breath and then exhaled slowly. "Okay, Jeff. I'll adjourn the staff meeting and meet you in my office in five minutes.

"Thank you, sir."

When DDI Walsh entered his office Jeff Becker was already seated. He started to rise. "Stay seated, Jeff." Walsh sat behind his large cherry wood desk. The top was buried under volumes of recent intelligence reports, briefings and position papers. He noticed the dark wet patches under Jeff's arms and smiled. *Gotta lighten up a bit, you old son-of-a bitch*, he mused. "Okay. What do you have, Jeff?"

Becker produced two transcripts. He handed the DDI the original and opened his copy. "Our analyst translated these from a live satellite transmission we received from Pakistan. One of our special operatives, Anthony Delgado, set up a listening post near an Al Queda encampment. He up-linked one of our new mini parabolic microphones to a satellite and called in coordinates for a Predator air strike believing he had spotted Bin Laden in the camp. Senior officer Stephen Andrews was monitoring the video feed and gave permission to fire."

"And? Did we send the bastard to Paradise? Or rather to Hell, I hope?"

"No sir. We heard what sounded like gunfire. Synchronizing the timing of the audio transmission and the air strike video, it appears the shots alerted the targets and they retreated into their cave seconds before the Hellfire missile struck."

"Shit!"

"Yes sir. We believe Delgado was killed shortly thereafter."

"May God bless him and his family," Walsh replied, shaking his head. "At some point I hope we can recover his body."

"This transcript continues from the point they resumed their meeting. Evidently they didn't realize Delgado had set up monitoring equipment so they never disabled it." Becker watched his boss adjust his reading glasses and begin reading the transcript.

"It's difficult to follow, Jeff. What do these characters signify?"

"The pound signs indicate static, transmission breakup, or unintelligible clutter. We're submitting the recordings for further analysis to decipher additional words. As you can see there are numerous general comments, what sounds like praying, discussing our attack on their encampment, how they killed Delgado, and some unimportant conversation. But turn to the section I noted on page five." Becker bit his lip impatiently as the DDI thumbed to page five. He saw Walsh's eyes narrow as he read the key section Becker had highlighted.

> ######Ahmed #### the result #### this plan ######### huge loss of life #####economic disruption ######### British and American interests will ############### When ##### hang the necklace########## queen ##########never leave New York Ahmed ########### wonderful ##### #### Allah will ###############

Walsh finished reading and looked at Becker. "Is this it?"

"Yes sir. The remainder of the transcript contains additional general conversation, vague references to destroying America, which they call "The Great Satan," bragging about past achievements, including the 2001 World Trade Center attack, but nothing else actionable or threatening."

"Has anyone else read this transcript, Jeff?" asked Walsh.

"No sir. Just the analyst who translated it, me, and now you."

"Alright. I'll schedule a staff meeting with my senior aides. Eight o'clock tomorrow morning here in my office. We'll make it a breakfast meeting. Bring four copies and mark them top secret."

Chapter 6
Cozumel

May 12th

Terry had finished cooking paella, a family favorite, and also Jaime's favorite meal. Jackie and Peter were setting the table when the doorbell rang. "Door's open, Jaime," shouted Joe. "Come on in."

"Hola, everyone," said Jaime as he and Joe embraced in a typical warm Spanish greeting. Then he walked into the kitchen, kissed Terry and handed her a chilled bottle of Chardonnay.

"Thank you, Jaime, but you shouldn't have."

"You mean not the wine or not the kiss?" he asked, laughing.

"I'm referring to the wine, of course. You know you can kiss me anytime, Jaime."

"Hey Joe, did you hear that? Your wife wants me!"

"Well, she may be free tonight, depending on how dinner goes," replied Joe, laughing.

"Hola Uncle Jaime," said Peter, mixing Spanish and English fluently, as he hugged Jaime.

"Hola, Peter, and you too, Jackie," he replied, as she rushed into the room and kissed him.

"Terry, the house looks great. You've done so much remodeling the past three years, I wouldn't recognize it."

"Joe and I can't thank you enough for finding it for us before you left the real estate business."

"Well, with your dive business so successful you deserve your dream house."

"Come outside to the patio and salute the sunset with a margarita," Joe beckoned.

"Go ahead, Jaime, I'll join you guys in a minute," Terry said.

"Okay, but you better hurry," replied Joe. "Sun'll be down soon." Joe quickly pulled three large goblets from an overhead cabinet, sliced a juicy lime into three parts and smeared the rims. Then he flipped the goblets over and rubbed the lime-sticky rims into a flat dish with salt. Next he filled the glasses halfway with crushed ice and added one part tequila to three parts of his own custom blended margarita mix. He handed a drink to Jaime and they stepped outside. "Salud," said Jaime, as they clinked glasses. Joe returned the toast and turned to face the sea and the sunset. "This view is incredible, isn't it?" asked Joe, watching cotton-white puffy clouds turn purple, then fiery red.

"Si, mi amigo. I never tire of watching the sun disappear over the Yucatan," replied Jaime.

"Do you miss the real estate business?" asked Terry, joining them with her margarita.

"Well, I miss meeting wonderful people like you and developing meaningful friendships. But I enjoy my little glass-bottom boat business now. No pressure, you can't beat the hours, and my office is on the water."

"I can relate," agreed Joe. "And I support Terry's comment. We really appreciate you finding us a larger house here on a beautiful, quiet part of the island."

"De nada," replied Jaime, raising his glass again.

"Well, there goes the sun," Terry said watching the glowing red ball sink below the horizon. "Let's go inside and eat. The children can't wait to tell us about their dolphin encounter today."

"Oh it was so cool," said Peter. "Notchka and Gemini swam with us. We haven't seen them in so long, ever since they stopped visiting our beach."

"You mean the dolphins come to the beach here?" asked Jaime.

"Well, you may have noticed our beach forms a natural cove," explained Terry, pointing out the curving sweep of sand. "Evidently, Notchka and her pod used to herd fish here and enjoy a leisurely snack. After we moved here they saw us snorkeling one day while they were hunting and understood that we live here. The children would play with them when they visited. Between the natural food source and our companionship, the dolphins seemed to love the place. But we haven't seen them here for several months. Perhaps the fish have learned to avoid the area."

"And we saw more dolphins today, but they didn't come very close," Jackie said.

"Well, don't forget they're wild animals. They probably have better things to do than hang out with humans," replied Terry.

"Today I saw the large dolphin with the notch in her tail. Is what they say about her true?" asked Jaime.

"You mean about how she saved Terry's life almost ten years ago by ramming the guts of that drug lord Oscar, seconds before he almost knifed her?" asked Joe.

"Si. Is the story true?"

"Every word," replied Terry. "I just regret that Oscar killed Notchka's calf, Lucky, just before she saved me. I feel so responsible."

"I guess Lucky wasn't so lucky, commented Jaime.

"Well, Terry did save Lucky's life once," mentioned Joe. "Without her he would have died much earlier. That's how he got his name."

"Really? How?" asked Jaime.

"Well," continued Terry, "I came upon two dolphins one day while diving, a mother and her calf. The young dolphin was in distress, swimming in circles, entangled by a fishing net. It would have eventually killed him. I removed it, and he recovered. So I named him Lucky. I named the mother Notchka because she had a distinctive notch in her tail fluke, probably from a shark encounter. She learned to trust me and always sought me out when she was in the area. We had many encounters and became friends."

"Amazing! And who is Gemini?"

"Well, as soon as Joe and I were married we tried starting a family. I had difficulty conceiving, and when I finally did I suffered a miscarriage. Several months later Joe and I traveled to Iceland, where we had a run-in with pirate whalers. But that's a whole other story. I became pregnant toward the end of our trip but didn't know it. About a month later, Notchka and her new calf swam by when I was diving here. We hadn't seen her for a long time, almost half a year. After Lucky was killed I never thought she would trust humans enough to bring any other offspring near us. It was amazing. I felt a tingling sensation from Notchka's sonar, and she kept swimming near me, acting strangely. I realized later that by scanning me she learned I was pregnant, even before I did. And she probably knew I was carrying these twins no less," she said, nodding toward Jackie and Peter, who were beaming. "So I named her calf Gemini, after the constellation of the twins."

"An incredible story," Jaime replied, smiling.

"Can we go with Uncle Jaime and see Notchka and Gemini again, Mom? Please?" begged Peter.

"Well, I don't . . ."

"Oh it's no problem," replied Jaime. "The dolphins have been in the area for a week now. We'll probably see them again. And I'll get huge tips from the tourists if they see dolphins."

"Well, okay," she said, looking at Joe, who nodded his assent. "We're scheduled to dive near Punta Sur in two days, but we probably won't tackle the Devil's Throat. I only do challenging dives with my regular customers. The divers are from a cruise ship, and I don't know their skill levels or certifications. If it's no trouble we can meet you in the area and you can take Jackie and Peter snorkeling. I know you'll keep an eye on them."

"No trouble at all, Terry. Now let's enjoy your delicious paella. It smells wonderful!" said Jaime, licking his lips.

Chapter 7
Pakistan

May 13th

W hen will you leave for the United States, Ahmed?"
asked Bin Laden.

"Not for several weeks. With all their increased security, penetrating the Great Satan's homeland is more difficult. I need better false documentation. I'll change my appearance by shaving my beard and cutting my hair in Western style, in case the Americans or Israelis have a file on me. Most important, I must find several dedicated men with specific technical skills."

"What skills?"

"I need one experienced scuba diver, preferably two if I need a backup. Then, I need a specialist in remote controlled explosive techniques, and finally a skilled bomb maker, like me."

"So, a team of four besides you?"

"Yes. But actually I prefer a smaller team. I'm hoping to find dedicated people with overlapping skills. I would prefer traveling with only three other people."

"I agree. The fewer the better. But take sufficient resources to carry out your very ambitious plan. I will provide whatever financial assistance you require."

"Yes, many thanks," said Ahmed. "Without the information your contacts in America provided I could not have developed my plan."

"Do you believe our enemies maintain a dossier on you?"

"It would not surprise me. There was much publicity and worldwide condemnation after the Israeli jets bombed our school several years ago, killing twenty-three children, including my son and daughter. Newspapers around the world published pictures of the demonstrations. I'm sure my photo appeared many times. Who knows what those jackals do with their photos? When American air strikes killed my wife and her family the following year, along with several of your trusted aides, my photo probably appeared again. Many news organizations photographed us removing mountains of rubble, trying vainly to save our families with our bare, bleeding hands. The Americans arrogantly dismissed the bloody carnage as 'acceptable collateral damage.' If they recognized the same man in photos after both attacks what would they think?"

"They would think this man endured severe personal loss, and somehow he will avenge the deaths of his wife and children."

"And they would be correct, Osama. Public condemnation will not bring back my family. I will extract my revenge on the Americans and their British lackeys, who lick the Americans' heels like cowardly dogs."

Bin Laden sighed. "Ahmed, if I had an army of men as determined and dedicated as you I would easily wipe the infidels from the earth. I truly believe Allah wills your success. I wish you well, though I fear I will never lay eyes on you again."

"If my plan succeeds as I envision, and if it is Allah's will, I will see you again. However, there are many risks so you may be correct. We may never see each other again. Goodbye, my brother."

"Bissalama (Have a safe journey)," replied Bin Laden. But Ahmed definitely planned to return. While lacking his leader's physical stature, he nevertheless saw himself as a leader. He aspired to assume Bin Laden's mantle as the world's number one terrorist. Leading a bold, gloriously successful mission would bring him closer to his goal.

Chapter 8
CIA Headquarters, Langley Virginia

May 13th

Deputy Director of Intelligence Walsh arrived at 7:30a.m. sharp, intending to prepare for his 8:00 meeting. "Good morning, sir," said Elise Deaver, his secretary of sixteen years. "Everyone is already in your office."

"Thank you, Elise," Walsh replied, with a warm smile. He appreciated her efficiency and, more importantly, her loyalty. He thought, *I trained my staff too damn well. From now on I'll have to come in an hour early if I want some prep time.* Walsh entered his office, where four senior CIA officers were seated at a round conference table. His presence immediately filled the room.

"Good morning gentlemen, and lady," he nodded toward Agent Susan Wilson. "Please remain seated," he said, as they began to rise. "There are rolls, pastries, bagels on the table, and coffee. High-test, naturally. Help yourselves." He waited until each officer had poured coffee and selected some food. "Jeff, please distribute the folders." Jeff Becker handed each officer a plain manila envelope, taped shut with the words *Top Secret* stamped in red across each folder.

"The information you are about to read cost an agent his life. I don't want his sacrifice to be in vain." The tinkling of china cups on saucers ceased immediately. The room became silent. "Please open your folders."

The only sound was tape snapping and paper sliding from envelopes. "This document is the transcript of a recorded Al Qaeda meeting relayed via satellite uplink from Pakistan. Please read the entire six-page document for context, but pay particular attention to the highlighted section on page five." The DDI reached for his coffee and buttered his toast while the agents read. After several minutes, he spoke. "Impressions? Miller?" he asked the youngest intelligence officer, seated to his left.

"Well, except for the highlighted section on page five, the document contains the usual chatter about their cause, how much they hate the U.S. and Western society in general, nothing significant as far as I can determine."

"Anyone else have a different take?" he asked, making eye contact with each individual. After a round of "No Sirs," he proceeded. "I agree. Then let's analyze the highlighted section on page five." He waited until each agent thumbed to that page and re-read the critical five lines.

> ######Ahmed #### the result #### this plan ######### huge loss of life #####economic disruption ######### British and American interests will ############### When ##### hang the necklace########## queen ##########never leave New York Ahmed ########### wonderful ##### #### Allah will ###############

"Jeff, you've had the advantage of thinking about this the longest. Any ideas?"

"Well, their focus on *"huge loss of life"* and *"economic disruption"* clearly means they're aiming for an impact as lethal and massive as 9/11. But this time the event involves Britain, not just the U.S."

"They mention New York, but we don't know if it's New York City or somewhere else in New York State. And there's no timeframe reference," said Agent Miller.

"Donaldson?" asked the DDI.

"I agree with Agents Becker and Miller, sir. I don't see any other interpretation. The way I read it the plan involves the Queen of England, Elizabeth. Perhaps it's an assassination attempt. But killing the Queen, as horrible as that would be, won't cause huge loss of life and major economic disruption."

"Unless it's done in spectacular fashion," replied Susan Wilson. "Like a nuclear explosion, a dirty bomb, that sort of thing. The Queen would be killed along with thousands more, including many high-ranking political officials. And in a location like New York City, massive economic disruption would be a certainty. A dirty bomb could impact the financial center severely, even though many companies decentralized their operations centers and facilities after 9/11."

"Good analysis, Wilson. That dovetails pretty much with my opinion," said the DDI, intentionally revealing his thoughts last to avoid intimidating more junior staff members.

"But what's this reference about *hanging the necklace?*" interjected Jeff Becker. "Juxtaposed to the reference about the Queen it sounds like an assassination attempt, possibly strangling her with her necklace, or her jewels, or something else. It's a very personal one-on-one reference, though it sounds ridiculous."

"Yes, it sounds ridiculous, at least on the surface," replied Walsh. "But, remember two things. First, we're dealing with fanatics. What seems irrational to us may be perfectly rational in their paradigm. Second, there may be a hidden meaning to that necklace phrase." He looked around the table and smiled. "After all, the CIA selected you for your uncanny abilities to ferret out and decipher hidden meanings in the information we receive. That's how seemingly disjointed information becomes good intelligence." He glanced at his watch. "8:30. Good timing." He pressed a button on his intercom as the four agents exchanged inquiring glances. "Elise, is that New York call ready?"

"Yes sir. I have Mayor Williamson and Director Bilboa on hold."

"Thank you. Please put them through."

The conference phone in the middle of the table rang and he pressed the "all-talk" button. "Mayor Williamson, thank you for joining us this morning."

"My pleasure, Tom. Good to hear from you. As you requested, I've asked our recently appointed Director of New York State Homeland Security, Michael Bilboa, to join the call."

"Thank you for meeting with us gentlemen. Nice to meet you, Michael."

"Thank you, sir, but please call me Mike," Bilboa replied.

"Okay, Mike. Let me get right to the point, gentlemen. I'm here with four of my best analysts. We've obtained intelligence that is both specific and general in nature. I am not at liberty to disclose how we obtained the information, other than saying our field agent made the ultimate sacrifice obtaining it." The DDI paused for effect, letting that fact register, and then continued. "The intelligence indicates a possible assassination attempt against Queen Elizabeth. No date, time, or specific method is mentioned. But there is a New York reference. Can you help us?"

"Yes, I believe so," replied Mayor Williamson. "The Queen is scheduled to visit New York City for about a week during the July Fourth holiday. I don't recall all the particulars, but I believe she arrives in D.C. in late June, meets with the president, then flies to New York several days later, stays in town through July Fourth, and then returns to England. Does that help?"

"Yes, Mr. Mayor it does. We now have a probable location and general timeframe. We'll continue analyzing the information and contact you as soon as possible. Good day, gentlemen."

"Good bye, Tom. I'll obtain more details on the Queen's itinerary."

"Thank you. Goodbye." Walsh turned to his team. "Well, we now have significantly more information than we had several minutes ago. Let's get to work."

Chapter 9
Cozumel

May 14th

At seven in the morning Terry, Joe, the twins, and Manuel arrived at Caleta Marina, where the *Dorado II* was docked. It took almost an hour preparing the boat for the day's diving. Terry inventoried the equipment, counting the silver scuba tanks lined up in tank racks along both sides of the boat. "Okay, five divers plus Joe and me, so we need fourteen tanks for two dives. Today's customers don't have their own regs or BCs, so we brought seven plus a spare. We have weights, belts, emergency equipment, and I know food and drinks are in the cooler. Fuel topped off, Manuel?"

"We have three-quarters of a tank. That's plenty to reach Punta Sur and return."

"Okay, so now we can relax and wait for our customers. I told them to arrive by eight-thirty, but they could be delayed leaving their cruise ship."

Peter sighed. Joe affectionately tousled his son's wavy brown hair, which complemented his even darker large brown eyes. "Hey, tiger, while we have spare time get aboard and arrange your snorkel gear. You know the first rule: A good diver is always prepared. You too, young lady" he told Jackie.

"Okay, Dad," she replied cheerfully, looking up at her father with sharp green eyes that matched her mother's perfectly. Jackie turned and followed her brother. Her auburn ponytail whipped across her shoulders. The twins scampered onto the boat as Joe smiled at Terry. "Jackie's a mini you."

"Well that's only fair," she replied. "After all, whenever I look at Peter I see aminiature version of you. And all signs indicate he'll be a strapping six-footer, just like his dad."

"We sure are lucky, hon. Two great kids and a life most people would die for,especially my friends back in New York."

"Anything else you feel lucky for, sailor?" Terry replied, coyly, sliding next to Joe.

"How could I forget? And a very lovely, very sexy wife!" he said, slipping his arm around Terry's slim waist, pulling her close and kissing her lips.

"There they go again," Jackie said, shaking her head. Her brother replied characteristically.

"Ugh! Mush!"

Ten minutes later a dented white van pulled into the marina, screeching to a dusty halt near the *Dorado II*. "Are you Terry?" asked a passenger, leaning out a window.

"You found me," she replied, smiling.

"Great! I was afraid we were late. We paid the boat tender a little extra to be first in line off our cruise ship."

"I wish they'd repair those cruise ship piers. It'd make life much easier for you passengers," said Terry. "Okay, hop aboard and we'll get going. First, we have some paperwork. Please fill out these forms while I check your certification cards."

The passengers found seats, and Manuel skillfully eased the *Dorado* through the crowded marina, passing several half-submerged wrecks, remnants of Hurricane Wilma. Then he headed south, toward the reefs. Ten minutes later, they arrived at Paradise Beach, where Jaime had moored the *Jolly Mon* and was picking up nine passengers. "Hola," he shouted, waving to the approaching *Dorado*.

"Where are you snorkeling today, Jaime?" Terry asked, as Manuel cut the engines and maneuvered next to the *Jolly Mon*.

"The dolphins have been sighted just north of Palancar Point, so I'll try there first."

"Okay, please keep a close eye on the kids. The current's been quite strong there recently."

"Si, Terry, I will," he said. "With so many snorkelers today I brought my assistant, Gavin, today. He'll be in the water leading them."

"Hi, Gavin, good to see you today," Terry hailed. Gavin waved back. A tall, husky ex-patriated Canadian, Gavin had traded the frozen tundra for Cozumel's hot sand ten years ago and never looked back. Jaime hired him whenever he had a large snorkel group.

Jackie and Peter grabbed their gear bags containing snorkel fins, masks and floatation vests. "Bye, Mom. Bye, Dad," said Peter, waving.

"Obey Uncle Jaime and Gavin! Don't cause them any trouble," Joe shouted as the *Jolly Mon* pulled away. "Okay, Manuel, let's head for Punta Sur."

"Uncommon name for a boat," commented Alex Benson, one of the divers. "Sounds like a Jamaican or West Indian name, more Calypso than Mexican."

"Interesting story about the boat's origin and its name," said Joe. "The boat actually came from the Bahamas. I don't know if it was sailed to Cozumel or transported here. Supposedly the owner was a Parrothead, you know, a Jimmy Buffett fan. He named the boat after Buffett's hit song, *The Jolly Mon*. Jaime feared changing the name might jinx the boat so he kept the name."

"Oh yeah, I recall the song, a real fun tune," said Alex. "About a Calypso singer attacked by pirates but saved by a dolphin, and somehow they all became a constellation in the sky or something like that."

Joe glanced at Terry. She appeared concerned watching the *Jolly Mon* disappear toward the distant bay. She was biting her lip, and her brow was furrowed as she squinted, looking back toward the sun. Joe felt the children were safe with Jaime. But he also knew Terry had an uncanny intuition for sensing trouble looming ahead.

Chapter 10

May 14th

May 14th

Jaime carefully piloted the *Jolly Mon* into the bay south of Palancar Point, less than three knots to avoid causing a wake, which might disturb the fish and other creatures inhabiting the shallow water. The surface near the white sandy shore was calm, a mirror of the clear azure sky. Farther out near the Point, the sea was choppy. Whitecaps dotted the surface as the prevailing northbound current pulled the water along against a steady southbound breeze. The tourists were fascinated, watching colorful, round brain coral, spiky stag horn coral and purple tube sponges pass under the glass bottom. They ooh'd and aah'd when multi-colored parrotfish swam into view under the boat, and laughed when an aggressive school of sergeant major fish, resplendent in their shimmering gold scales and vertical black stripes, pecked at the *Jolly Mon's* glass bottom.

After watching the sea life below them for thirty minutes, the tourists were eager to join the fish. Jaime passed floatation vests to his nine customers and fins, masks and snorkels to several who hadn't brought any snorkeling gear. Jackie and Peter felt superior as everyone watched them pull their equipment from their gear bags.

"Okay everyone, please listen carefully. We'll snorkel here for about an hour. Gavin will lead you around and point out interesting things. He'll be dragging a red buoy with a red and white dive flag so you can follow him. Please only swim between the boat and the shore. Currents sweeping past the point might pull you out and separate the group. Stay close to each other. If anyone is having difficulty wave one arm over your head and I'll come and pick you up. If you hear me blowing the boat horn repeatedly like this," Jaime demonstrated, pulling the air horn cord, *BLAAT, BLAAT, BLAAT,* "that means return to the boat immediately. Does everyone understand?" Everyone nodded affirmatively. Jaime turned to the children. "Jackie, Peter, the same rules apply to you. Understand?"

"Sure thing, Uncle Jaime," said Jackie, as Peter nodded. Gavin splashed in first.

"Alright then. When you're ready climb in using the ladder or simply roll off the side." He watched Peter and Jackie leap from the stern while the others sat on the side, then slipped in. He counted eleven snorkels in the water and watched the group begin exploring the shallow reef. Ten minutes later he spotted several dorsal fins breaking the calm surface just beyond the point. As they came closer he smiled, realizing their curved shape meant they were dolphins. He counted five. "Look!" he shouted to the snorkelers. "The dolphins are here!" Everyone finned toward them. The dolphins were busy chasing baitfish and kept their distance. But two came closer. Jaime noted a v-shaped notch in the larger dolphin's tail and recognized Notchka and her calf, Gemini.

Peter and Jackie swam farther out to meet the two dolphins, and Notchka scanned them with her natural sonar. The returning echo-location vibrations registered them as familiar in her dolphin memory. She remembered the two small humans from previous encounters. Notchka made a close pass and communicated instructions to Gemini by emitting clicks and whistles, then rejoined the other three dolphins. Gemini stayed near Peter and Jackie. Jaime, preoccupied keeping his excited customers from venturing into deeper water, did not notice Peter and Jackie swimming away from the group. The current was slowly pulling them farther out past Palancar Point while they played with Gemini.

Fifteen minutes later, Jaime noticed two additional dorsal fins slicing the water. Something else was chasing baitfish. But these dorsals were not softly curved like a dolphin's. These were pointy and triangular. Jaime realized these were shark fins. Immediately he pulled the cord, repeatedly blowing the *Jolly Mon's* horn. *BLAAT; BLAAT; BLAAT.* He maneuvered the boat near the swimmers and avoided panic by not mentioning the sharks until everyone was safely aboard. But then, someone pointed toward the two dorsal fins and shouted, "Sharks!" Everyone turned and watched a school of yellow-tail snappers leaping from the water vainly seeking safety. Shark fins roiled the surface as they consumed the slowest and weakest fish.

"Are there many sharks in Cozumel?" asked one passenger.

"Mostly harmless nurse sharks," replied Jaime. "These might be hammerheads. We see them here once in a while. But they never bother people. They eat fish, and stingrays are their favorite food."

"You mean they prefer sushi to prime rib," joked the passenger, watching the action.

"Si," replied Jaime, laughing. "But these sharks don't look like hammerheads," he said, watching one shark break the surface and seize a fish. The panicked snappers turned, and swam beneath the *Jolly Mon* with the sharks close behind, giving all aboard a good view of the attack.

"Oh my!" exclaimed one tourist, watching two streamlined torpedoes shoot past, under the boat's glass bottom.

"Those are Caribbean reef sharks," remarked Jaime. "A school of several young reef sharks appeared just after the hurricanes last year. They were just babies then, only three or four-footers. I guess they stayed and grew. These two look almost five feet long. And they're very aggressive!"

"Fascinating. I never . . . hey, what's that shark pulling behind it?" another tourist asked.

Jaime shielded his eyes from the sun and squinted. "Looks like he's hooked and trailing a line and some small floats."

"I guess he won a tug of war with a local fisherman," remarked his passenger.

"Yes, perhaps long-liners or poachers illegally shark finning. They catch sharks, cut off their fins and toss them overboard to die. They're the scum of the ocean. Pulling that line isn't good for that shark. It'll tire and have difficulty catching food. Eventually, it may even . . ."

"Hey where're Jackie and Peter?" interrupted Gavin. Jaime looked around, first the boat, then at the water and realized Jackie and Peter were missing, out of sight.

"Oh, madre mio!" he exclaimed. He noticed the current was flowing north past the point. After quickly counting that all other nine passengers were safely aboard, he headed with the current.

Jackie and Peter were preoccupied playing with Gemini and had drifted almost a mile. They heard the *Jolly Mon's* horn bleating repeatedly in the distance. "Peter we have to swim back to the boat, now!" exclaimed Jackie. They turned and tried snorkeling toward the boat. After several minutes they looked around and realized they were not making any progress.

"We can't get back. The current's too strong," replied Peter, winded after finning hard against the current. "Let's just swim closer to shore. The point should block the current, like Mom taught us. Then we can swim to the beach or float until Uncle Jaime comes."

They snorkeled toward shore, making headway as the point shielded them from the swift current. "Hey, look at all these little fish," said Jackie.

"Yeah, snappers. They sure are moving fast," replied Peter. "I wonder what's chasing . . ."

"EEEK! Sharks!" screamed Jackie. Peter turned where Jackie was pointing and saw two triangular fins rounding the point. The fleeing school separated, and one shark chased some fish into deeper water. But Peter's eyes widened as one dorsal fin veered toward the remaining snappers, heading toward his sister and him. The fish fled toward the beach and the shark herded them toward shore, where there was no escape. "The shark's between us and the beach. Where should we go?"

"I don't know!" her brother shouted. They watched the hungry shark charge through the school, attempting to catch fish with each pass. However, dragging the fishing line and floats hampered the shark's feeding. The faster, more agile snappers evaded its jaws. But its lateral line, the nerve pathway running along its body from head to tail, sensed the children's vibrations as they thrashed the water. Instinctively the frustrated shark turned toward these different vibrations, indicating another food source that might be larger and slower than the snappers.

"Peter!" screamed Jackie as the shark approached her. She froze, eyes wide, mouth agape, watching the dorsal fin sink like a diving submarine's periscope, leaving only ripples in the calm bay.

"Where'd it go?" asked Peter, spinning around, expecting a mouthful of white daggers to erupt from the blue glassy surface.

"I don't . . . ooph!" gasped Jackie as the shark bumped her stomach, rubbing its flat snout against her nylon floatation vest. Another sensory system, tiny nerve receptors called the ampullae of Lorenzini, transmitted a conflicting message to the shark's primitive but efficient brain: *Inedible; Not food.* It bumped Jackie's vest a second time confirming the information, and then circled both children as they screamed. The beach was 200 yards away, but Peter noticed the point's pock-marked rocky wall, formed of wave-gouged limestone, was much closer, only about 50 feet away.

"C'mon. This way!" he shouted to Jackie. They turned and swam toward the safety of the rock wall, furiously kicking their fins and wind-milling their arms. Jackie's left fin slipped off her foot and sank, but she ignored it and continued swimming toward the wall. The shark, excited by their frantic splashing, focused its attention on Peter and circled him, cutting off escape. Jackie looked back at her brother and stopped, but Peter shouted, "Keep going!" The shark approached, then dived beneath him and bumped his leg. "OW!" He screamed as the shark's rasp-like skin, abrasive as rough sandpaper, scraped his thigh. This time the ampullae of Lorenzini, rubbing against bare flesh, sent the shark's brain a different message. *Food.* Peter rubbed his leg and saw blood on his hand. Panicked, he ignored the pain and finned toward the rock wall. He saw Jackie reach the wall and swim into an opening, the top of which was several feet above the surface. She swam inside the tiny cave and pulled herself onto a ledge. Peter swam toward the same opening. *A few more feet and I'm safe*, but the menacing dorsal fin surfaced between him and the wall.

Cut off again, he reflexively finned backwards as the shark swam purposefully toward him. Peter saw the mouth open, a flash of white, and he lunged backward, scissor-kicking his legs as fast has he could. The shark accelerated, and clamped its jaws on Peter's fin. Its triangular, serrated teeth missed his toes by inches. The shark violently shook its head, shaking Peter like a rag doll, dragging him under. Peter clawed for the surface until his lungs burned. But suddenly he was free, shooting upward when the shark tore his fin loose. Gasping for air, he screamed, "Help! Shark!" Jackie heard him and cried inside her tiny sanctuary, the vivid image of the shark tearing her brother apart seared her imagination. The shark dropped the fin and followed Peter to the surface continuing the attack. He watched, horrified, as it circled. He kept turning, keeping the shark in view as it circled tighter and then closed in. Peter ripped off his mask and snorkel and pounded the shark's flat snout with the hard faceplate. The water foamed as it thrashed, trying to sink its teeth into an arm, leg, anything. Peter grabbed his snorkel and jammed it into the shark's eye. It broke off the attack momentarily, and Peter turned toward the wall, swimming as fast as he could. The shark circled, and then followed Peter, closing the distance rapidly. It opened its jaws but, blinded in one eye, razor-sharp teeth snapped on air. The shark accelerated and was about to seize Peter's bare foot, when it was violently rammed. The collision propelled it airborne, fully out of the water. Peter reached the cave and ducked inside the opening, unaware how he had escaped death.

"Peter! Here!" shouted Jackie, extending her hand. He grasped her hand and she pulled him onto the ledge. "Are you okay?" she asked, crying when she saw the angry red bruise on his thigh oozing blood.

"I, I think so," Peter replied, now crying himself.

The shark settled in the water, trying to recover from the brutal ramming when it was struck again. Notchka, alerted by Gemini's frantic clicking and squealing had realized her calf and the two small humans were in danger, and had left the pod to help them. Seeing the shark attacking Peter, she accelerated and rammed it with her rostrum, pulverizing its organs. She had killed the drug lord Oscar the same way years ago, when he had killed her calf and then was about to kill Terry. Fatally injured, the shark turned its stomach inside out, a stress reflex to eliminate indigestible objects swallowed while feeding. Then its underwater world faded. Negatively buoyant, it slowly sank.

Moments earlier, the *Jolly Mon* had cleared Palancar Point with Jaime, Gavin and the nine vacationers scanning the water, searching for the children. A loud gasp arose when they saw the shark summersault from the water. They watched in morbid fascination as a large dolphin circled the shark and then rammed it again. But they hadn't seen Peter and Jackie duck into the cave. Jaime turned the *Jolly Mon* into the bay and, as the two dolphins swam away, he spotted the notched fluke of the larger adult. He radioed the *Dorado*.

Terry, Joe and their divers were halfway through their surface interval when his call came. "Terry, it's for you," said Manuel.

"Yes, Jaime, what's up? Slow down, you're talking too fast. What? Oh my God! We'll be right there."

"What's up, Ter?" asked Joe.

Terry half shouted, half cried, "Jackie and Peter were following dolphins and got separated from the group. Sharks were in the area, and they saw Notchka kill one. But now they can't find the kids!" She yelled to her divers standing on the pier. "We're leaving immediately! Everyone on board right now! We have an emergency!"

"Peter, I think the tide's coming in. Look!" Jackie exclaimed. Peter saw the cave opening shrinking as the water slowly rose. They inched farther back on their tiny ledge. "We better get out or we'll be trapped."

"No way I'm going out there with that shark waiting," he sniffled, sitting on the ledge in the dimming light. He pulled his knees under his chin watching the rising tide lapping higher and higher. Soon, it would reach the top of the cave.

Chapter 11

May 14th

Jaime noticed a boat approaching at high speed. He saw Terry and Joe standing on the bow, scanning the surface shielding their eyes from sun glare. The *Dorado* pulled alongside the *Jolly Mon* and Terry jumped aboard. She ran up to Jaime and grabbed his arm. "What happened? Where are my kids?" she asked, in a panicked parent's frantic tone.

Jaime, distraught and wracked with guilt, began babbling.

"Terry it happened so quickly. One minute they were snorkeling with the group, and then they were gone. I'm sorry, I'm . . ."

"Okay Jaime," said Joe, sharply. "Blaming yourself now won't help find the kids. Think! Where did you see them last? What about the sharks?"

"I saw Jackie and Peter paddle farther out, playing with some dolphins," said a snorkeler.

"Then we left the water because of sharks," another said.

"Gavin and I searched for them, Terry, but the current was going past the point and swept them toward this bay," said Jaime. "When we arrived we saw a dolphin kill a shark. I'm sure it was Notchka, but we couldn't find Jackie or Peter."

"Hopefully they swam into the shelter of the point instead of fighting the current, like I taught them," said Terry. "Otherwise they would have tired and . . ."

She bit her lip and tears welled up but she couldn't express the thought of her children drowning.

"Terry, don't forget they were wearing floatation vests. They couldn't drown," said Joe trying to reassure her.

"Then we should have passed them on the way here." She looked at Joe, who appeared blurry through her tears. "But sharks! Oh not again," Terry sobbed, shaking her head, recalling the day twelve years ago when a great white off the California coast had brutally ended her future with her fiancé, the late Mark Stafford.

"Okay, I'm going in. Get my tank and gear," said Joe. "If we didn't pass them they must be near."

Terry wiped tears away and drew a deep breath. "I'm coming with you. Get my stuff." Joe knew better than to dissuade Terry when she had decided to act. He silently prayed this would be a rescue mission, not a recovery effort. "We'll swim a box pattern," she said, "about 200 yards toward the shore, right ninety degrees toward the rock wall, right again along the wall for a couple of hundred yards, then a last right back to our starting point." They jumped from the *Dorado's* stern, descended to the sandy bottom and headed toward the beach, with the open bay on their left and the rocky point on their right. Visibility was almost one hundred feet, typical Cozumel gin-clear water.

Five minutes into the dive Terry spotted a small yellow snorkel fin on the bottom. She retrieved it and saw bite indentations. A shark tooth was imbedded in the fin. The tip was shredded. She turned it over and saw the initials *PM* in white paint. She handed it to Joe. He saw fear in her eyes. Joe tucked the fin under his arm and they continued their search pattern. A minute later Joe tapped his tank with his dive knife's metal handle, gaining Terry's attention. She looked toward Joe and then turned where he was pointing. Fifty feet away on the bottom they saw a Caribbean reef shark contorted in a permanent spasm, a spark of life still convulsing its body. The float line suspended its head so the shark appeared to be standing on its tail. Its stomach protruded from its mouth like a bizarre balloon. Joe left Terry and swam toward the dying shark. He searched the sandy bottom, looking for human body parts the shark may have regurgitated. Relieved finding none, he glanced toward the shark again. He observed the float line and large hook piercing the left corner of its gaping maw. A broken hook's rusty shank protruded from the right side of the shark's mouth. *Looks like this poor guy's had a tough time,* Joe thought. He made the diver's OK sign, three fingers up with the thumb and forefinger in a circle. Terry acknowledged with the same sign, pointed to her right and swam toward the rock wall.

They saw nothing as they reached the wall, then made another right-angle turn swimming along the wall, the next-to-last leg of their search pattern. After a hundred yards Joe saw Terry jackknife, dive down and insert her hand between two pieces of elk horn coral. She pulled out a child-size pink fin, with the initials *JM*. She examined it for shark teeth, found none and handed the fin to Joe. They continued for the last hundred yards but found nothing. Joe turned, making the last ninety-degree right turn back toward their starting point, when he heard Terry banging her tank. He turned and saw her shaking her head, pointing back from where they came. Joe sensed Terry's intuition was sending her a message she would not ignore. He followed her back to the coral formation where she had found the pink fin. Then she swam toward the rock wall and slowly ascended. Just below the surface an opening in the wall appeared. She swam inside.

Huddled together on the ledge in near darkness, Jackie and Peter shivered. With the cave opening now underwater, the only illumination was a thin light beam shining through a three-inch wide hole extending through the porous limestone. They sat silently, watching the water slowly rising, lapping at their ledge, wondering how long until their sanctuary became flooded. Suddenly, bubbles exploded from the calm black water. Startled, they jumped back against the wall. A diver's head appeared, but the children were too stunned to speak. Then, recognizing Terry's eyes through her facemask, they simultaneously yelled, "MOM!" Terry kicked her fins, rose and boosted herself onto the ledge, wrapping her arms around her children.

Seconds later, another bubble eruption occurred, and Joe broke the surface. Spitting out his regulator he exclaimed, "KIDS!"

"DAD!" Peter shouted. They embraced and the children began a rambling account of their adventure, recounting the details in a non-stop sentence.

"Okay, tell us all about it later. For now let's get out of here and go home," said Terry.

"But mom, the shark's out there," cried Jackie.

"The shark's dead, princess," replied Joe. "Notchka killed it. Didn't you know?"

"No, Dad. We couldn't see what was happening outside," replied Peter. "Wow! She killed it? How? I never knew a dolphin could kill a shark. I thought sharks kill dolphins."

"Well, sometimes they try. That's probably how Notchka got that notch in her fluke. But dolphins are pretty smart. They know ramming a shark destroys their internal organs and . . ."

"You mean it turns their guts to jelly?" asked Peter, grinning as he wiped away tears.

"That's a good way to put it, tiger," Joe said, laughing, tousling Peter's wet hair. Let's go home, kids. Just take a deep breath, dive under and we're out of here. Follow me."

Joe went first, followed by the children and Terry. Surfacing a moment later, they shouted and waved to the *Jolly Mon* and *Dorado II*. As the boats approached, Joe and Terry held Peter and Jackie up. Terry's divers and Jaime's snorkelers erupted with cheers.

Chapter 12

May 14ᵗʰ

Jackie and Peter became instant celebrities soon after Jaime's and Terry's customers arrived in San Miguel to catch motor launches returning to their cruise ship. Waiting on the pier, they recounted the children's exciting adventure to locals and tourists alike. The story spread throughout Cozumel, blossoming into an exaggerated adventure about two brave children swept away by raging currents, saved from the jaws of death by a courageous dolphin who killed a giant shark, and finally rescued by their heroic scuba diving parents, moments before drowning in an underwater cave.

Terry saw the children telling their ordeal to several friends. She was concerned they carried themselves with too much swagger, given that their own poor judgment caused their brush with death. She watched Peter pantomiming fending off the shark with his mask and snorkel. "Joe, I think we need a family meeting after dinner."

"Huh?"

Terry pointed and Joe turned. They watched Peter jabbing an imaginary shark with an imaginary snorkel, like Peter Pan dueling Captain Hook.

"Take that! And that! I told that big old shark," they heard Peter exclaim, as his wide-eyed friends hung on his every word. Joe smiled and shook his head.

"I see what you mean, hon. You know, I was so relieved finding the kids unharmed I didn't think about the lesson this incident should have taught them." He walked over, interrupting Peter's performance. "Sorry kids. We've had a busy day and we have to get home."

After an early dinner Jackie and Peter were exhausted. They started upstairs when Joe called them back. "Just a minute, tiger. You too, princess. We need to discuss what happened today." The children looked at each other apprehensively, sensing trouble ahead. They looked at their mother, hoping for a reprieve.

"Your father has something to say, and I agree with him."

"Do you two realize you could have been killed today?" Joe began, gently.

"But Dad, the current was . . ."

"No buts, Peter!" Joe continued in a firmer tone. "Uncle Jaime told you not to swim away from the boat. You both disobeyed . . ."

Several minutes later the discussion ended with a two-week snorkeling ban, but also with their parents' reassuring hugs and kisses. Chastised but still feeling loved, Jackie and Peter slowly climbed the stairs to their rooms. They soon fell into a restless sleep, their dreams populated by friendly dolphins and ferocious sharks. Friends and reporters called all night requesting additional details, but Joe and Terry downplayed the events.

The next morning, however, their story appeared in several local newspapers: the *Playa Maya News, Por Esto* and *Diario Quintana Roo*. "Oh well," Joe said, smiling as he read various newspaper accounts describing his children's close brush with death. "No harm letting the kids enjoy their fifteen minutes of fame. Hey, we should get their front-page photo framed."

"Sure, maybe they'll even autograph it for us," replied Terry, sarcastically.

"Hmm, looks like the Associated Press also picked up the story," said Joe. "That means it'll be in U.S. newspapers, foreign ones, too. Probably on the internet by now."

"Hey Mom, does this mean we're heroes?" asked Peter, hopefully.

"Amazing!" said Terry, shaking her head. "A family of four could be wiped out riding a motor scooter in downtown Cozumel and the story probably wouldn't get mentioned. But the whole world goes wild over a single shark encounter."

"It wasn't just an *encounter*, Mom," objected Jackie. "It was an *attack*!"

The phone rang and Joe answered. "Hello, Manetta's home of heroes," he said, smiling as Terry rolled her large green eyes. "Hola, Jaime. How are you today? What? No, they haven't called us yet. Really? Oh, Terry will be thrilled," he said laughing. "Adios, Jaime. I'll tell her now."

"Tell me what, dear?"

"Producers from the *Today Show* in New York just called Jaime. They want to interview all of us together on the show tomorrow morning."

"WHAT? You must be joking!" Terry exclaimed, as Jackie and Peter smacked palms, high-fiving each other. "No way we're going on TV."

"Oh come on, Ter, it'll be a hoot. Think about the free publicity for the business."

"Sure! I can see the headlines now: *Come to Cozumel and get attacked by sharks!* That'll be great for our business."

"Oh, we can spin it, talk about how rare shark attacks are here. In fact I don't recall ever seeing aggressive reef sharks in these waters."

"Well, they show up occasionally, perhaps somewhat more frequently since last year's hurricanes. But as you said, it's very rare to even see them, and they've never attacked anyone."

"So let's do the interview, Ter. Don't be a party pooper," Joe said, grinning.

"Yeah, Mom. Don't be a pooper," agreed Peter.

"Okay, okay. I know when I'm outnumbered," Terry said, throwing up her hands in surrender. "But my intuition tells me we'll regret it."

At seven the next morning, Terry, Joe, Jackie, Peter and Jaime were seated in a local television studio in Cozumel's Municipal Building, anxiously waiting for the live feed from NBC headquarters in New York. A make-up woman powdered Jaime's bald head, reducing the glare from the bright studio lights. Terry laughed as he sneezed, momentarily engulfed in a puff of talcum. A technician entered the room and asked, "Everyone ready? You're on after the next commercial." They all breathed deeply, trying to relax. Then the technician began counting. "5, 4, 3, 2, 1, you're on," he crisply pointed to them.

"Good morning everyone," began Matt Lasker, whose familiar image suddenly appeared on the television monitor. Soon, New York and the entire nation heard their harrowing adventure and learned about a bottlenose dolphin named Notchka, the hero of the story. Co-host Meredith Vincent focused on Terry's feelings from a mother's perspective. The interview went smoothly. The trickiest part was managing the three-second delay between New York and Cozumel as questions were asked, answered and new questions posed. Just before concluding, Matt Lasker surprised Terry with a final question.

"Terry, our researchers informed me that this same dolphin, Notchka, saved your life several years ago in a similar fashion. Evidently she rammed someone attempting to kill you. Is that true?" Terry was stunned, unprepared to relive the traumatic event for several million television viewers.

"I, ah, well. . ." she groped, but the words caught in her throat. Joe intervened.

"Yes, Matt, that's accurate. But as you can imagine that was quite a terrifying experience. If you don't mind we'd rather not discuss it today."

"I can understand how you both feel, Joe," Lasker said, sensing Terry's discomfort. "We appreciate you sharing your latest adventure with us," he said, concluding the interview.

Minutes later, Matt and Meredith thanked everyone for appearing on the program. They signed off and the monitor went blank.

"Wow!" exclaimed Terry, regaining her composure. "The interview went so fast. Seemed like we had just started and then it was over."

"Well, Jaime, you're famous now," laughed Joe. "After this you'll probably need a bigger boat."

"I hope so, amigo," Jaime said, smiling.

In Brooklyn, a New York City borough, Lieutenant Bill Ryan, Joe Manetta's former NYPD partner, was watching the *Today Show* before leaving for work. He called his wife into the living room. "Hey, look honey! I'll be damned! There's my friend, good old Joe-boy, Terry and the kids!" he exclaimed. Bill watched the segment with rapt attention. "What a story! I didn't realize that dolphin was still around."

Chapter 13
Pakistan

June 1st

Ahmed's immediate concern was recruiting his team. After leaving his mentor, he had traveled through Pakistan's poor rural sections, avoiding large cities and towns. Even in remote locations he was known and respected as a senior Al Qaeda member. The local populace regarded him as a leader. When he revealed his intentions to recruit several men who would carry jihad into the Great Satan's homeland he had numerous volunteers. But his plan required men with specialized skills.

One warm, sunny afternoon Ahmed relaxed in the garden of a friend's home. The two sipped tea under the protective shade of an olive tree, discussing where Ahmed might find the men he needed. They did not notice two young men approaching on foot until the men entered the garden. They turned, facing the men. One looked directly at Ahmed and addressed him. "Excuse us. We know why you are here. May we speak with you?"

"Sit. Be comfortable," Ahmed replied, gesturing toward a wooden bench near his table. He glanced at his friend. A subtle nod indicated he wished to interview the two men alone. His friend rose, smiled and excused himself. The taller man spoke first.

"Ahmed Mohammed, my name is Waleed Alomari. This is my cousin, Salen Hanjour. We have heard you need brave men to help you carry out a holy mission, to bring jihad to Islam's greatest enemy. We are ready to fight with you." Ahmed carefully assessed the two men with a trained eye. His cold dark eyes moved from one man to the other. They shifted uneasily under his gaze. He had recruited fighters before. He could tell these two possessed the desire and the spirit. *But do they have the skills I need?* he wondered. They were shabbily dressed. Their shirts were old and tattered. Their pants were threadbare and baggy, at least one size too large. Their sandals were worn out, stringy weeds replaced missing leather straps. Ahmed sighed. *They're probably illiterate goat herders, well intentioned but uneducated.*

"Why do you think you can help me? Why should I be interested in you?" He expected them to shrink from his sharp questioning. But Waleed surprised him, replying self-assuredly.

"I can help you because I am an expert in radio controlled explosives." Then Salen spoke for the first time.

"And I am an explosives expert, like you. I have admired your brave deeds, but I think my bomb making skills are better than yours." Ahmed was taken aback by their audacious demeanor and by Salen's brash assertion regarding his bomb making ability. Ahmed's body language reflected his revised assessment. Intrigued, he sat erect for the first time since they had arrived.

"Tell me more about your background and experience," he inquired. He marveled at what they told him. The cousins were experienced jihad fighters, recently returned from Iraq. Together they were responsible for designing and planting scores of improvised explosive devices used by insurgent fighters. Both men had participated in attacks on U.S. troop convoys and had destroyed numerous American armored vehicles and killed many Iraqi civilians with their uniquely designed explosives. Best of all, from Ahmed's perspective, they hated Americans, British and Israelis. In fact, they hated anything Western. And they were fanatical, cold-blooded killers. They had the exact skills Ahmed had been seeking, unsuccessfully until now. He mused. *Clearly Allah must favor me, for he has dropped these two men into my lap.*

"Please wait here." Ahmed went into the house, where his friend had been observing the meeting through a window. He repeated what the two men had told him. "Are these two who they say they are?" he asked his friend.

"I have heard the names Salen and Waleed mentioned many times, regarding bold attacks on Americans, but I have never met them. I believe they live in a nearby village. A friend told me they were away, fighting in Iraq."

"Come outside with me," Ahmed beckoned. He looked at the two men and made an immediate decision. "I welcome you to join my holy mission. But I must warn you. It is dangerous, and you may become martyrs." Waleed looked at Salen. They made eye contact for a short moment. Ahmed watched them carefully, assessing their commitment. He would dismiss them at their first indication of wavering. Then Waleed spoke.

"Ahmed Mohammed, we welcome the chance to sacrifice ourselves for such a noble purpose." The three men embraced. Ahmed turned to his friend.

"Please bring these holy warriors some hot tea, bread and fruit. We must celebrate our alliance." He smiled, noting there was just one more piece left in his puzzle: finding a skilled scuba diver. He was certain there were no scuba divers in the land-locked mountains of Pakistan. But Ahmed was confident he would find one at his next destination, Karachi, Pakistan's largest city, located on the Arabian Sea coast. "I have only one more question. Can you leave within the week?" he asked.

"We are at your disposal," replied Waleed. "We can leave tomorrow if you need us." Ahmed looked at Salen who smiled and nodded.

Ahmed Mohammed and his two-member terrorist team traveled south, eventually crossing the Afghanistan border. They traveled mostly at night, on foot, by horse or camel, through rugged mountain terrain, evading American and British search teams combing the country for Taliban fighters. During the day, sympathetic tribal lords loyal to the Taliban sheltered them. They traveled a route east of Kabul and Kandahar. During their journey they told no one about their mission. Maintaining secrecy was extremely important, especially with the American CIA offering substantial sums to the local population for details about Taliban positions, future terrorist attacks and other information. Several nights later they would cross back into Pakistan, continuing south toward Karachi, their final destination in Asia.

"How many more bitter cold nights must we suffer, Ahmed?" asked Waleed. "My back aches from riding this lame horse."

"Pray to Allah for patience and strength, Waleed. In two more nights we will cross back into Pakistan, safe from enemy troops. Then we can travel by day, and you'll be rid of the horse. We can travel in comfort by bus and train to Karachi."

"I hope my back can last that long," sighed Waleed.

"How long do we remain in Karachi?" asked Salen.

"Just long enough to complete our business," replied Ahmed. "I must recruit a scuba diver for our team. I hope to find one there since the city borders the sea. We'll also meet good friends, senior Al Qaeda members. They'll provide money, plane tickets, forged U.S. passports, driver's licenses, and any other documentation we need for our mission. We won't bring any equipment with us. Once we reach New York, more friends will supply the materials I requested, additional money and anything else we need.

"You've thought of everything," replied Waleed.

Ahmed smiled, envisioning the death and destruction he would soon inflict on his enemies. *Ah, Waleed, there is so much more that you don't yet know,* he thought.

Chapter 14
CIA Headquarters, Langley, Virginia

June 10th

Deputy Director Walsh began his weekly staff meeting promptly at eight o'clock. "Okay, Jeff, what have you guys learned?"

"Well, sir, yesterday we spoke with Mike Bilboa, head of New York Homeland Security. He provided more details. Susan?" Jeff said, nodding toward agent Susan Wilson.

"He told us Queen Elizabeth will visit New York City from June 29th to July 5th. It's a busy trip. First she flies into D.C. aboard British Airways on June 27th. She meets with the President on June 28th, and addresses a special joint session of Congress the morning of the 29th. She leaves for New York that afternoon, where she combines some official business with a little sight seeing. On June 30th she hosts a reception aboard the liner Queen Mary 2. That'll be a major event, attended by numerous dignitaries. She has two days to rest and recoup, then on July 3rd she addresses the U.N. General Assembly. On the Fourth, she attends several Independence Day celebrations and a fireworks display in Battery Park. She'll probably tell the usual jokes about how proud she is that England's colonies have accomplished so much in the last 231 years, that sort of stuff. She flies home to England the next day, July 5th."

"That's a packed itinerary, especially for an 82-year-old queen," said the DDI, as everyone nodded.

"And a security nightmare for the NYPD and Secret Service. Not only is the Queen in New York, but you'll have the President of the United States and other dignitaries attending the UN General Assembly meeting," added Jeff Becker.

"It does mesh with our intelligence though, you know, about the Queen and New York," replied agent Wilson.

"But we're still in the dark about this *hanging the necklace* reference," added agent Donaldson. "It sure sounds like an assassination attempt."

"By using her necklace? Choking or strangling her?" asked Wilson.

"I can't believe they could ever get that close to her," interjected agent Miller.

"Neither can I," agreed DDI Walsh. "But, team, you haven't considered another potential target." All eyes focused on the boss as he continued. "The Queen Mary 2, pride of the Cunard line, and Great Britain. I did some research on her last night."

He pulled a printout from his inside jacket pocket, unfolded it, adjusted his bi-focal glasses and began reading. "One of the largest passenger ships afloat, 1,132 feet in length, 113 feet longer than the original Queen Mary and 147 feet longer than the height of the Eiffel tower. Weight, 151,400 gross tons. Crew size 1,253. Maximum capacity 3,056 passengers. She's one of the fastest ocean liners in the world. Cruising speed 28.5 knots, more than 30 miles per hour."

He placed the information sheet on the desk, removed his glasses and looked at the group. "But June 30th she'll be a sitting target, moored at Pier 92 on the Hudson River. And the Queen of England will be aboard. Think of the multi-national symbolism. Of course, we shouldn't discount the reference about strangling the Queen with her jewels, or necklace, or whatever the hell they're planning. With a crew exceeding 1,200, mostly foreign nationals from many countries, Al Qaeda might use an infiltrator for an assassination. But when you consider the other intelligence information, references mentioning *huge loss of life* and *economic chaos*, my bet is they'll kill two birds with one stone. Or one bomb. I think they're going to blow the ship with the Queen aboard."

DDI Walsh looked into the agents' eyes, noting their agreement. He read their facial expressions, indicating personal frustration because they failed to make the same connection. He thought, *Well, that's why I'm the boss*. Then he turned and pressed the intercom. "Elise, please call the mayor's office in New York."

Chapter 15
Pakistan

June 14th

Several nights later, Ahmed Mohammed and his terrorist team crossed the Pakistan border on horseback, once again enjoying relative safety. Here, they would not have to evade American and British search and destroy teams, or constantly watch the sky fearing deadly Predator drones. President Mushariff's Pakistani government had repeatedly stated its commitment to eliminate Al Qaeda terrorists. But many feared it was mostly lip service from a government needing to accommodate opposition forces to remain in power.

Eventually, the men reached Quetta, a small village high in the mountains. They searched for a place to buy cool water, welcoming the opportunity to walk. Several hours later, a loud engine backfire and cloud of blue-white smoke signaled the arrival of the twice-weekly bus. The team looked toward the smoke and noise and watched a mustard-yellow, rickety vehicle sway on worn out shocks and bald tires as it turned a corner. The bus' aging brakes moaned and steam hissed from a rusty radiator, as it halted next to a small building serving as the local bus terminal. Many of the bus' windows were cracked and all were smeared with dirt. The driver's window was mud-streaked from the last time he used a dirty wet cloth to wipe away road dust. "You expect us to ride in that?" Asked Saleen, incredulous. Ahmed simply ended the conversation with a cold stare. The team boarded the bus for a 250-mile, seven-hour journey to Moenjodaro. From there they would board a train for the 200-mile ride to Karachi.

Ahmed watched his weary team settle into thinly padded seats, most with straw spilling from torn vinyl. He smiled. "Did I not promise you would eventually ride in comfort, in the sun's warmth?"

"A thousand thanks, my brother," replied Waleed, his eyelids drooping. Ahmed looked at Salen, but he was already asleep. Not even the 22-year-old diesel engine's loud droning kept them awake. Seven hours later the old bus lurched to a halt. The driver stood up, turned around and shouted, "Moenjodaro! Whoever is continuing with us to the next stop, please return in one hour."

Ahmed woke from a light sleep and shook each man's shoulder. "We've arrived. Everyone up! We have two hours to eat before our train arrives." Groggy after their first good sleep in days, each gathered his belongings and staggered off the bus. They squinted in the bright sun, shielding their eyes with their hands. "This way," shouted Ahmed as he spotted a small restaurant near the train station. They staggered into the restaurant and sat at a long table with wooden bench seats. They threw their baggage under the table, called the proprietor over and ordered lunch.

Three hours later Ahmed was paying the bill when he heard a distant train whistle, echoing through the mountains. He looked at his watch. "Amazing. Only one hour late. Let's go!"

The team walked across the street to the station, little more than a wooden platform protected by a rusted corrugated tin roof. A single track approached the station from either direction and a switch separated the tracks at each end of the platform, forming a passing siding so opposing trains could pass without colliding head-on. Waleed and Salen looked at the track, pointed out several missing spikes and shook their heads. The train, an old diesel chugging oily blue smoke pulling two passenger cars, rounded a bend and eased into the station. It squealed to a halt as metal brakes clamped onto rusty metal wheels. After a short delay the train departed with a lurch.

In a land where it seemed fiction writers wrote the timetables, it pulled into the bustling city of Karachi that evening only two hours behind schedule, better than its usual performance.

Ahmed spotted their contact, an old friend, leaning against a wall in the rear of the Karachi train station. He guessed his forty-ish, balding acquaintance had gained about ten kilos since they last met, but he recognized him immediately with his trademark drooping cigarette dangling from the left corner of his mouth, always the left corner. They acknowledged each other with a subtle hand wave. Ahmed and his team followed the man to a dark limousine and drove off into the night.

Thirty minutes later they arrived at a secluded house, large but not ostentatious. It was set back 100 feet from the road, surrounded by a six-foot high stone wall. It blended with the other stone houses in the neighborhood, except for several antennas sprouting from the slate roof. A tall man came outside and greeted them. "Ahmed, so good to see you again," he said, embracing him.

"And good to see you also, Rahim. How long has it been? Two years?"

"Yes, almost two years since we worked together, but it seems longer. And now you are going to carry out a direct attack against the Great Satan's homeland?"

"Yes, Rahim, with my team. This is Waleed Alomari and Salen Hanjour. I chose them for their dedication and their specialized skills."

Rahim nodded to the three men. "Come inside. Relax, have some tea and dinner. You must be famished after your long journey." They smiled and each carried a small pack into the house. The men took positions around a rectangle table, with Rahim at one end and Ahmed at the other. Two women appeared from the kitchen carrying large steaming platters of lamb and vegetables.

After dinner Rahim said, "I'm eager to discuss your mission and how we can assist you. But I see you are tired. My servant will show you your sleeping quarters. I'm sure you will find them satisfactory. Have a good night's sleep. We'll talk tomorrow morning."

Chapter 16
One Police Plaza, New York City

June 14th

The six senior NYPD police detectives and their department chiefs rose as Police Commissioner Richard Jackson entered the conference room. Even at sixty-two, Jackson's six-foot-three, heavily muscled frame filled the room, any room in fact, with his presence. His close-cut, thinning hair showed some salt mixed in with the pepper. His piercing dark eyes were never still, constantly darting from person to person. It was an ingrained habit from his early years as a beat cop, when noticing every crime scene detail meant the difference between missing or finding minute traces of evidence. And it frequently meant the difference between life and death while patrolling a dark street.

Jackson was the first African-American NYPD commissioner appointed since Lee Brown in 1990. Jackson's on-street accomplishments quickly propelled him up the ranks and into administrative positions, where his uncanny ability to navigate big-city political minefields caught the mayor's attention. He repeatedly deflated highly charged issues, which had ambushed equally competent but less politically savvy peers. Consequently, the mayor appointed Jackson Police as commissioner two years earlier.

"Please be seated, gentlemen," Jackson began, in his sonorous voice. He waited until all the detectives were seated and the squeaky sound of chairs sliding on linoleum had ceased. He addressed the detectives directly.

"I know having you attend a chief's meeting is departure from protocol, but since they handpicked you for this assignment, with my personal approval, I wanted everyone to hear the same information simultaneously." Jackson made eye contact with each officer, and then continued. "I just spoke with Mayor Williamson and New York State Homeland Security Director Mike Bilboa. We have a significant challenge ahead. We already knew we'd have our hands full in July protecting Queen Elizabeth, the president, and other foreign dignitaries visiting New York. Now it seems the Feds have received intelligence that Al Qaeda is planning to assassinate the Queen and possibly blow up the Queen Mary 2, which will be docked here from June 24th to July 4th."

The six officers exchanged glances, shifting in their chairs. "Sir, do they have hard evidence, or is this some vague threat they heard third-hand from some unreliable contact trying to score a few bucks?" challenged Lieutenant Mike Leonetti.

"Well, Mike, the information came directly from their field operative in Afghanistan. In fact, he was killed obtaining it."

"Anything more specific about the plan itself?" asked Lieutenant Bill Ryan, Joe Manetta's former partner.

"They believe June 30th is the key date. The Queen will host a reception aboard the QM2 that day. If someone wanted to sink the ship and kill the Queen that makes for a very convenient, efficient scenario. However, the intelligence also indicates the possible use of a necklace or some other jewelry in an assassination attempt against the Queen. So that means the attack could occur somewhere else. In fact the whole ship angle is just an assumption. The QM2 was never specifically mentioned in the original intelligence report."

"Did they share the context of their intelligence?" asked Sergeant Pete Ainello.

Commissioner Jackson opened a 9 by 12-inch envelope and handed each officer a single sheet of paper. "Yes they did, Pete. This page is the primary source of their intelligence. Consider it for your eyes only. Please read and return it before you leave." The room fell silent as the detectives read the terrorists' disjointed comments from page five of the original report.

> **######Ahmed #### the result #### this plan ######### huge loss of life #####economic disruption ######### British and American interests will ############### When ##### hang the necklace########## queen ##########never leave New York Ahmed ########## wonderful #### #### Allah will ###############**

"That's all? It's not much to go on," commented Lt. Ryan.

"True, but that's what these CIA spooks do, Bill," replied Jackson. "They take disjointed information, apply assumptions and background information and determine a logical context. These lines don't seem like much at first glance. But when you combine this with the information we gave them it makes a whole lot of sense. Al Qaeda wants to damage the U.S. and Britain. They plan to make sure the Queen doesn't leave New York alive. They know she always wears jewels, so perhaps they're planning to kill her with her own necklace. That would certainly make a powerful statement about how they view our financial excesses and those of our allies."

"But that doesn't translate into these other comments about huge loss of life and economic disruption," replied Ryan.

"True, but that's why Washington feels the ship angle comes into play." Jackson saw Ryan raise his eyebrows, skeptically. "Hey, Bill, I don't know. Maybe they're planning separate attacks. Who the hell really knows? The point is, we must act on this information."

"And are the Feds gonna pony up some extra cash and help pay for all this additional security we'll need?" asked Lt. Leonetti.

"I'm afraid not," replied Jackson. "The Secret Service will protect the president, and the Queen, of course, with help from British Secret Service, MI5. But they're confident the current Homeland Security budget allocation provides sufficient security funding."

"Yeah. After all, they do have to allocate sufficient money protecting the annual 4-H convention in nowhere's-ville Kansas from terrorists," sighed Ainello, as everyone laughed.

"Point well taken, Pete," said Jackson, smiling. "But nevertheless, we have to get down to work. I'm dividing the responsibility among you six. Each of you will develop security plans for the areas I assign, within budgetary guidelines of course. Pete, you'll handle the East side. That includes the area around the United Nations. Mike, the Queen will be in Lower Manhattan most of July Fourth. That's your responsibility. She hosts a luncheon at Fraunces Tavern, where Washington gave his farewell address to the troops. Then she attends a reception at Castle Clinton, the Revolutionary War fort located in Battery Park. The Statue of Liberty and Ellis Island are nearby in the harbor. That's a lot of symbolism in a relatively small geographic area. That evening she'll watch a Grucci fireworks display over the Hudson from a reviewing stand set up along Battery Park's seawall. Bill, you have the West side, including security for the QM2 itself. Jerry, you're responsible for . . ."

After delegating security assignments, Commissioner Jackson adjourned the meeting. "I'm scheduling a follow-up meeting for Friday, three days from now. I'll review your preliminary plans at that meeting. Good day, gentlemen. And good luck."

Chapter 17
Pakistan

June 15th

Ahmed, his team and his Al Qaeda hosts sat around a low table. Rahim's servant gave each man a cup of steaming hot tea. Biscuits and assorted fruits were passed around. Ahmed saw his hosts were eager to discuss his plan. "First, let me say how grateful we are for your continued support, my brothers. Without your assistance, difficult missions like this could never succeed. But I regret for security purposes I cannot discuss specific details." Ahmed saw Rahim was visibly disappointed, reaching out with his hands, palms up, as if he wanted to literally pull information from Ahmed's body.

"Well, Ahmed, since you requested airline tickets to New York, can we assume you are planning your attack there?" Rahim asked, gently probing.

"Here is what I can share with you. Yes, our attack will occur in New York during the summer. We will rub the noses of the Americans and the British in the mud. We hope to kill as many infidels as we did in the World Trade Center attack and cause the greedy capitalists significant financial loss. Please understand, however, I cannot share our specific targets or attack method. One unintentional slip of the tongue, an intercepted phone call, anything like that could result in failure."

"We understand, Ahmed," replied Rahim with a resigned sigh. "What you have just told us whets our appetite for our enemies' blood, and we will pray to Allah for your success."

"Well, our success depends on me finding one more man, critical to our mission. That is my goal today."

"What kind of man are you seeking?" Ahmed paused before answering. The more details he revealed about the mission, the greater the chance a foreign intelligence service might intercept the information. But if Rahim or his associates could help him, it was worth the risk. Ahmed had decided to recruit only a single scuba diver, foregoing a backup, even though the diver's role was crucial to his plan's success.

"I need a scuba diver, a skilled commercial diver, not a casual recreational diver who just likes watching little fish swimming around. With so much construction in the port area I hope to find someone here. I don't suppose you would know such a man?"

"Unfortunately, no. But I can have someone drive you to the docks. Al Qaeda actually owns a marine salvage and construction company."

"I had no idea we were so diversified," replied Ahmed.

"Well, it provides us additional income. But more importantly, it's a training ground. With so many potential targets located in or under the world's oceans we need the capability to attack them," Rahim said, smiling. "I believe someone there can help you."

After they had finished tea and a light meal, Rahim motioned to one of his associates. He left with Ahmed and drove him to Al Qaeda's marine salvage company, located on a nearby pier.

After a 30-minute drive they arrived at a small, shabby building. "Not very impressive," remarked Ahmed.

"It is intended that way, to avoid unwanted attention," the driver replied. Ahmed nodded, realizing the strategy made sense. The driver opened the door, and they stepped inside. The large, dimly lit room contained dive helmets, hoses, boots and other commercial dive equipment, carelessly scattered about. Ahmed wrinkled his nose as if he smelled dead fish, looking around the room, decidedly unimpressed. The driver smiled at his reaction and beckoned Ahmed to follow. They walked down a narrow hallway and through a second door, which opened into another room inside a larger building. Ahmed's mood improved, noticing this room was well lit, air conditioned, and the dive equipment was stored in organized fashion. Wet suits and dry suits hung from racks in size order. On an opposing wall, various types of buoyancy vests hung, arranged by style and size. Regulators with depth and pressure gauges were stored on special racks at the far end of the room. Ahmed turned and saw an array of scuba tanks, he estimated at least 60, arranged upright along a long wall in an adjoining room. Most were single tanks, but he also saw several double-rigged tanks. Curious, he walked closer and noticed the tanks were grouped according to special markings and labels. Not being a diver, Ahmed had no idea what the labels meant. In fact, the tanks were segregated according to the gas they were designed to carry. Those containing regular air were sorted to the left. Tanks containing nitrox, a special blend, with less nitrogen and more oxygen than normal air, were in the center. Those containing more exotic tri-mix blends for deep diving, incorporating helium as a third gas, were grouped to the right. The divers would select the tank containing the appropriate air mix for their required depth or dive time.

Several men sat quietly at workbenches, assembling and repairing dive equipment. The driver approached an older man, Ahmed guessed about sixty-five, adjusting a dive helmet's faceplate. Ahmed watched him whisper in the man's ear. The older man smiled and motioned for the driver and Ahmed to follow him toward a small room. Inside, two young men were locked in an intense chess game. Ahmed, the driver and the older man watched and waited patiently. Twenty minutes later one player capitulated, tipping over his king. The older man tapped the winner's shoulder and spoke softly in his ear.

"Kalid, would you please speak with a special friend privately?" Kalid eyed Ahmed curiously as he rose. The two men stepped to a far corner of the room and sat at a table, directly across from each other.

They spoke quietly for several minutes. Across the room Ahmed's driver and the older man waited and watched, like expectant parents. Finally, they saw Kalid smile and nod affirmatively. Ahmed and Kalid rose and embraced.

Ahmed had found the last piece to his bizarre puzzle. Kalid Moqed was a highly skilled technical diver. But more importantly, he had assisted in the attack on the American destroyer USS Cole in Yemen seven years earlier, killing seventeen American sailors. Ahmed was pleased to have found the man he needed.

"I will pack my dive gear and be ready to leave immediately," Kalid said enthusiastically.

Ahmed smiled, appreciating the young man's eagerness. "I'm sorry Kalid. We have a long journey and must carry as little as possible. Furthermore, bringing dive equipment through our enemy's border could attract unwanted attention. Our contacts in America will help you purchase whatever you need." Ahmed saw Kalid frown and worried the young man might change his mind. Like most experienced divers, Kalid preferred using his own, familiar equipment. After a moment of silence, he spoke.

"I understand your concern, Ahmed. And I have faith that Allah would not let me follow you unless you could properly equip me for my mission." Smiling, they shook hands.

"I will pick you up at dawn tomorrow," Ahmed said.

The next morning Ahmed and his three-man terrorist team sat at a large table in Rahim's home. Rahim reached behind him and opened a large envelope, containing four smaller envelopes. He handed each man an envelope. "Inside are your plane tickets to America."

"These are roundtrip tickets, Rahim. You know we will probably not return," said Ahmed.

"Yes, we are aware you may sacrifice your lives for Allah. We purchased roundtrip because one-way tickets would call attention to you. That is a security flag, which may prompt additional scrutiny. You will fly from Jinnah airport in Karachi to Singapore to Frankfurt to JFK." As Ahmed nodded Rahim, continued. "Also inside each envelope is one thousand American dollars in cash. Any more might arouse suspicion if you are searched. If you need more money your New York contacts can give you all you need. You will also find passports, social security cards, driver's licenses and credit cards. That should be everything you require. Please sign everything before you leave for the airport." Each man studied his counterfeit identity documents.

"Rahim, how can we thank you?" asked Ahmed.

"By succeeding in your mission, Ahmed Mohammed," Rahim replied.

Chapter 18
Cozumel

June 17th

Joe was home alone, answering customer's e-mails when the telephone rang. "Hello," he said.

"Hey, Joe-boy, it's your former partner!"

"Bill? How the hell are you? I never expected to hear your voice today."

"You know I always pop up when you least expect it. How are you and the family?"

"We're all fine. The kids are in school and Terry should be home soon. She took a group out this afternoon for a single-tank wreck dive on the C-53, that old sunken minesweeper, where Oscar and his gang stashed their drugs several years ago. Remember?"

"How could I forget, old buddy? That was the most exciting adventure of my otherwise boring life," Bill said, laughing. "What are you doing now?"

"I dived with a large group this morning so I'm just catching up on some business."

"Ahh, you and your mermaid lead the perfect life."

"By the way, Bill, belated congratulations on your promotion. Do I call you Lieutenant Ryan now?"

"No, just Looey will do. But don't forget to kiss my ring next time you see me," answered Bill, laughing.

"So to what do I owe the honor of this call?" asked Joe.

"Well, Joe-boy, I'm calling in a chip. I figure you owe me a favor after the help I gave you restoring that damaged videotape during your murder investigation involving those pirate whalers in Iceland eight years ago."

"You have some memory, buddy. How can I help?"

"I need your assistance, and probably Terry's, regarding a security issue here in New York."

"That's a little out of our line, Bill. Investigating homicides and catching drug smugglers is where we shine," teased Joe. "Security's not really our bag. But we'll be happy to help if we can. What's up?"

"I need to speak with you in person, Joe," replied Bill, turning serious. "There's a a lot of information I can't divulge over a non-secure line. I'm flying to Cozumel tomorrow. Can you meet me at the airport?"

"You don't believe in giving much advance notice, do you," said Joe laughing. When Bill did not return the laugh, Joe realized the situation was grave. "Okay. We have a dive group tomorrow, but Terry can handle it alone. I'll pick you up. What time do you land?"

"US Airways, flight 1025 arriving at 1:15."

"Okay, I'll be waiting. Hey, say hello to my beautiful mermaid. She just walked in. Honey, it's Bill Ryan." Terry eagerly grabbed the phone.

"Bill! Great to hear from you. How've you been? When are we going to see you again?"

"Hello, Terry. I'm fine. Is tomorrow soon enough?" Terry blinked and looked at Joe. "Sorry it won't be a social visit. And apologies for the short notice. But I need some help from that ex-detective you married, and maybe from you, too."

"Well, whatever the reason you're coming it'll be good to see you again. You won't believe how much the children have grown since you saw them."

"Oh, I saw all of you on the *Today Show* recently. I almost forgot I'm talking to the Hollywood jet-set."

Terry laughed. "Blame these publicity hounds I live with. I had nothing to do with that fiasco."

"Anyway, it sounds like you had an exciting adventure. I can't wait to hear all about it in person. I'll see you tomorrow."

"Okay, Bill, see you then. Bye." Terry hung up the phone and turned to Joe. "What was that all about?" she asked.

"Bill needs help on a security assignment he's working on in New York. He couldn't talk about it over the phone. That's why he's flying down. How was your dive?"

"Great! Since Hurricane Wilma dragged the C-53 along the bottom the props are bent and the hull is split so now it looks more like a genuine shipwreck, less pristine than before. Everyone enjoyed swimming around inside the ship. It's still a safe dive, especially with the large entry and exit holes they cut into the ship. It'll be good to see Bill again, but I'm really puzzled about why he thinks we could help him."

"Well, I suppose we'll find out tomorrow." Joe stepped toward Terry, put his hands around her waist and nuzzled her ear. He whispered, "Hey, did I ever tell you how sexy you look in a tight wet suit and your long hair all wet?"

Terry drew a quick breath as her spine tingled responding to Joe's touch. "No, mister ex-detective, but you can show me." She arched her neck and held Joe tightly against her body, kissing him, darting her tongue between his lips. "The children won't be home for at least an hour." They went into the bedroom holding hands, and Terry closed the door.

Chapter 19

June 18th

Joe entered Cozumel's small international terminal just as the US Airways Airbus from Charlotte skimmed above the trees and touched down on the airport's single runway. *Good timing,* he thought. Then he noticed that the American Airlines flight from Dallas and the Delta flight from Atlanta had landed minutes earlier and were offloading passengers. There were no jetways, so he watched the tourists clambering down the portable metal stairways the ground crews had maneuvered into place. *This island is sure getting popular. With two planes ahead of Bill's it'll take him a while to clear immigration and customs. I better find a comfortable seat.* Joe was reading a magazine when Bill appeared minutes later. "Hey Joe!" he called out. Joe looked up, surprised.

"Bill! How did you clear immigrations and customs so . . . ," then he remembered. "Oh yeah, I forgot. You're on official business." The shook hands, and embraced warmly. "Good to see you, Bill."

"You too, buddy," replied Bill, recalling all the cases they had worked together. "I just waved my badge and eased through with the flight crew. Can't wait to see Terry."

"She'll be home from this morning's dives when we get back." They stepped from the air-conditioned terminal into the muggy afternoon heat; it was like walking through a steam bath. The strong Caribbean sun beat down, piercing puffy, cotton-like cumulous clouds. Bill squinted, fumbling for his sunglasses as Joe loaded

Bill's luggage, a single roll-aboard, into his car. "You sure travel light these days."

"It's a short visit. You and Terry today, Mexican officials tomorrow morning, then home the same night." Joe drove out of the airport and decided to take a route along the water. Bill gazed out the window. "What a view! Those Caribbean colors never cease to amaze me. Kinda like a painter on Prozac," he said, laughing. "And I can't wait to see your new digs. Not that your other place was too shabby, but from what you described this must be your dream home."

"Yeah, we were pretty lucky to find it. Actually our real estate agent Jaime found it for us."

"Really? You think he could find me and the wife a little vacation hideaway on a secluded beach?"

"Well, he's out of that business now, more or less semi-retired. He runs a glass-bottom boat for tourists who want to see the fish, coral and sponges without getting wet."

"Interesting. Maybe I'll take a boat ride with him time permitting." Their small talk continued as they drove along. *Wonder what kind of help Bill needs? Guess I'll wait until he's ready to tell us,* Joe thought, suppressing his not totally extinct interrogative instinct. They drove past the resorts along the southern beaches, the Allegro, the Grande, and finally a mile past the Iberostar resort they turned off the road onto a small path. They bounced along a choppy dirt road cut through the jungle for a couple of hundred yards and then broke into the open. Facing them was a two-story white stucco house with a Spanish tile roof and a sun deck facing the water. A large, kidney-shaped pool with a hot tub was near the house. Several tall palm trees shaded the pool deck. "Wow, what a shack! You did well, Joe-boy!" exclaimed Bill enthusiastically, slapping Joe's back.

"Thanks, Bill. We really enjoy it here. It's a great life. Let's go inside, have a drink and relax."

Terry greeted them at the door wearing a light, low-cut blouse, flowered tropical skirt and open-toed sandals. The ensemble flattered her tall athletic figure. Her long auburn hair was pulled back in a pony-tail. "Bill! Great to see you!"

"Hello, Terry. You look fabulous as usual," Bill said, lifting her off her toes and swinging her around. "Been battling any more drug dealers or pirate whalers since I saw you last?" he said laughing.

"Oh no, life's been pretty tame lately. Just been rescuing little lost children from undersea caves, that sort of boring stuff," she smiled back. "Drop your bag by the stairs and join us for margaritas on the patio. I just made a batch. On the rocks with salt okay?"

"Perfect. I always say, when in Rome, do as the Mexicans do," Bill replied, as Terry handed him a foamy margarita in a large frosted goblet. "Cheers!" he said, sipping his cold drink through a straw.

"Salud," replied Joe as the three clinked glasses.

Bill leaned back on the chaise lounge, rolled up his sleeves and basked in the warm sun. "This feels great, but I can't overdo it. Gotta be careful with this high-test sun, you know. My name doesn't end in a vowel like you *eye-talians*," he said, smiling at Joe.

"Just another jealous Mick," Joe replied, looking at Terry, who was laughing.

"You guys are too much. I wish I could have seen you two patrolling the mean streets of New York City together."

"Well, little lady," said Bill performing his best John Wayne imitation, "We made the streets safe for you women-folk and the young-uns."

"That right, Kemo Sabe," said Joe, not letting his former partner outperform him.

"Enough, you two! You guys can reminisce about your gun-slinging, wild-west days in the Big Apple by yourselves. Even though tonight it's Joe's turn to cook I'm granting him a reprieve in your honor, Bill."

Several minutes later Terry heard a van pull up. Jackie and Peter bounded through the door. "We're home!" Peter announced to the house.

"Hi kids," Terry said, kissing them. "Run outside and say hello to Dad and Uncle Bill. You haven't seen him for two years." The children ran past their father and into Bill's arms.

"Whoa, you two sure are a lot bigger than last time I saw you. I can't just scoop you up anymore," Bill said. "I heard all about your recent adventures. What else are you guys are up to these days?" He listened, wide-eyed as the children recounted their shark adventure.

Forty minutes later Terry called everyone inside for dinner. She had prepared lobster tails over fettuccini with alfredo sauce. Bill inhaled the aroma, and his eyes went wide admiring his plate. Then he twirled some fettuccini on his fork before plunging it into a juicy chunk of lobster. Jackie and Peter finished eating before the adults. "Children, please go into the family room and start your homework. When you're finished, right to bed." said Terry.

"Good night kids," said Bill, as Jackie and Peter hugged him and left the table. He glanced at Terry, then Bill. "Beautiful, and she can cook, too. What a combination. Hey Joe-boy, what did you do right to deserve her?"

"That's what happens when you rescue the damsel in distress," interjected Terry, stroking Joe's hair and playing off Bill's compliments.

"I better find some dragons to slay and damsels to rescue," remarked Bill.

"I won't tell your wife you said that," Terry said, laughing.

Joe poured properly chilled chardonnay, glanced at Terry, then asked Bill, "So how are things in New York these days, old buddy?"

"I see you haven't forgotten how to steer a conversation," said Bill. Joe smiled but just cocked his head, maintained eye contact and said nothing, one of his favorite former interrogation techniques. It still worked.

"Well, things are really hopping back home," replied Bill, not sure how to begin. He glanced at the children, busy doing their homework in the next room. He made eye contact with Terry, then Joe, drew a deep breath and leaned forward. "Okay, here's the scoop. We're dealing with a major terrorist threat. It seems the Feds, CIA specifically, received intelligence from a reliable source, one of their ground agents in Pakistan. Al Qaeda is planning to assassinate Queen Elizabeth when she visits New York City this coming July. A bizarre reference was made about strangling her with her necklace, or some other jewelry." He read Terry's and Joe's disbelieving expressions.

"Hey, it sounds weird to me, too. The threat also included comments about causing a large loss of life, economic disruption, and retaliation against the United States and Britain. But no specific targets were mentioned other than the Queen. Complicating the issue is that while she's in town so is the president, and numerous foreign dignitaries attending the Queen's United Nations address. Then, other U.S. politicians and diplomats will be officiating at various July Fourth celebrations around New York."

"So I gather they assigned you the unenviable task of defending multiple potential targets with limited resources," said Joe.

"Right. And there's one other potential target I forgot to mention. This is where I come in. On June 30th the Queen will visit the Queen Mary 2, which will have docked in New York several days earlier. She'll be hosting a reception aboard the ship. Some CIA big wig concluded that makes the QM2 a prime target."

"Sounds like a logical assumption," said Joe. "Imagine the world-wide impact of terrorists killing the Queen of England and sinking Britain's most famous ocean liner in New York City, right around America's Independence Day celebration."

"Thanks a lot for agreeing with him. Well, yours truly is responsible for that piece of security. I have to devise a plan protecting the QM2, at least until the Queen has left the ship. We certainly don't want the legacy of Queen Elizabeth's assassination in U.S. history books."

"And what's your plan?" asked Terry.

"Well, they could attack the ship several ways, by land, air or sea. Someone else is coordinating air coverage with the FAA, so that's not my concern. The land coverage I have pretty well figured out. That mainly involves blocking access from the West Side Highway and local streets. I can also close access from adjoining piers, isolating the QM2. But sea access is the problem. I can block boats from entering a restricted zone, at least above the water. But I need divers patrolling under the ship. It wouldn't be too difficult for a scuba diver to attach a mine to the hull."

"Hey Mom, what's *sasnation* mean?" asked Peter. Terry blinked, not realizing the children were listening from the next room. She jumped up.

"You two can finish your homework upstairs. Say good night!" she ordered.

"Aw Mom!" protested Peter.

"Kids! Up to your rooms. Now," said Joe, firmly. They reluctantly started up the stairs.

"You had to ask that stupid question," said Jackie frowning, scolding her brother.

After the children left, Joe and Terry glanced at each other. "Bill, you don't seriously expect Terry and me to . . ."

"Oh no, Joe, at least not directly. I have authority to utilize NYPD divers. They can cover the ship adequately. But it has to be a 24 by 7 effort. The problem comes at night. Underwater visibility in the Hudson River is poor enough during the day, five or ten feet at most. It's not like Cozumel, with your crystal clear water. At night it's even worse. Trying to cover an entire 1,000-foot ship in the dark is a nightmare. Underwater lights are almost useless. The water's too damn murky." Terry and Joe looked at Bill, puzzled. "What I need for night coverage are dolphins. Specifically, one particular dolphin."

Chapter 20
New York, JFK Airport

June 18th

Ahmed and his team were dispersed on the huge Singapore Airlines 747, as if each man traveled alone. Entering New York airspace the aircraft descended below 3,000 feet, passing over Montauk and following Long Island's south shore, heading west, toward JFK airport. Kalid dozed while Waleed and Salen looked down and watched rolling blue surf break along the Hamptons. Minutes later, at 2,000 feet, they flew over Fire Island, and then Jones Beach. Numerous beach umbrellas dotted the sand, appearing as little more than colorful periods on a page. Beneath the cheerful umbrellas were people they had never met and did not know, but hated anyway. Seated on the aircraft's left side, Ahmed looked down at the sea and the distant New Jersey coastline. Flying over Long Beach, the plane banked right, beginning its final landing approach, and Ahmed saw the Verrazano Bridge towers spanning the boroughs of Brooklyn and Staten Island. Farther in the distance he saw the steel, glass and concrete towers of Manhattan Island. Glancing at lower Manhattan he smiled, seeing a gap where he knew the World Trade Center's twin towers had once stood. *May Allah make my mission as successful,* he silently prayed. Ahmed felt a vibration as the landing gear extended and locked. The huge plane appeared to lumber through the sky as it slowed and descended, passing over the borough of Queens. Moments later, the tires screeched as the 300-ton aircraft hit the runway, bounced once, then settled into a roll. Four powerful General Electric engines roared as the pilot applied full reverse thrust, rapidly slowing the aircraft.

The four terrorists filed out separately, blending with the passengers moving through the International Arrivals terminal. They followed ramps leading to Immigration and Customs. Ceiling cameras recorded the passengers, feeding the video into a new facial recognition system. But the computers failed to match Ahmed's close-cut hair and beardless face to his image originally scanned from news photos and stored into the massive database over a year ago. Approaching Immigration they entered separate lines, passed cursory questions by Immigration Officers and proceeded to baggage claim. After retrieving their minimal luggage the four men followed arrows directing them toward the Customs line. But a Customs Inspector, who noticed a tick mark on Salen's immigration card, diverted Salen to a screening room. A suspicious Immigration Officer had marked his card with Immigration's secret daily code, recommending a thorough luggage search. Ahmed watched the officer accompany Salen into the private room. He and the team casually proceeded to the taxi stand and took separate cabs. Although Salen was the team's explosive expert, the mission would still continue if he were captured since Ahmed could also perform those tasks.

The Customs inspector instructed Salen to place his bags on a table. Salen spoke passable English but pretended not to understand, forcing the inspector to pantomime placing the bags on the table. Instructions were to play dumb and act pleasant if detained. He stepped back and watched the inspector rummage through his luggage, thankful he had followed orders to carry as little as possible. He would purchase what he needed for his mission in the U.S. Several minutes later the inspector repacked Salen's bags and pointed toward the exit. "Okay, you can go," he said.

Salen nodded, smiled and quietly said "thank you." His simple, friendly smile camouflaged deadly thoughts about slitting the inspector's throat. Salen walked outside, still smiling, and proceeded to the taxi line. Entering the first cab, he handed the driver a slip of paper. "Take me to this Brooklyn address, please."

Chapter 21
Cozumel

June 18th

Why do you need *one particular dolphin*, Bill," asked Terry warily, her internal threat senses heightened. She felt the tiny hairs on her freckled arms tingle.

Bill took another deep breath and paused, sensing he was treading on dangerous ground. "Well, several weeks ago I watched the *Today Show* story about how Notchka killed that shark, ramming it to death. So did many other people in New York. When Matt Lasker asked you about that earlier attack I remembered what happened during our drug investigation ten years ago. When I got this assignment I checked the files and refreshed my memory." Bill avoided eye contact with Terry and looked at Joe. "When that drug guy Oscar tried to kill Terry, Notchka killed him the same way she did that shark. So, I showed the old files to my boss, and also told him about what just happened recently. Seems he saw the *Today Show* story, too. He requested a copy of the tape from NBC and we watched it again, together. At first he thought I was nuts, but then he thought about it and agreed it could work."

"I agree with your boss' first assessment. You are nuts!" exclaimed Terry, her anger rising. "What are you going to do?

Kidnap a dolphin and fly it to New York?" Joe knew Terry was a moment from exploding and tried defusing the situation.

"Bill, this area is a national marine park. Taking wildlife or anything out of it, even a seashell, is strictly prohibited. The government would never allow it." Joe glanced at Terry and noticed she was calmer.

"Well, that's why I'm here. The U.S. State Department and Department of Homeland Security have already cleared it with the Mexican government. We already have permission to take a wild dolphin." Joe and Terry sat mute, staring at Bill, not believing what they had just heard. After several seconds Bill continued. "Of course, we don't know how to catch a wild dolphin. That's why we need your help."

Terry slammed her fist on the table so hard that Bill's half-full wine glass toppled into his lap. He grabbed a napkin as she exploded. "No fucking way, Bill!" He looked up, startled by the fury in her eyes, and her language. "You need our help because you'd never get close enough to catch Notchka. You know we could get close because she trusts us. I will never violate her trust. She saved my life. She saved my children's' lives. Now you're asking me to repay her kindness and devotion by dragging her into in your hare-brained scheme? I should risk her life by involving her in a human conflict? You're out of your . . ."

"Bill," Joe interjected, "Doesn't the U.S. Navy already have a dolphin or marine mammal program for this very purpose? I recall stories about dolphins trained to harpoon enemy divers in 'Nam."

"Yes, Joe. After I came up with my so-called 'hare-brained scheme'," Bill glanced at Terry, still glaring at him, "I did some research. Seems I wasn't far off the mark and not even the original thinker I thought I was. Besides dolphins the Navy has used pilot whales, beluga whales, even California sea lions, for many different tasks as far back as the 1960s. Even the Soviets used dolphins during the Cold War. The Navy uses them now for retrieving lost objects, underwater photography, planting mines, and marking hostile divers by attaching some sort of tag."

"Just *marking* divers?" asked Joe.

"Yes, although rumor has it the Navy has developed a swimmer nullification program, the Navy publicly denies dolphins are trained to kill hostile divers."

"What the hell is 'swimmer nullification'?" asked Terry.

Bill took a deep breath and continued. "Well, according to the rumor, a long hypodermic needle is fitted over the dolphins' snouts, and the needle is attached to a CO2 gas cartridge. They train the dolphins to ram enemy divers, automatically injecting them with gas, causing fatal damage."

"Nullification. A euphemism if I ever heard one," Terry said, rolling her eyes.

"Supposedly, now they're trained to just locate and mark suspicious divers for retrieval and questioning by authorities, who determine the captured subject's intentions and then take appropriate action."

"So if the U.S. Navy already has dolphins why your interest in Notchka?" asked Terry in an inquisitional tone.

"Well, as a first option we asked the Navy for assistance. But the Navy's interest in dolphins had been heightened after the October 2000 attack on the USS Cole in Yemen. Dolphins have been deployed to critical areas, and currently they're all slotted for the Middle East. The Navy just can't spare any dolphins on such short notice. Based on this situation we'll probably put in a standing order for future assistance. Due to restrictive U.S. laws we can't obtain any dolphins from marine parks like Sea World. . ."

"Thank God," remarked Terry

Bill continued, "and organizations like PETA . . ."

"People for the Ethical Treatment of Animals?" Terry asked, rhetorically, as Bill nodded.

". . . would be all over us and raise a public stink. We can't afford that now. And we don't have the luxury of time to catch and train a wild dolphin. I know Notchka's technically a wild dolphin, but she's used to people, at least to you two, and she already possesses the skills we need." After a moment of silence the volcano finally erupted.

"I'll never help you get your hands on her," Terry shouted, angrily pushing her chair back and leaving the table. "You two cowboys can wash the dishes. Good night," she said, storming upstairs and slamming the bedroom door.

Terry's outburst stunned Bill, and he turned to his friend. "Joe, we're talking about using an animal to save thousands of human lives. Can't you get that point through to her?"

"Bill, I understand what's at stake. But to Terry, Notchka's not just an animal. They have a personal relationship. I'll talk to her later. Give her a chance to cool down." He changed the topic. "What else has been going on since I left the Department?"

The two friends talked and reminisced late into the night. Finally, Joe said, "I'm turning in. See you tomorrow, buddy. Your room's at the top of the stairs on the left. But you better lock your door tonight," Joe said, grinning. "If something should happen to you there'd only be two suspects in the house, and I wouldn't be the guilty one."

Joe opened the door and stepped into the dark bedroom. He saw Terry sitting up in bed, her face lit by the television's reflected bluish glow. She still had not changed from her dinner outfit. "Joe, can you believe Bill's nerve? I'll never . . ."

"Terry, calm down. We have to discuss this."

"Discuss what, Joe? We'll never help him. We can't put Notchka's life at risk. What if . . ."

"Terry, I understand how you feel, but there's a much bigger picture to consider. We just can't . . ."

"*Bigger picture*! Joe, what the hell are you talking about? You sound just like him now. You can't be serious. You can't think that I'd ever endanger Notch . . ."

"All I'm saying is let's think about it. See what this entails, what assurances we can get that . . .'

"*Assurances*! You honestly think they can guarantee Notchka's safety? That she won't get hurt or killed?"

"Hon, I don't know yet. All I'm saying is . . ." Joe put his hand on Terry's shoulder, but she pulled away, turning her back. Her gesture shook him. In eight years of marriage she had never rejected his touch. "Terry, we can't dismiss the fact that there's a real threat out there. Thousands of people in New York might get killed, and Bill's doing his best to prevent that from happening. Who's to say someday we won't be facing the same threat? In fact, we already are. Look at all the airport security here now. Do you enjoy having strangers searching your luggage, piece by piece every time you board a plane? We never used to have Mexican Navy ships patrolling outside town." The automatic timer turned off the television. In the dark bedroom Joe heard Terry sobbing.

Joe undressed and slipped into bed. Normally, Terry would roll over, envelop him in her arms, kiss and snuggle. But tonight she remained on her side of the bed, her back toward him. Joe took a deep breath and sighed. This was the first major crisis of their otherwise storybook marriage. From the beginning, their relationship had been based on mutual trust, faith and respect. At that moment he didn't know how to restore the love that seemed to disappear in one angry evening.

Chapter 22
Brooklyn

June 18th

The taxi driver stopped at the address Ahmed had given him: 225 Nevins St., in downtown Brooklyn near Atlantic Avenue, the heart of Brooklyn's predominantly Arab section. The non-descript, three-story red brick apartment building in the middle of the block was attached to buildings on both sides. The street-level storefront had been converted to a garage, secured by a slide-down graffiti-covered steel door. Ahmed checked the address, walked to a door just left of the garage and pressed the buzzer. Seconds later an intercom in the doorframe above his head sparked alive. "Yes, who is it?"

Ahmed looked up at the intercom speaker. "My name is Ahmed Mohammed. I have brought you a gift."

"What kind of gift?" asked the owner of the intercom's voice.

"A beautiful necklace," Ahmed replied.

Satisfied that the correct code words had been exchanged, the intercom's electronic voice said, "Please wait. I'll be right down." Moments later Ahmed noticed a flicker behind a peephole, then heard a bolt slide and a lock turn. The door opened and Ahmed stepped inside. Ashur Sharib, a 73-year-old Syrian gentleman, the building's owner, warmly embraced him. "Welcome, my brother. I have heard much about you." The two had never met. Sharib's massive arms engulfed the physically diminutive Ahmed. Six-foot-two and robust, with a shock of wavy steel-colored hair, Sharib could easily pass for a man ten years younger. He led Ahmed upstairs to a large second-floor room. "We have been expecting you. Your team arrived a half-hour earlier. We were concerned you had gotten lost."

"My taxi driver was confused by the directions, but I finally arrived. We expected to meet a larger group," replied Ahmed.

"Others will join us for this evening's prayers. My job is to make you comfortable. We will support your needs."

"What we need most is sleep. We've had a long journey," he said, noticing Kalid, Salen and Waleed relaxing on plush sofas, their tired eyes reduced to slits. They appeared as if they might fall asleep at any moment. "Thank you for your hospitality and for offering us the use of your home."

"This is not my home. I prefer thinking of this as my office," replied Ashur, smiling. "I also own another building a short distance away on Sackett Street. That is my home."

"I see," said Ahmed. Refocusing on his mission, he said, "I will prepare a list."

"Fine," replied Ashur, handing Ahmed a notebook and pen. "Just write down what you need, and then rest. We will obtain whatever you require."

Ashur Sharib was the front man for the Al Qaeda terror cell, which had financed the building's purchase. The cell also financed building renovations, far beyond cosmetic and structural repairs. All entrances and exits had been fortified with bulletproof doors. The top two floors had been completely gutted and re-built with sleeping quarters for twenty men, with separate accommodations for women. Microwave relay antennas were hidden inside false chimneys and roof-top vent pipes. The main floor had been converted into a small garage and work area. Behind the garage was a large open space, used for prayer, dining and socializing. The basement had been lined with lead sheathing to defeat nuclear detection devices. The rear half was walled off for mixing explosives and assembling detonating devices.

Later that evening, young men in their twenties and thirties began filtering in from the street. Many held low-profile jobs in the community. Others did not work, at least not in the usual definition of work. Their jobs consisted of gathering information and developing plans for when Al Qaeda would activate their cell. The men assembled in the large main room. They spread prayer rugs on the floor, and Ashur Sharib led them in evening prayers. Upstairs, the four-man terrorist team slept soundly, though Ahmed tossed and turned while he dreamed. Images of explosions, bloody limbs flying through the air, and dying men, women and children screaming, floated through his sleeping brain, a nightmare for a sane person. For Ahmed, these were sweet dreams.

Chapter 23
Brooklyn

June 19th

The next morning Ahmed handed Ashur his shopping list. "This is what we need. Waleed, Salen and I must scout the actual locations so I can refine my plans. There is only so much you can determine from reconnaissance photos and video."

"I agree," replied Ashur, scanning Ahmed's list. "We can easily obtain most of these items. But you need such large quantities of some materials it may take additional time."

"Unfortunately, time is a luxury we do not have. Our target date is only two weeks away." Ashur took the list, read it and tore it into two pieces. He called in two of his most reliable and resourceful men.

"This is Hossein and Ali. They will procure what you need." He turned, facing the two men, and gave each part of Ahmed's shopping list. "Okay, here is what you must get for our brothers. Ahmed's mission depends on you obtaining this material. Go." After they left Ashur called another cell member into the room. He fished in his pocket and withdrew a set of car keys and a business card with the name of a scuba shop. "Here, Fahid. Use my car. Take Kalid to this store to buy his dive equipment." The cell members left separately.

Fahid drove along Atlantic Avenue to the Brooklyn-Queens Expressway, known to New Yorkers as the BQE, then took the eastbound Long Island Expressway. Looking out the window as they drove through Brooklyn, Queens and into Long Island, Kalid was amazed at the dense traffic and numerous stores filled with shoppers. Smiling, he thought, *So many targets for future missions.* Forty minutes later, they arrived at Scuba Network, a popular scuba shop located in the Long Island hamlet of Carle Place. Martha, the owner, was speaking with a customer purchasing a set of split fins when they entered the store.

"Good morning," she said, smiling as they passed the cash register. Fahid avoided eye contact, looking straight ahead. Kalid ignored Martha's friendly welcome and simply threw her a dismissive glance as he walked toward a wall display of buoyancy compensator vests. Bob, the store manager, was arranging a display of newly arrived scuba fins. A grizzled diver on the wrong side of sixty, Bob was happiest when underwater exploring a deep wreck, or throwing lobsters into his bug-bag for dinner. His idea of heaven was an eternal dive in Truk Lagoon. He approached Fahid and Kalid.

"Can I help you?" Bob offered, in a friendly manner.

"If I need your help I'll let you know," replied Kalid, rudely. Bob hadn't been underwater in three weeks and hadn't tasted lobster in a month. Consequently, he was unusually cantankerous and short on patience. Bob turned on his heels and walked away. "What a jerk," he muttered, under his breath. Kalid knew exactly what he wanted. He preferred Italian equipment, so he selected a weight-integrated Cressi BC vest. Then he stepped over to a rack of wetsuits. Even in July, Northeast water is cool below the surface. So he bought a 7-mil (one-quarter-inch) thick Henderson wetsuit, their more expensive, but very comfortable, *hyperstretch* model. Then, Kalid looked around the store but did not see the one piece of equipment he really wanted. He turned, looking for Bob. But Bob had decided to busy himself inspecting tanks. Kalid beckoned Martha. His unfriendly manner had piqued her curiosity, and she was watching him from the corner of her eye. She noticed him waving her over.

"Hello, I'm Martha. How can I help you?"

"Yes. I need a re-breather. I want a self-contained system with a full-face mask that can be equipped with a communications module. Do you carry such equipment?" he asked sharply. Martha noticed the two men were very serious. They did not exude the usual carefree, happy demeanor of most dive customers, who are purchasing equipment for an upcoming tropical vacation or local wreck diving. She attempted lightening the mood with some humor.

"A re-breather? Are you looking for extra bottom-time or just trying to hide your bubbles from someone?" she inquired, laughing. Kalid did not laugh but froze her with an icy stare. Martha felt a chill run up her spine. She decided humor was not appropriate with this customer. She simply replied, "I'm sorry, but I don't stock re-breathers. I can order one for you, however, and have it here within a week."

"Not good enough. I need it immediately." Kalid said, abruptly. He did not want to leave his name or contact information. Annoyed, he thought, *So much for Ahmed's thorough planning. If I couldn't bring my own equipment he should have let me order what I need earlier.* He walked over to the scuba tank display and selected a black steel 120 cubic foot tank, instead of a smaller, standard aluminum 80 cubic foot capacity tank. "I'll take that one," he pointed. *That should give me enough air for my mission. I'll just risk that my bubbles won't be seen at night*, he thought, shaking his head.

Turning back to Martha, Kalid asked, "Do you have an AGA MKII full-face mask?"

"Not in stock. I can order it for you." As he began shaking his head Martha continued enthusiastically, trying to close a major sale. "But I do have an excellent Poseidon full-face mask. It includes a second stage regulator and can be fitted with a communications module."

"I suppose that will do," Kalid sighed. He turned to a wall display and selected additional gear. "I want that, and that," Kalid said matter-of-factly, pointing to a Cressi octopus rig with gauges and an air-integrated computer. While Martha was pulling the items from stock Kalid selected a set of Mares open-heel fins and booties. Finally he purchased a spare-air pony bottle, used for out-of-air emergencies. Kalid was a careful diver who always prepared himself for unforeseen situations. He intended living through his mission. Martha was surprised someone would purchase so much equipment at once. She was shocked when the diver paid cash for the entire purchase, $2,969.75, including tax. Very few divers walked into her store and peeled off thirty $100 bills paying for equipment. She was thrilled with a major cash sale, since no percentage would be siphoned off to MasterCard. But the disturbing vibrations she felt from her encounter with Kalid unsettled her. Consequently, she was not above engaging in some politically incorrect racial profiling. She observed the two men appeared Middle Eastern. Martha noted Kalid's accent, but she couldn't place the country. After they left the store, she rummaged through her business card Rolodex file until she found the card she was looking for: Special Agent Thomas McHale, Federal Bureau of Investigation.

The FBI had started visiting scuba shops in the New York area after 9/11, requesting they collect social security numbers of customers signing up for diving lessons and report anything suspicious. New York City is a potential terrorist shooting gallery. First, there are obvious aboveground targets: bridges, government and private buildings and landmarks, like the Statue of Liberty. In addition, there are numerous underwater targets: the Lincoln Tunnel, the Holland Tunnel, the Brooklyn-Battery Tunnel, the Queens-Midtown Tunnel, and train tunnels under the Hudson and East Rivers servicing Amtrak, the Long Island Railroad, and New Jersey Transit, each carrying tens of thousands of commuters daily.

"Special Agent McHale, how can I help you?" he said, answering on the second ring.

"Hello Tommy? Martha from Scuba Network."

"Martha! Good to hear from you. What's up?"

"I just thought you should know two men I've never seen before bought over $2,900 worth of dive equipment just now. In cash."

"Interesting. Anything else unusual about them?"

"Well, they looked like, you know, Middle–Eastern, early to mid-twenties. They were very serious, not like my usual customers.

And one man asked me about purchasing a re-breather. I just caught some bad vibes, you know?"

"Interesting. Okay, did you get their social security numbers?"

"No. If you recall you stopped asking us for that information last year. But when I helped them carry their stuff to their car, I got the license plate number."

"Hey, good girl! Read it to me." Agent McHale copied the New York State plate number. "Great. Let me know if they come back. Bye, Martha, and thanks."

Ali stopped at a Radio Shack electronic store. Reading Ahmed's list he asked for long cable wire, certain types of communication equipment, batteries, electronic transmitters and receivers. The manager noticed the customer didn't know much about the equipment he was purchasing. The manager tried to help and inquired about the intended use, so he could suggest the best brands or type of equipment. He thought it strange that the customer became evasive, paid cash and left quickly.

Hossein, drove his van along the Brooklyn-Queens Expressway, over the Williamsburgh Bridge to Manhattan, then took the Holland Tunnel to the New Jersey Turnpike to Route 80 and then headed west toward Pennsylvania farmland. His shopping list called for ammonium nitrate fertilizer, diesel fuel and steel barrels. He purchased small amounts at several different farm supply outlets to avoid suspicion about buying a large amount of potential bomb-making material at one time. He repeated the trip several times during the week, purchasing more material in Pennsylvania, and western New Jersey, until he had finally procured the required amounts.

Chapter 24
Cozumel

June 20th

The next morning, Joe and Bill rose early and ate breakfast on the patio. The breezeless morning turned the sea glassy smooth. For several moments neither spoke, each privately contemplating the scene. The rising sun reflecting off the varying sea bottom through crystal water produced intermingled color shades, unlike any on a painter's palette. Pale turquoise indicated a shallow, white sandy bottom. Dark blue water broken by green hues meant a sea-grass meadow grew below. Royal blue water was deep. Both men turned hearing a loud splash as a brown pelican dove like a missile, capturing a seafood breakfast in his basket-like bill. They watched as the bird wriggled a fish down his gullet. Finally, Bill inquired, "Did Terry say anything else last night?"

"No. In fact she avoided me all night. In the entire time we've been married I've never seen her so upset," Joe replied, shaking his head.

"I truly hope I haven't caused a problem between you two, Joe." Just then Terry walked out on the patio with a cup of coffee. She passed the two men without saying a word and sat on a chaise lounge, quietly staring at the ocean. For several awkward minutes no one spoke. Then she turned to Bill.

"If, and I'm just saying if, we decide to help you, what would be involved?" Terry asked.

"Well, with your assistance, we'd locate Notchka. Then we'd transport her to New York."

"How?"

"The Navy has detailed procedures for transporting marine mammals long distances. Dolphins are placed in soft, fleece-lined stretchers to avoid abrading their sensitive skin. The stretchers are suspended in fiberglass containers filled with sufficient water to support the animal's weight. A vet also accompanies the animal and monitors its condition the entire trip."

"What happens when you reach New York?"

"We've made arrangements to keep her in a large holding tank at the New York Aquarium in Coney Island. They used the tank for dolphin performances, but there are no dolphins there anymore. After acclimating, she'd be transported to a netted area in the Hudson River, next to the pier where the QM2 is berthed. Then she'd patrol the area around the ship at night and return to her enclosure during the day."

Will she survive the environment? I can't imagine Notchka swimming in cold, polluted water."

"Well, in July the water's not extremely cold in New York. It ranges from the mid-60s to the mid-70s. And with all the pollution control, the water's pretty clean now. In fact, during summer it's not unusual to see dolphins off Long Island or even in New York Harbor occasionally."

Terry raised an eyebrow, skeptically. "What about food? Notchka's a wild dolphin. She won't eat dead fish like captive dolphins."

"She'll have the best live fish available, every day."

"What about crowds. When they hear about a live dolphin living in the Hudson you'll have mobs swarming continually."

"That part's easy. We'll cut off waterfront access for the duration the QM2 is docked. This is a top-secret operation, anyway. We won't be advertising the fact she's even there. In addition, we'll cover her enclosure with an opaque tent, like a tennis bubble."

"What about Joe and me? Remember, Notchka trusts *us*. We need to be with her."

"No problem, Terry. You and Joe can certainly accompany her to New York and back."

"Sorry, Bill. Not good enough." Bill looked at Joe, and then Terry. He waited for Terry to explain. "One of us will be in the water with her when she's on duty. I won't let her patrol that ship alone."

"Well, Terry, I don't know. We have a large team of very skilled NYPD divers. They'll be in charge and they have procedures, rules and regula . . ." Terry cut him off sharply.

"That's it, Bill. Either we're in the water with Notchka or no deal. Take it or leave it." Terry rose and left the patio. Bill just stared at her as she closed the door, then he turned to Joe.

"Joe. . ."

"Sorry, Bill. I know my wife. When she makes up her mind, that's it. Negotiations are over. You'd better escalate that issue back at the ranch."

"I guess I'll have to," he said.

"Come on, I'll give you a lift to your meeting with the Federales." Bill looked for Terry to say goodbye, but she had gone upstairs on the sundeck. He let out a deep breath, feeling as though he had just been grilled by a congressional committee.

Returning home, Joe walked upstairs where Terry was meditating, staring at the sea. "Penny for your thoughts," he said.

"I was just remembering the days when Notchka and her pod visited our cove during their fishing expeditions and played with us and the children. I was almost afraid they'd appear while Bill was giving us his pitch. I'm wondering if I made the right decision to help them."

"You did, Ter. I know it wasn't easy. It's not pleasant, but it's something we must face. And if they don't agree to your final condition we won't do it. I'll back you 100 percent."

"Still, if anything happens to Notchka, I'll never forgive myself. Or you," she said, locking eyes with Joe.

Chapter 25

For the next three days, The *Dorado* and the *Santa Rosa*, a larger boat used by Chankanaab National Park personnel to catch dolphins for their popular, and profitable, S*wim With Dolphins Program* patrolled Cozumel's southern tip and east toward the open Caribbean. The dolphin catcher had a small crane for hoisting marine mammals from the water into a specially designed water-filled tank in its hold. "Three days and no dolphins, Terry," said Manuel, the *Dorado's* captain. "Perhaps they know we're trying to take Notchka away from them."

"I don't think so, Manuel. Dolphins are pretty smart creatures, but I don't think they're clairvoyant." Manuel stared at her with an inquiring look. "I mean they can't read your mind," Terry explained as Manuel nodded, comprehending. Terry checked her watch. "Well, it's getting late. Let's head home. It'll be seven by the time we reach the marina." Suddenly the radio crackled. Jaime Rameriz's voice shouted through the speaker. "*Dorado, Dorado,* this is the *Jolly Mon.* Over." Manuel picked up the receiver.

"*Jolly Mon* this is *Dorado.* Hola, Jaime. Over."

"Dolphins just passed us near Palancar Reef heading south. Over." Terry ran to the bow and ripped the microphone from Manuel's hand.

"Jaime, it's Terry! Can you tell if Notchka is with them? Over."

"Hola, Terry. I think so. One dolphin had a notch in its fluke. Over."

"Gracias, Jaime. Well try to intercept them. Okay, Manuel, turn north. We should see them in about ten minutes."

Joe waved to the *Santa Rosa* and shouted. "Dolphins! Follow us." The *Dorado* heeled around 90 degrees and the *Santa Rosa* followed. Terry and Joe donned wetsuits, masks and snorkels, and weight belts to offset their wetsuits' buoyancy. Fifteen minutes later Joe pointed and shouted, "Dolphins at two o'clock!" Ahead, four dorsal fins broke the surface off *Dorado's* starboard bow. Soon, five additional dorsal fins joined them. "Looks like they're feeding," Joe observed, as the dolphins dived repeatedly in one location. Terry and Joe jumped off the stern and swam toward the dolphins. Without the annoying bubbles from scuba tanks the dolphins readily accepted their company. Suddenly Terry was gently bumped. She turned and saw a large dolphin next to her. The dolphin swam to the bottom, 40 feet below. Terry saw the familiar notched fluke. She sucked a deep breath and followed Notchka down to 20 feet. The dolphin returned carrying a two-foot long seaweed strand in her mouth. She released it in front of Terry, who grabbed it, surfaced for a quick breath and swam away. Notchka followed but did not swipe the seaweed back until Terry intentionally dropped it. This was the game of *keep away*, according to dolphin etiquette.

The game continued for 15 minutes. Finally, Terry rested at the surface, swimming close to the *Santa Rosa*. She slapped the water with her open palm, and Notchka swam to her. She stroked the dolphin, holding her close until the *Santa Rosa* had lowered the sling in front of them. Terry swam through the sling. Notchka followed, but when she was inside Terry stopped, blocking her exit. The sling was raised and Notchka was caught. She flapped her tail fluke, squealed and whistled, agitated by her confinement in the strange object. Terry stroked her forehead calming her and pulled her pectoral fins through holes in the side of the sling. The dolphin calmed, trusting Terry would not harm her. Then the sling was slowly hoisted and swung over the tank in the *Santa Rosa's* hold. By the time the sling was lowered into the tank, Terry was beside Notchka, speaking softly and stroking her. Gemini and the other dolphins squawked and chirped, confused by their matriarch's disappearance. The *Santa Rosa* pulled away from the *Dorado* and headed toward the Navy Pier in San Miguel. The dolphin pod followed for a mile, then broke off and departed for deeper water. In San Miguel, Notchka's specially designed tank was transferred to a truck. The captive dolphin, Terry and Joe rode to Cozumel Airport, where a U.S. Navy Hercules C-130 cargo plane whisked them on the first leg of their New York City journey.

Chapter 26
Washington, D.C.
F.B.I. Headquarters, The J. Edgar Hoover Building

June 23rd

Hello, this is Special Agent Tom McHale. Bill Ryan, NYPD, are you on the line?"

"Yes, Tom, I'm here."

"Jeff Becker, CIA, are you there?"

"Yes, I'm patched in."

"Great! Glad you both could join us. By the way, today's call is on a special STE line."

"Please enlighten us," requested Bill.

"Stands for Secure Telephone Equipment," explained Tom. "It's encrypting our conversation as we speak. The Bureau's using it more frequently. You never know who's listening to whom these days."

"I get it. Kind of like, *Spy versus Spy*," cracked Bill.

"Who?" asked Jeff.

"You know, the *Spy versus Spy* cartoons in *MAD* magazine," Bill said, chuckling.

"Don't think I ever read . . ."

"Anyway, gentlemen!" Tom interjected, regaining control of the conversation, "I initiated this call to keep everyone in the loop regarding information I learned last week. A Long Island scuba shop owner called me and reported two people who appeared Middle Eastern bought a lot of diving equipment."

"What's unusual about that?" Bill asked. "Just because people with an olive complexion buy dive equipment, that doesn't make them terrorists."

"Several things were unusual. First, they bought a lot of equipment all at once.

Most people purchase a few items at a time. Buying all your equipment at once is a pretty substantial investment. Second, the owner had never met either one before. Divers usually patronize a store where they know the staff and feel comfortable with their recommendations. You know, it's a relationship thing. Third, they paid cash for everything, almost 3,000 bucks. One guy just peeled off thirty crisp 100-dollar bills. And one more thing. The guy who was actually selecting the stuff purchased some very specialized equipment. He bought a type of full-face mask rigged so he could talk to another diver underwater or someone on the surface. He also wanted a re-breather. Either of you know anything about that type of equipment?"

"A little," replied Jeff Becker, laconically.

"I don't," said Bill Ryan. "But I know someone I can ask and get back to you."

"Okay, thanks. That'll be helpful," replied McHale. "Oh, and one more thing, Jeff. Tell your boss his hunch about an underwater attack against the QM2 is currently in first place on our betting list."

"Will do. He'll appreciate that. Nice guy, but he loves gloating," said Becker laughing. "What about next steps?"

"Well, the scuba shop owner got the license plate while they were loading the equipment into their car. We ran the number, and the car is registered to some guy in Brooklyn. We're applying for a search warrant."

"That was a lucky break," replied Becker.

"Yeah. Luck helps. Well, thanks for making time for the call, everyone," said FBI Special Agent McHale. "We'll keep you posted."

"Hey, we appreciate the information," replied Ryan.

"Yeah, looks like these new inter-agency communication policies are working after all. Too bad it took 9/11 to make it happen," said CIA Agent Becker.

"Ditto. 'Till next time, gentlemen."

Chapter 27
Houston, Texas

June 23ʳᵈ

The Navy Hercules prop plane touched down at Houston International Airport, a short stopover to transfer its live cargo to a faster military cargo jet for the longer New York leg of the trip. Terry and Joe deplaned through a special area where they could clear Immigration and Customs quickly and stopped at a restaurant for a late supper. Spreading ketchup over a medium-rare burger, Terry said, "Notchka seems okay, Joe. I was worried the air pressure changes might bother her."

"Yeah, me too, but the vet onboard said she's taking it like a trooper. You should relax a little."

"I'm trying, but worrying about her, how the kids are doing back home and our dive business. It's our livelihood, Joe. I . . ."

"The kids are fine. They're in their own house and Jaime is looking after them. And your buddy Cozumel Kelly said she'd give Jaime a hand, cooking, getting the kids settled for bed, whatever help he needs."

"Yes, she's been a godsend. Whenever I've needed help Coz has always been right there."

"I've always been fascinated with her name. She sounds like a Caribbean legend or something."

"Well, she just made the name up for business purposes. The alliteration works and people remember it. Her real name's Kelly McGuire."

"And you know her from the states?"

"Yes, from my USC undergrad days. We were just casual friends, not real close. We lost track of each other, but one day I ran into her in San Miguel. She's done pretty well with her condo rental business, giving tourists an alternative to bland hotels. She's become quite the American ex-pat. Speaks Spanish almost like a native, and she really loves Cozumel."

"Well the kids like her, and she likes them, so I'm okay with the four of them being back home together. As far as our dive business is concerned we're in good shape. We referred our customers to good dive operators, and Manuel can transfer new bookings to them."

"You're right. But you know *DiveWithTerry* is more than just a business to me. I started it, and it's like my other baby."

Joe smiled and looked at his watch. "I know. Hey, the pilot said the other aircraft should be ready to leave in an hour. We should head over there."

"Okay, let me call home first. I'll catch up with you." Fifteen minutes later Terry joined Joe as he was boarding the military cargo jet. "All's okay back home. Kelly cooked up one of her famous seafood pasta dishes and left after she and Jaime put the kids to bed. Jaime'll sleep in the guest room."

"See? I told you not to worry. Get aboard, and we're out of here."

Three and a-half hours later they landed at New York's JFK airport. Notchka was transferred to a specially designed truck and whisked away to the New York Aquarium, in Brooklyn's Coney Island section. Bill Ryan met Terry and Joe, and they followed the truck in his unmarked police cruiser. The aquarium's director, William Hartford, met them. "Greetings. Mr. and Mrs. Manetta, let me show you your dolphin's temporary accommodations."

"Thank you, but please, call us Terry and Joe, all right?" requested Joe.

"Fine by me. Come this way." Hartford led them to a large oval tank, 30 feet across and 90 feet long, in a stadium setting. "This is where we used to hold our dolphin shows, but we haven't kept dolphins here for several years. Now we use it for sea lion shows and other exhibitions. Notchka will have plenty of room, and we can quickly train her for her assignment."

"I thought you told us there wasn't sufficient time to train a wild dolphin," Terry asked Bill.

"There isn't," he replied. "Although Notchka has some relevant experience in similar situations, we need to train her to recognize an enemy diver. In her wild setting she can identify natural threats under specific conditions. For example, when her son was killed and when you were in danger. And more recently, when the shark threatened Gemini and attacked your children. But this is different. We need to train her to recognize what *we* identify as a threat. She wouldn't recognize a diver carrying a limpet mine as an enemy or a threat unless we conditioned her to identify it as such and act accordingly."

"What do you mean by 'act accordingly,' Bill? I won't let you turn Notchka into a killing machine."

"Oh, we might train her to perform a specific action, such as signaling an enemy is below by leaping over his location. Or, maybe take direct action by bumping the diver. She already knows how to do that."

Terry looked hard at Bill, pursing her lips as she assessed his answer, hoping she could trust him. "Well, she'll arrive in a few minutes. I'll put my wet suit on and get into the water."

Minutes later, a truck rumbled through the entrance and pulled into the stadium. A wide gate swung open and the truck backed up to the pool edge. The truck bed tilted slightly and the tank slid slowly into the pool. Hinged sides opened, and Notchka slipped out. She remained still, just floating, confused by unfamiliar surroundings. Then she saw Terry and swam to her, clicking and whistling. Terry stroked Notchka's skin, whispering to her. They swam together, exploring the pool. Several small live sea bass and mackerel were tossed in. They watched her dive to the bottom and snap up two fish. "Guess she was hungry. I think she'll be okay tonight. It's warm so I'll dry off and sleep out here next to the tank."

Chapter 28
The Atlantic Ocean

June 24th

S hortly after sunrise, Commodore Ian Smyth, cut the Queen Mary 2's 157,000 horsepower gas turbine engine, slowing the massive ship. Then he blew her foghorn. Anyone within a ten-mile radius heard the deep bass tone. The sleek black and white ship was nearing New York Harbor after a transatlantic crossing from her homeport, Southampton, England. From several miles at sea the passengers' only indication they were approaching New York was the sight of two thin towers jutting from the ocean's surface at the horizon. Nearing the harbor they saw the towers were joined by a long, graceful steel span, the Verrazano-Narrows Bridge, linking Brooklyn and Staten Island at a location called 'The Narrows.' Appropriately named, the site forms the bay's narrowest point, forming a natural gateway through which virtually all passenger vessels, freighters and tankers pass into New York harbor.

As the ship approached Ambrose Light, off the New Jersey coastline, passengers crowding the outside decks watched a small grey boat rapidly approach. Aboard was a New York harbor pilot who would guide the QM2's Commodore safely through the harbor's shoals and tricky currents, ensuring an uneventful docking. The pilot boat approached the ocean liner, now almost still, kept pace, and 34-year-old harbor pilot Jim Archer nimbly jumped into an open hatch in the ship's side. "Welcome aboard, sir," saluted a young seaman, sent to escort Archer to the QM2's bridge.

"Good day, sir," Archer said, as Commodore Smyth turned to greet him. Smyth had been a Cunard Lines employee his entire 40 year career, working his way up from seaman to First Officer, and had commanded ocean liners for the past 20 years. Now, nearing retirement, he had been named the QM2's Commodore. Archer thought Smyth resembled old news photos of the Titanic's Captain, projecting a stern countenance but minus the old Captain's abundant facial hair. Smyth was just over six feet tall, stout, with a ruddy complexion, thick, neatly styled hair white hair and long, sharply trimmed sideburns.

"I have a schedule to maintain, Mr. Archer. Let's get moving," ordered Smyth, brusquely. The harbor pilot assisted him navigating past Sandy Hook, New Jersey, a spit of land protruding into the outer bay. Keeping the QM2 in the middle of Ambrose channel, they skirted the dangerously shallow Romer shoal. The Verrazano's 4,260-foot span, 60 feet longer than San Francisco's fabled Golden Gate Bridge, loomed ahead. Passengers looked up, gawking, expecting the QM2's tall red stack to scrape the bridge's bottom deck. Entering the harbor at high tide, the ship eased under the bridge's double-decked roadway, suspended 280 feet above the choppy bay, with only 18 feet to spare. The Brooklyn waterfront was on the right, Staten Island to the left, and Manhattan Island lay dead ahead.

Nearing the southern tip of Manhattan, the harbor pilot instructed Smyth to steer slightly to port, toward the Hudson River. The ship passed the Statue of Liberty, the folds of its green copper sheathing vividly detailed by the golden morning sun. Several minutes later the QM2 slowly brushed past Ellis Island, the entry point for nearly 12 million immigrants between 1852 and 1954. Dozens of returning American passengers stood along the ship's left side, staring silently at Ellis Island's restored landmark buildings. Many wondered how their grandparents must have felt arriving from Europe, packed aboard much more humble ships a hundred years earlier. Passengers glimpsed the East River on the right, technically an estuary branching off from New York harbor, along Manhattan's east side. Looking up the East River they enjoyed a postcard view of the picturesque Brooklyn Bridge, spanning lower Manhattan and Brooklyn. Completed in 1883, it is the oldest and most distinctive of New York's bridges, supported by stone towers and spider web of steel cables. Entering the Hudson, the ship passed Manhattan's financial district. The passengers crossed the deck and lined the ship's starboard rails to view New York's West side and famous skyscrapers. The crowd became hushed, almost reverent, as the QM2 passed the World Trade Center complex at Ground Zero. As the ship proceeding up the Hudson River and passed West 34th Street, cameras clicked and beeped as first-time tourists and returning New Yorkers snapped photos of the Empire State Building's elegant, slim profile. After Al Qaeda destroyed the Trade Center's Twin Towers, the landmark building reclaimed its status as New York's tallest and most famous skyscraper. Several minutes later the ship reached her final destination, pier 92, located at the foot of 52nd St. and 12th Avenue. She eased into her berth bow-first as three small but powerful red McAllister tugs helped the QM2's hi-tech directional propellers perform a tight ninety-degree pivot. After the liner completed the intricate docking maneuver, longshoremen secured the giant ship to the pier with huge ropes, each thicker than a man's fist. Her stern overhung the pier, like a tall basketball player trying to fit into a standard-sized bed.

Chapter 29
Downtown Brooklyn

June 24th

In the basement of their safe house, Ahmed and his operatives examined the equipment procured with Ashur Sharib's assistance. Kalid familiarized himself with his dive equipment, assembling and disassembling the pieces. He spent considerable time carefully filing off serial numbers and other identifying markings. In another corner, Salen worked on the magnetic limpet mine that Kalid would attach to the QM2's steel hull. "Look at this," he said holding the circular thirteen-pound deadly device like a proud father. "They were able to get us a Meindeka mine, the most technologically advanced mine available on the international market. It's so beautiful I almost hate blowing it up," he said caressing its gray fiberglass housing. Next to him, Waleed tested the specialized electronic transmitting and receiving equipment, crucial to Ahmed's plan.

In the garage several men mixed diesel fuel and ammonium nitrate in special barrels, according to Ahmed's instructions. Others shaped Semtex, a plastique explosive, to fit around the barrels and into key structural areas. Ahmed, Ashur and a third conspirator, a respected physics professor at a local university, were hunched over a table covered with blueprints and schematic drawings.

Ahmed anxiously watched the professor entering information into a Hewlett Packard scientific calculator. Finally the professor declared, "According to these blueprint specifications, you will need almost double the amount of explosives you estimated."

"Impossible!" exclaimed Ahmed. "I checked my calculations three times. I could not have been wrong by such a large amount."

The professor shrugged. "My analysis is based on what these blueprints indicate.

I believe you will need much more explosive energy to achieve your desired results, given the density and strength of these structures. Of course, I'm assuming the builders followed the blueprint requirements during construction. You see, for your plan to succeed you must pulverize structural concrete into sand. Concrete has a yield strength of about 3,500 pounds per square inch. You need to counteract that by a factor of almost 200 times. So, generating the required force, a blast wave of, say, 600,000 to 700,000 pounds per square inch, requires approximately 5,000 pounds of ammonium nitrate. You only have 3,000 pounds."

"I don't know if we can get that much. Is there no other way?" Ashur asked the professor.

"Well, you will need less ammonium nitrate if you can obtain additional plastique explosive, because you can shape the plastique, maximizing its power toward specific critical structural areas."

"Then we need more plastique," Ahmed said, turning to Ashur.

"Even this much Semtex was very difficult to obtain, Ahmed. We've been smuggling small amounts into the U.S. over the last two years, and you have almost our entire supply. I will try, but we should obtain both explosives to ensure your success."

"What about using C-4?" asked Salen, listening to their conversation. "That's what I used to blow a hole in the USS Cole and also to destroy the American's military barracks in Saudi Arabia in 1996. It's easy to use and very powerful."

"That's a possible option. I'll see what I can do," replied Ashur. "Tomorrow I'll send Salen out with my van."

"What about the motor boat I requested?" asked Ahmed. "Because of the Americans' security precautions Kalid must approach his target from the river, and he won't have sufficient air for a long swim."

Ashur reached into his pocket and with a flourish withdrew a key dangling from a lanyard. "I've secured the cooperation of a wealthy sympathizer. He docks his boat in a marina at Riverside Drive and 79th Street, in Manhattan," he said, grinning.

"Good. But I want to inspect it tomorrow morning. We may need to install modifications, like an underwater towing platform. The weather will be very nice tomorrow. I think we should go for a boat ride. I read in the newspapers the Queen Mary 2 docked earlier today."

Chapter 30
Downtown Brooklyn

June 25ᵗʰ

The safe house bustled with activity the next morning. Ashur and his cell members met Ahmed and his team for breakfast. "My heart beats faster as we near the date for your bold strike," said Ashur. Ahmed said nothing but just smiled, nodding his head. *Your rapidly beating heart would explode out of your chest if you knew the true magnitude of my plan,* he thought. After breakfast Hossein drove off in Ashur's van to purchase additional explosive material. This time, his route was the eastbound Brooklyn Queens Expressway, then the Long Island Expressway toward the few remaining farms on eastern Long Island. He planned to drive along the Island's South Fork first, stopping at as many farm suppliers as he could find. Then he would cross over to the North Fork, doing the same thing. He needed another ton of ammonium nitrate fertilizer, but his strategy required purchasing small amounts to avoid raising the curiosity of the patriotic populace.

Ashur sent Ali to buy whichever plastique explosive his clandestine contacts could secure quickly, either Semtex or C-4. Both materials were highly controlled and monitored because of their destructive nature. Only several ounces of Semtex hidden inside a hand-held radio had brought down a Pan Am 747 over Lockerbie Scotland in 1988, killing 259 people, including 189 Americans.

Ashur drove Ahmed, Kalid, Salen and Waleed to examine the boat he had procured and to scout the location where the QM2 was docked. His car entered the BQE at Atlantic Avenue and he drove across the Brooklyn Bridge to Manhattan. Then he proceeded south on the FDR Drive, around Manhattan's southern tip and up the west side. "I chose this route so you could see what Americans call 'Ground Zero', where the World Trade Center towers stood, the site of Islam's biggest victory." Ashur said proudly.

"Thank you," replied Ahmed. "Watch me spit on their so-called holy ground when we drive by." All five men shared a hearty laugh as Ahmed opened the car window and spit several times as they drove past the site. Continuing up the west side highway they passed the QM2's tall bow at the 52nd Street pier. The men craned their necks to catch a glimpse of the huge ship.

"An impressive target. In fact the most ambitious target of my life," remarked Kalid, the scuba diver. They exited the highway at 72nd Street and drove along Riverside Drive, passing the 79th Street boat basin looking for the most precious commodity in New York City: a legal parking spot. At 81st Street Ashur swerved quickly toward the curb, throwing the men to one side.

"My apologies, but I almost missed this parking space," he said. The men exited the car and crossed to the opposite curb, failing to notice a common bane of New York living: parking signs so confusing one needed an advanced degree to decipher them. They walked two blocks to the boat basin searching for a particular boat. "There!" exclaimed Ashur, pointing toward a sleek 40-foot motorboat. The name was painted on the transom in gold leaf script, bordered in black: *Crescent Moon*. They walked slowly to the mooring, avoiding attention, and stepped aboard. "What do you think, Ahmed?" asked Ashur.

"I think you did very well," he replied, smiling. "This craft suits our needs perfectly. It has sufficient space for equipment storage, enough power and range, and we can easily suspend a small platform beneath the hull so we can tow Kalid toward his target in comfort."

"I am pleased that you are pleased, my brother. Help me untie the lines and we'll depart for a short cruise." The men cast off the mooring lines and Ashur eased the *Crescent Moon* from the cramped marina, entered the Hudson River and turned south.

"Slowly, Ashur," said Kalid. "I know this is a fast boat, but remember, I will be underneath. Underwater, even a four-knot current feels like a fierce windstorm. You cannot go faster than five knots or I may be swept away." Ahmed and Kalid checked their watches, timing the one-and-a-quarter mile journey to the QM2. "We would arouse too much suspicion if we stopped behind the ship. We'll check the current's direction that day and drop you about a quarter-mile up-current, so you can drift toward the ship as you swim toward her. Continue a couple of miles down the river, Ashur. We should appear like typical boaters enjoying a pleasure cruise."

Cruising farther down the Hudson, Ahmed saw a U.S. Navy destroyer docked near a Navy cruiser. Moored at the next pier was a Navy transport. Then he saw another destroyer heading up the river in their direction. "Ashur, what's going on? Do the Americans know we're here?"

"Relax, Ahmed. I read in the newspaper this is called 'Fleet Week.' This cursed nation celebrates its birthday in several days. Many Navy ships are here letting their sailors enjoy a holiday. Look over there." He handed Ahmed a strong pair of binoculars. As the *Crescent Moon* approached the mouth of the Hudson, Ahmed looked where Ashur was pointing, south, toward Staten Island. He saw several small tugboats maneuvering the huge aircraft carrier U.S.S. Ronald Reagan toward the Navy pier at Stapleton. "Those little boats look like ants pushing a giant elephant," he remarked.

After Ahmed recovered from the initial shock of seeing so much American naval power in one place he sighed. "I wish I had known about this earlier. With so many targets we could have brought more weapons to kill these sailors and sink their ships." Ashur drove the *Crescent Moon* past another marina at the World Financial Center near Battery Park City. Then he slowly circled and cruised back the same way they came. Passing the QM2 again, Kalid stared at the giant ship, lost in meditation. "What are you thinking about?" asked Ahmed.

"I'm thinking about my mission, blowing up that ship. I am confident I'll succeed. I can feel Allah smiling down on me," said Kalid. *And you'll be joining Allah sooner than you realize*, thought Ahmed.

Chapter 31
Coney Island, the New York Aquarium

June 26ᵗʰ

Hey, toss her a fat, juicy mackerel!" shouted Joe after Notchka leaped almost eight feet from the water over an "enemy" diver. The trainers had spent the morning teaching Notchka her first assignment: jumping as high as possible over a submerged diver she had been trained to recognize as the enemy.

"Okay, my turn as enemy," said Terry. Conditioning Notchka to react to a profile and not to a recognizable personality, each diver, Joe, Terry, and NYPD diver Hans Bauer, took turns assuming the hostile profile. That profile was a diver carrying a round object resembling an underwater mine and not wearing a specially modified vest, which reflected Notchka's sonar in a specific frequency range. Hans had been plucked from the NYPD dive team for this assignment because he was also a former U.S. Navy diver, with experience training dolphins for the Navy's Marine Mammal Program. Hans and Joe circled the pool bottom wearing their vests, and Notchka swam between them. Terry slipped into the water without a reflective vest and carried an actual disarmed limpet mine. The twelve-pound device, about six inches thick and shaped like two large dinner plates stuck together, was fitted with a magnetic ring on one side for attachment to a ship's steel hull. Terry swam to the pool's deep end, and Notchka immediately swam past her. Terry felt a tingling sensation as Notchka scanned her and then shot to the surface, performing a high summersault before splashing back, her own version of an exclamation point. An aquarium trainer threw two live mackerel into the pool, which Notchka consumed in one pass.

Joe became the enemy and then Hans one last time. "Well, I think she definitely gets the idea identifying a particular diver profile, and she has the jumping maneuver down very well," remarked Hans after Notchka performed successfully four consecutive times. "Now we'll proceed to the next level and see if she can carry out a direct attack. I've heard she has experience in that area." Hans flashed a wry grin at Terry.

"Yes, she's knows how to kill who *she* perceives as a true enemy. You know, like a shark or someone directly threatening her or someone she cares about," replied Terry. "I don't know if you can condition Notchka to fatally attack someone who's playing a game like this. As I said, I don't want you turning her into a killing machine."

"Well, here's what we'll do," replied Hans, ignoring Terry's editorial comment. "I'll assume the enemy profile. Terry you swim at me carrying this." He took a rubber mold of a dolphin's head and snout from the pool deck and handed it to Terry. "Swim toward me as fast as you can holding the rubber dolphin with your arms extended and bump my rib cage. Swim away and do it again. Then back off and see what Notchka does.

Hans removed his vest, grabbed the limpet mine and swam down to the deep end. Before Terry could react, Notchka swam toward Hans, scanned him, then shot to the surface, leaping almost ten feet. She splashed, then waited for her mackerel reward. When it didn't come she assumed she had not performed the task properly and was about to repeat it when she saw Terry swim toward Hans carrying the dolphin head. Curious, she watched Terry bump Hans once, then again. When Terry surfaced, Notchka, bored and ready for a new game, copied what she had seen Terry do. Then she received her reward. Each diver took turns getting bumped.

"Hey, she's doing pretty well!" exclaimed Joe.

"Now we'll put the two exercises together," said Hans. "I'll start as the enemy. If she bumps me first, she gets no reward. If she jumps first and then bumps me, she gets her treat." Notchka finally performed the sequence correctly after several attempts. Then she performed flawlessly, six consecutive times. "Okay, let's take a break," said Hans. "There's one last piece to the puzzle. She has to ram the enemy diver hard enough so he drops the mine, not just bump him. Like most dolphins after a long training session, she's probably getting tired. Let's have lunch and resume later."

After lunch they met at the pool. "Okay, I don't want anyone to end up with broken ribs, or worse," said Hans. "I'll go first. If I'm still alive after a few hits, it's your turn," he said, smiling at Terry. After an hour Hans was frustrated. I don't know what to do. I can't make her bump hard enough to injure a true enemy diver."

"I'm not surprised," Terry replied. "What constitutes an enemy to us doesn't translate into her frame of reference. Dolphins aren't political. She's too gentle."

Hans shook his head. "I could train her if I had more time. But we don't. The QM2 is already here."

"Look, isn't it enough if she marks a diver's location by jumping and then disrupting his mission but not killing him?" asked Terry.

Hans thought for a moment. "I suppose so. What are you getting at?"

"Notchka thinks this is some kind of game. So, let's just modify the game. She won't get her reward unless whoever is playing the enemy diver drops the mine. I'll demonstrate, bumping you twice. On the third bump you just drop the mine. Notchka won't know how hard I bump you, but if you keep holding it, she'll eventually keep bumping you harder until you drop it."

"Pretty good idea, Terry. We may find you a new career," he said.

Notchka watched Terry bump Hans repeatedly with the dolphin head until he dropped the mine. Notchka tried it, each time bumping Hans a little harder. On the fifth bump she knocked the wind out of him, and he dropped the mine. Gasping for air at the surface, he said, "Don't try to hold it for five bumps! She's a very strong girl."

Joe went next, releasing the mine after a strong bump on Notchka's fourth attempt. Watching the two men holding their sore ribs, Terry laughed. "I think I'll sit out this part of the training. After all, this was all your idea, dear," she said massaging Joe's aching chest.

After an hour of training Hans said, "I think this will work fine. Locating a diver's position and making him drop the mine should give us time to retrieve and disable it and capture him for interrogation. We'll resume tomorrow morning. If Notchka hasn't forgotten what she's learned today we'll transfer her to a large pen in the Hudson River, next to the QM2."

Chapter 32
The New York Aquarium

June 27th

After breakfast Terry, Joe, Hans and several trainers met at the pool. "Good morning, big girl," said Joe, slapping the water with his palm. Notchka swam over and squirted everyone with a stream of water. "Well, now that we're wet we may as well start today's training session," he said, laughing.

"Good morning, everyone!" They turned and saw Lieutenant Bill Ryan approaching.

"Hi Bill. I think you'll be pleased. Notchka's a fast learner. Watch today's session. If she passes we'll transport her to the pen next to the QM2," Joe said.

"Great! Let's see what she's got."

They jumped into the pool, and Hans played the enemy diver. Notchka swam above him, leaped into the air with her signature summersault, landing with a loud splash. Then she dived, circled Hans and bumped him. He held onto the mine, and she circled and bumped him a second time. Hans dropped the mine and Notchka surfaced for a reward. After two successful runs Joe repeated the exercise, and then Terry tried it for the first time. She dropped the mine on Notchka's first bump.

"Chicken!" teased Joe. "You got off easy."

"Sorry dear. Suffering bruised ribs isn't my idea of fun."

"Hey Joe, I have a question," asked Bill. "The FBI reported some persons of interest bought scuba equipment recently. One item they purchased was a full-face mask. Why would someone buy that type instead of a regular mask?"

"Well, depending on how it was rigged, it could enable divers to talk to each other or communicate with someone at the surface. Commercial divers performing underwater tasks like excavations, boat and pier repairs use them."

"What about divers attaching underwater mines to a ship's hull?" Bill asked.

"Definitely a possibility," replied Joe.

"We heard they also wanted to buy a re-breather." Terry's ears perked up.

"Well, divers use re-breathers to extend their bottom time," she said. "But more importantly, they also eliminate the tell-tale bubbles so no one knows a diver's below. That's why the military uses them."

"Okay, where are we on this?" Bill asked Hans.

"Notchka's ready to go. She learned her skills yesterday and repeated them this morning. Once she got it, she never missed. You can take her to the pier whenever you need her."

"We need her right now. Let's go."

They fed Notchka several live striped bass. Then the aquarium staff lowered the transport sling into the pool. Terry guided her into the sling, making sure her pectoral fins fit through the side holes while the transport truck backed into the pool area and swung its crane over the edge. Then she was hoisted into the air and gently guided into the water-filled tank on the truck bed for the hour ride to the Hudson River pen. Terry accompanied her, stroking her skin and talking to her while she calmly floated in her tank. The truck wound its way through the Brooklyn streets with a police escort, proceeding along 3rd Avenue underneath the always crowded Gowanus Expressway, through the Brooklyn-Battery Tunnel and up the West Side Highway to Pier 92 at the foot of 52nd St. Notchka was lowered in her sling into the Hudson. Terry, Joe and Hans guided her into a holding pen across from the Queen Mary 2, and then let her swim out of the sling. She acclimated to her new environment, a rope-mesh pen, 30 feet wide and 100 feet long topped by an opaque bubble like an outdoor tennis court, which let sunlight in but kept prying eyes out.

"She seems comfortable," Terry said, leaning over the edge of the holding pen. She wrinkled her nose watching some garbage, pieces of lumber and paper objects, float in the swells. "But you can't see the bottom through this murk. I hope she'll be okay swimming in this pea soup."

"Yes," replied Hans. "We'll watch her carefully for signs of stress. The water temperature is about the same as the aquarium, and the river is brackish so it's salty enough for her. The fact that the water's murky shouldn't bother her too much. She relies on her sonar to get a clear sense of her surroundings. The mesh enclosure allows small fish to swim through, but we'll supplement her diet since there aren't enough fish here to sustain her. We'll keep her inside during the day and release her at night to patrol the ship."

"Joe and I will take turns with her during her night watches," said Terry, firmly.

"Oh yes, Bill Ryan told me about your terms," said Hans, smiling. "Well, you have several hours before the first watch so why don't you eat lunch and then rest."

Terry changed into dry clothes and met Joe, Bill Ryan and Sergeant Phil Barone, NYPD dive team supervisor, on the pier. Forty-eight year old Barone was heavily muscled, with a sturdy six-foot frame and as fit as the men he commanded, many twenty years younger. He was a throwback to diving's early days, relying on training and instinct and the most basic equipment. He eschewed modern paraphernalia, such as dive computers. Barone routinely teased younger divers. "Whatta ya gonna do if your batteries crap out, sonny? Cry for momma?" Some thought Barone resembled macho Lloyd Bridges, who played diver Mike Nelson in the popular 1950's television series, *Sea Hunt.* They watched divers entering and exiting the water from an NYPD dive boat anchored next to the QM2. "We've got everything under control for now," said Sergeant Barone. They're constantly swimming the length of the ship visually inspecting the hull, and one diver has a LIMIS system."

"LIMIS?" asked Joe.

"Sorry. That's a Limpet Mine Imaging System. It's a sonar imaging system. The diver has a viewer attached to his mask and he points what we call an acoustic flashlight with one hand and operates the main electronic device and battery pack with his other hand. Depending on resolution settings, he can see an object from ten to thirty feet away, even when he can't see his hand in front of his face. The water here can be pretty turbid, not what you're used to in Cozumel," he said, turning to Terry. "Depending on the tide's direction and weather conditions, visibility on a good day occasionally approaches ten, maybe fifteen feet, but most days it's less than five feet. We'll constantly sweep the QM2's hull for anything that doesn't belong there."

"Pretty impressive," she said.

"Yes it is, but we can use all the help we can get. I understand you two'll be diving with us."

"Yes we will, along with Notchka," Terry replied. "How do you plan to use her?" Terry asked.

"Well, I've given it a lot of thought," replied Barone, running his hand through his hair. "I don't think continually patrolling the length of the QM2's hull will be productive. Over 1.100 feet is a lot of area to cover, especially considering the ship's width. I think focusing on the aft section, say the rear one or two hundred feet near the props is the best plan. The stern is the most vulnerable section, given how it juts past the pier into the Hudson. That's where an enemy diver would approach."

"Makes sense," Terry agreed, glancing at Joe, who nodded affirmatively.

"I've heard a lot about your dolphin. I also heard about your creative training method. We just received the reflective vests our divers will wear when she's in the water. I'm looking forward to meeting her."

"Well, come over and get acquainted," said Terry, leading Barone toward Notchka's holding pen.

"I'll catch you guys later," Bill said. "I have a meeting downtown at Police Headquarters."

Chapter 33
NYPD Headquarters, Downtown Manhattan

June 27th

Glad you could join us, Bill," Commissioner Jackson remarked sarcastically, as Bill Ryan rushed into the meeting almost fifteen minutes late.

"Sorry, Commissioner. Stopped by my office for an update and then hit heavy traffic in Chinatown."

"Okay, take a seat. I have Tom McHale, FBI, on the phone."

"Hi, Tom," said Ryan.

"Hello, Bill. How are things in the Big Apple?"

"Pretty busy, Tom. We have everything in place to cover the Queen Mary 2. She docked a couple of days ago, and we have divers in the water now on a 24 by 7 basis, along with a dolphin for additional nighttime surveillance."

"Before you strolled in," commented Commissioner Jackson, "I was just telling Tom we've coordinated full coverage with the Secret Service and their British counterparts, MI5. That'll be a big help as Queen Elizabeth moves around town. We'll shift additional resources to the QM2 for the Queen's June 30th reception. Once we get past that event we'll shift resources to cover other celebrations, to the U.N. for her address on July 3rd and her attendance at celebrations downtown on the Fourth."

"Sounds like the Queen's very secure," said Special Agent McHale.

"Yes," replied Jackson. "Our approach is pretty basic but sound. We've established classical multi-layered protection. A potential assassin will have to penetrate several security layers to get near her. By the way, did the CIA ever come up with any further analysis on this necklace reference or the assassination attempt?"

"No, 'fraid not. They've hit a blank wall. Their recommendation was pretty much what you're already doing, to provide multiple layers of security. Oh, plus one other thing. They had the Secret Service ask the Queen not to wear any jewels around her neck."

'What was her reply?"

"Well, as I understand it she used some pretty salty language, especially for a queen. She reminded everyone that as a teenager during World War II she survived Hitler's London Blitz. Said she'd wear what she damn well pleased."

"Really?"

"Actually, she said, and I quote, 'At this point in my life I'm not letting any bloody terrorists intimidate me!'"

"Good for her," Jackson said, laughing. "Anything else, Bill?"

"Yes sir, just a question for Tom. Hey, Tom, any more details on the plate number the scuba store manager gave you?"

"Yes there are, Bill. The car's registered to a Mr. Ashur Sharib, a 73-year-old Syrian gentleman. Lives on Sackett Street in downtown Brooklyn, near Atlantic Avenue, a neighborhood some people call 'Little Arabia.' Somehow I don't think he'd have much use for scuba gear."

"I agree."

"And the store manager said the two guys who purchased the stuff were in their mid-to-late twenties, so obviously Sharib wasn't one of them. They fit the profile of the 9/11 hijackers, though, and just about every other terrorist we've ever captured or killed or who's still on the loose. All young Middle Eastern males in their twenties or early thirties. Classic Al Qaeda personnel."

"So tell me, Tom, how come we still waste time patting down 80-year old grannies from Indiana at the airports?"

"Sorry, Bill, profiling policy's not my department," said McHale, smiling. "But on the not so funny side, we requested a court order to search Mr. Sharib's house ,and we were denied."

"Why?"

"The short answer is, according to the judge, no probable cause. We even tried citing the Patriot Act for leverage, but he threw it back in our faces. Said as far as he was concerned certain Patriot Act provisions violate the Constitution, specifically the Fourth Amendment's guarantee against unreasonable search and seizure. Felt like I was back in law school again. He also informed us buying scuba equipment is not a crime. They didn't steal it and didn't pay for it with counterfeit cash or a stolen credit card. Furthermore, Sharib is a naturalized U.S. citizen, and he wasn't even buying the equipment himself. He could have lent his car to friends or relatives, so they could buy the stuff. The judge lectured us that we can't break into U.S. citizens' homes merely on suspicion. We got our hands slapped big time."

"Too bad. I guess probable cause is in the eye of the beholder."

"Well, we'll keep an eye on the place for a while. Nothing high profile, just a routine stake-out to see if anything interesting is going on."

"Good idea, Tom. Let me know if you need any help."

"Thanks. Will do. And Bill, I have a recommendation for you," said McHale. "Keep your dolphin well fed and happy. I have a funny feeling we're going to need her."

Chapter 34
Pier 92, Hudson River

June 27th

Terry watched the late afternoon sun dip below the New Jersey side of the Hudson. Then she slipped into the river, wearing an aluminum-100 tank, containing 100 cubic feet of air, instead of the standard aluminum-80, extending her dive time at least 30 minutes, to over an hour and a half. She floated for several minutes, checking her equipment one last time. She finned backward avoiding a small oil slick and bumped into a chunk of foam, discarded from an old pillow. She shoved the foam away and shivered momentarily as the cool water filled her wetsuit. The water temperature was just above 65 degrees. Even wearing a thick 7-mil wetsuit Terry felt chilled and unsettled by the floating debris. *Ugh! Give me the clean warm Caribbean,* she thought. *Hope I don't get a skin rash from whatever's in this water.* She planned diving no deeper than 30 feet, almost a permanent safety stop, so she could remain as long as her air held out and not worry about suffering the bends.

The pen's screen was raised, and Notchka swam out, exploring her surroundings. She followed Terry to the massive black hull floating motionless. Joe watched Notchka following Terry's bubbles, then saw her dorsal fin disappear as she dove, joining Terry just above the bottom.

Together they slowly swam from the bow toward the stern, over a thousand feet away. Per Barone's dive plan, they remained near the QM2's stern, patrolling the entrance to the berth. Visibility was almost ten feet, unusually clear for the Hudson River near shore. They swam close to the ship, keeping the hull in sight. A few more minutes of dusk remained, and visibility was declining. Terry shone her dive light on the hull, looking for any object attached that didn't belong there, like an underwater limpet mine. Notchka swam next to Terry but occasionally left to explore the area, snapping up an occasional small fish. *Lucky you can see with sound*, Terry mused, realizing Notchka was using her sonar to compensate for the dimming light and murky water. Occasionally Terry spotted the bubble trail of a nearby NYPD diver checking other sections of the ship.

After almost an hour and a half Terry surfaced and signaled Joe to relieve her. He slipped in and passed her before diving. "See anything interesting?"

"Nope. Pretty boring compared to diving in Cozumel. But, then again, this isn't a vacation. And that ship is awesome! It's like diving under a whale."

"Or maybe twenty whales, strung end to end," said Joe. "See ya later."

He pressed the deflate button on his BC and sank out of sight. Terry watched his bubble trail indicate he was headed toward the QM2's mid section. Joe reached the ship just as Notchka swam past to check if he was an enemy diver, or, in her frame of reference, a diver with whom to play the new game she had learned: jump and bump. She had scanned all the divers, but everyone wore a reflective vest and none carried a round pie-shaped object for her to knock loose and claim her reward. No one to play jump and bump with here. After an hour and a half, Notchka was bored and tired. Just as Terry jumped in to replace Joe she saw her dorsal fin swim into the pen. Joe surfaced nearby and saw Terry follow Notchka into the pen.

"I think Notchka's bored, Joe. She probably wants to sleep or rest."

"I didn't count on that. Too bad we don't have another dolphin to relieve her. It's only eleven o'clock. I had planned on her patrolling with us until dawn."

"Remember, Joe, as far as she's concerned this is only a game. Notchka's not political. She doesn't know we're patrolling this ship looking for a goddamned terrorist."

"Yeah, I think tomorrow we'll need to revise our action plan. I'll tell the NYPD guys we're through tonight."

Chapter 35
The Brooklyn Safe House

June 28th

A re you almost finished, Waleed?" asked Ahmed for the fourth time.

"Stop asking me! I will be finished when I am finished!" shouted Waleed.

Ahmed looked at Waleed but did not reply to his outburst. *As the final hour approaches I fear the strain is affecting us*, he thought. Ahmed took a deep breath and closed his eyes, visualizing the road the four had taken to arrive at this point. Hiding in the caves of Pakistan, hiking mountainous trails and crossing the Pakistan-Afghanistan border; dodging American and British patrols; the interminable horse and camel rides through rough, cold terrain at night; bumping along in a slow, aged bus and train; restless sleep during the long plane ride; and their final stress test: passing through U.S. Immigration and Customs authorities. But finally, they were in their sworn enemy's homeland.

Waleed's work required concentration, dexterity and skill. Without the electronics working perfectly, Ahmed's plan, still known only to him, would never succeed. Even then, success was still a long shot. Many events had to fall into place with precise timing. But he remained confident. He thought, *After all, Allah is on our side.*

"Okay, I'm finished," announced Waleed. "The communication mask works, and the antenna will carry communication signals even under water. The remote firing signal will detonate the mine, and the same mechanism will set off the plastique explosives and the fertilizer bombs, destroying our main target."

"Yes, assuming Hossein has found sufficient explosive material," said Ahmed. Just then he heard the garage door slide open and, as if on queue, the van rolled in. He left the assembly room and stepped into the garage. "Well?" he asked Hossein.

"I got it!" Hossein exclaimed. "Everything we need. And I bought an extra hundred pounds of ammonium nitrate for good measure."

"Wonderful," said Ahmed, his face a toothy, vicious grin. He enthusiastically slapped Hossein's back as Ashur walked into the garage. Ahmed turned to Ashur. "Tonight your men should finish mixing the fertilizer and diesel fuel. Then they can load it into the drums. I must move everything tomorrow morning."

June 29th

The next day, Ahmed and his team drove the explosive-laden van to their first target. The van's suspension groaned, objecting to 5,000 pounds of ammonium nitrate and diesel fuel packed into 30 steel drums about the size of residential garbage cans. Ahmed was concerned that the van, riding so low on its suspension and tires, might arouse police curiosity when they passed bridge and tunnel entrance checkpoints. He felt tense but appeared icy calm. His mind raced, planning for every eventuality. *The last thing we need is some suspicious cop ruining our mission with a simple inspection. But bold missions require risk,* he rationalized. Overnight they had re-painted the van with a local government agency's logo. Ahmed and his team had also secured excellent counterfeit government-issued ID cards and work clothes to eliminate suspicion should anyone challenge them.

An hour later they arrived at their first target. Ahmed smiled, seeing Waleed and Salen's shocked expressions as they finally realized the scope of his plan. "It looks just as it appeared in my photos. Al Qeada's intelligence contacts here did a wonderful job." Moving quickly and efficiently they entered the structure unobserved. "I can't believe there is no security here."

They forced a rusty padlock and pushed open two heavy metal doors, which creaked on hinges frozen by time and lack of use, and stepped inside the massive structure. They lit the interior with flashlights and set the drums where the blueprints indicated they would accomplish the most damage. Then they molded the plastique explosive Semtex onto massive supports and ran fuses to all the drums. Finaly, they attached the electronic communication detonators to the Semtex. Leaving quickly, they secured the steel doors with a new, stronger lock and drove to their second target.

They found the next target only slightly more secure than the first. Once again, no security guards were posted. A simple, flimsy, eight-foot chain-link fence and rusty gate surrounded the structure. The gate was secured by a lightweight lock and chain, which Ahmed easily snapped using a bolt cutter. An old lock, which yielded with only a little encouragement, secured a roll-down steel door. They placed the remaining steel drums containing their explosive contents according to Ahmed's instructions. Since they had already used their entire Semtex supply on the first target, C-4 plastique explosive was used to enhance their bomb's explosive power. Salen molded the pliable substance where it would do the most damage, then Waleed attached the electronic detonator. The team checked all the connections one last time, threaded the broken chain on the gate and left quickly. The broken chain was the only indication someone had entered the structure. "I wish I could replace the chain, but returning is too risky." said Ahmed. "I don't think anyone will notice the stupid chain is broken."

An hour later the empty van pulled into the garage below the safe house. As soon as Ahmed and his team stepped out, Ashur and his men besieged them for information.

"Everything went well," replied Ahmed. "We delivered the explosives you so diligently purchased for us." He slapped Hossein's back. "And you did well obtaining the C-4," he told Ali. "We needed it since we used all the Semtex."

He looked at their expectant faces, their eyes quietly beseeching him for more information. "I regret I cannot reveal the targets we selected. But soon you will all know."

"Come, let us share food and drink in the dining room," said Ashur, giddily. They celebrated their mission's successful initial stage. Soon they would kill thousands of innocent civilians, whom they considered infidels. They drank nothing stronger than tea, observing the Islamic law forbidding alcohol consumption.

Chapter 36

June 30th

Standing on the dock across from Pier 92, Terry and Joe observed the festivities while Queen Elizabeth held court aboard the QM2. Two days earlier, the Queen had met with Mayor Williamson at Gracie Mansion, the traditional home of New York City's mayors. Today's reception included numerous New York dignitaries, as well as national and international guests. Terry watched two NYPD helicopters circling protectively over the ship. Hearing a throaty roar, they looked skyward, squinting. Silhouetted against a bank of wispy cirrus clouds, a pair of Navy F/A-18 Super Hornets from the nearby aircraft carrier Ronald Reagan, temporarily operating from a land-base, patrolled high overhead. "Like Jackson said, layered protection," observed Joe.

"Here comes your buddy with the dive team supervisor," commented Terry.

"Good afternoon," said Bill as he and Sergeant Barone approached them. "I heard your dolphin had a problem a couple of nights ago."

"Well, it was something we should have anticipated," replied Terry. "Notchka had been trained, or conditioned, to expect continuous interaction and rewards for performing her tasks. To her it was a fun game. Instead, she was just patrolling back and forth. Dolphins are pretty intelligent. If you don't keep them stimulated they get bored and do whatever interests them. Back home she would just swim away and interact with her pod."

"I understand," said Barone. "So what do you suggest?"

"What's the most critical period for us? The time when we're most vulnerable or when someone may strike?" asked Joe.

"Well, as far as when they might strike, the time is right now. The Queen and many dignitaries are on board. However, it's still daylight and we have a tremendous amount of security." Barone pointed. "Divers are in the water, we have air coverage, boats are patrolling the river, and we sealed the pier off from pedestrian and vehicular traffic. But as far as vulnerability, I'd say later tonight when visibility is reduced. The Queen isn't scheduled to leave the ship until later this evening."

"In that case why don't we start Notchka patrolling about nine o'clock," responded Joe. "Also, let's keep playing her game to stimulate her. Every half hour or so we can send in someone she'll think is playing the game, a diver carrying a simulated mine and not wearing a reflective vest. She'll do what we trained her to do and get a reward. I think we can hold her interest longer, probably until dawn. What do you think?" Joe asked, turning to Terry.

"Sounds as good as any plan I could think of," she replied. "You can modify a wild dolphin's behavior only so much in a short period of time. We can't expect any more from her."

"Okay," said Bill. "I'll contact Hans and ask him to come over and play a bad guy. Why don't you two have dinner and report back at eight o'clock."

Chapter 37

June 30th

After dinner, Ahmed met with Kalid, Salen and Waleed, in a separate room. "Tonight we strike. I want to inspect all the equipment, but first let's review our plans. We arrive at the boat basin at midnight. I'll pilot the boat from the marina." He turned to the diver, Kalid. "And then what do you do?"

"I suit up and get in the water, holding onto the dive platform."

"Correct. I'll drive the boat slowly until we reach the spot where you will leave and carry out your attack."

"Yes. As soon as the boat stops I'll take a bearing on the ship, make sure my communications antenna and the electronic arming antenna are trailing behind me at the surface, descend ten meters and swim toward the ship. I'll tell you when I see the hull. Then I'll stop and wait for your instructions."

"Correct."

"But Ahmed, why can't I simply attach the magnetic mine to the ship's hull and leave?"

"Because that is not my plan, Kalid. Everything depends on precise timing. I must observe what is happening on the ship. That will determine where I want you to place the mine."

"All right, Ahmed. Then you will instruct me where to place the mine. After that I will swim with the current for 30 minutes and surface."

"Correct. We will pick you up and return to the marina. The electronic detonator's range is almost 2,000 meters. But we will explode the mine when we're less than a thousand meters from the ship to ensure we are well within range and the signal is strong. Does everyone understand?" Everyone nodded affirmatively. "Good. Let's go downstairs and inspect the equipment one last time." They assembled next to a table cluttered with dive equipment. They tested the dive mask and the communications equipment. Ahmed examined the 50-foot wire attached to the communications pack. It would function as an antenna floating along the surface, picking up the signal. Waleed camouflaged the wire, painting it dark mottled green instead of its solid black color. At another table Ahmed examined the limpet mine and confirmed that a similar antenna was properly connected to the device.

"I still think we should take advantage of the automatic arming feature instead of relying on your remote firing plan," suggested Kalid.

Ahmed's eyes flashed with cold anger and his voice rose. "I told you already that I have a reason for doing it this way. I will not be questioned anymore! Am I clear, Kalid?"

"As you said. This is your plan, Ahmed."

Ahmed nodded. "Fine. Let's load the equipment into Ashur's car."

Ashur came in to wish them good luck. He watched them trying to fit all the equipment into his car. "You'll be too crowded in my car. Take my van instead," he suggested.

An hour later, the four men arrived at the marina parking lot. There were no available parking spaces, so after transferring their equipment to the boat Ahmed parked on a nearby street and walked back to the dock. When all were aboard, the *Crescent Moon* quietly slipped out of the marina toward the Hudson River. Kalid looked into the clear night sky. He was not pleased to see a full moon shining a silver beam across the water. *Ahmed should have checked the calendar before scheduling the mission,* he thought. But a steady 10-mile per hour westerly breeze created some surface chop. *At least my bubbles will be more difficult to spot than if the river were smooth and calm,* he reasoned. Clearing the channel buoys, Ahmed turned the *Crescent Moon* south toward pier 92 and the QM2.

Chapter 38
Pier 92, the QM2

June 30th

Queen Elizabeth had departed the Queen Mary 2 at ten o'clock, but the festivities continued. Now, approaching 1 a.m. the party was winding down. Band members were packing their instruments, the remaining guests were exchanging goodbyes and business cards, and the crew was cleaning up. The security personnel, composed of U.S. Secret Service, British MI5, NYPD and the ship's security staff, were congratulating themselves on an uneventful evening. The air cover had been withdrawn, and the FAA had given New York Air Traffic Control permission to resume routing commercial traffic landing at La Guardia Airport up the Hudson River. Diver and trainer Hans Bauer climbed onto the dock across from the QM2 after serving as an enemy diver for the second time that evening, keeping Notchka interested in her game. She swam inside her pen enjoying a live sea bass treat before heading out again on patrol, this time with Terry replacing Joe as her partner. "Notchka gave me a pretty strong bump this time," remarked Hans, holding his side. "I think if we had more time we could train her to be a good military dolphin. She has all the right. . ." Terry cut him off.

"Forget it, Hans. Notchka returns to civilian life after that ship sails. And I know she prefers the clear, warm Caribbean to the soupy Hudson as much as I do. Looks like she's ready to go out on patrol again. C'mon girl," said Terry, slapping her palm against the surface. Notchka swam to her and Terry descended. Joe and Hans watched her bubble trail as she headed toward the QM2 with Notchka close behind.

Ahmed stopped the *Crescent Moon* a mile upstream. Kalid donned his scuba gear and slipped over the side. He swam below the boat and grabbed the underwater hang-bar. Informing Ahmed through his communication mask that he was secure, Ahmed resumed his southward course. He noticed several police boats patrolling the area behind the pier. He headed farther out toward the middle of the Hudson. It would mean a longer swim for Kalid, but he had no choice. A quarter-mile north of the QM2 Ahmed stopped the *Crescent Moon* again. Kalid let the underwater hang-bar go and surfaced, orienting his underwater compass and taking a bearing on the ship. Satisfied, he descended to 30 feet and swam toward the ship, helped by a moderate current. The deadly limpet mine hung from short lanyard attached to a "D" ring on his BC, freeing his hands. The *Crescent Moon* continued south with Ahmed, Waleed and Salen. Kalid looked back, making sure both 50-foot long antennas had properly deployed. He saw them disappear into the dark murk, and estimated 20 feet would trail at the surface. He turned forward, checked his compass and continued swimming through the black void. Kalid was like a pilot flying on instruments through dense fog, navigating according to his compass

Fifteen minutes later, Ahmed heard Kalid's excited voice through his headset. "I can see the propellers! The current is carrying me past the ship. I have to swim back." Ahmed heard Kalid's heavy breathing as he fought the current. Several minutes later, Kalid spoke. "Okay, I'm directly below the ship now, looking up at the hull. It's so big! I can place the mine here and blow the prop . . ."

"No, Kalid! Stay away from the propellers! Swim toward the bow about 100 meters. Then swim away from the ship, about 10 meters."

"But . . ."

"Do it, Kalid!" Ahmed commanded. *Blowing her propellers is the last thing I want*, he thought, shaking his head.

Notchka swam next to Terry, scanning two other divers, when she sensed a third diver out of visual range. She scanned the third diver. A weak sonar reflection returned, indicating this diver was not wearing a reflective vest. To her this meant the game was on, with a fish treat for her at the end. She bolted ahead to investigate. Swimming past Kalid she saw a round shape attached to him but hanging just below his body. Momentarily puzzled because he was not holding the round object in his hands, she made a second, closer pass. "Something large just swam past me!" Ahmed heard Kalid exclaim through his headset.

"What was it? Another diver?"

"No, I don't think so." In the murky darkness Kalid sensed a shape dart past him toward the surface. "There it goes again!" Notchka was satisfied that enough conditions were met to justify a leap and bump. The *Crescent Moon* had just passed the QM2 so Ahmed didn't see Notchka's leap, summersault and splash landing. But Joe, Hans and Sergeant Barone did.

"Over there!" shouted Joe, as Notchka broke through the surface like a Polaris missile and fell back with a loud splash. Barone fired a red flare in the direction where Notchka had landed, the agreed-upon signal that a possible enemy diver was in the area. A police launch sped toward the descending flair. Terry saw Notchka pass through the beam of her underwater light, a shadowy blur, only several feet away, diving toward the bottom. She immediately realized Notchka must have leaped. She knew Hans was not in the water, and no one else was playing the enemy, so this was the real thing. Terry surfaced to pandemonium breaking out around her. The smoky red flare was just reaching the surface, a police launch was approaching, and Sergeant Barone, Joe and Hans sped over in a Zodiac raft.

Notchka bore down on her target and bumped Kalid's rib cage hard.

Ahmed saw the flair in the distance and silently cursed, fearing Kalid had been spotted. Then he heard, "Ooph," through his headset.

"Kalid, was that you? What happened?"

"The thing hit me! I think it's a large fish, or maybe a porpoise! I can attach the mine now. I'm less than ten meters from the ship. I can swim to it and . . ."

"No. Stay where you are. Kalid, I want you to know that Allah and all Islam appreciates your sacrifice."

"What! Why? What are you . . ." Kalid's momentary confusion faded, crystallizing into the realization that Ahmed had decided to make him a martyr. "No! Please, Ahmed. I . . ." Kalid reached down and frantically pulled the antenna, attempting to dislodge it from the mine.

Ahmed put the microphone down and removed his headset. He picked up the transmitter, took a deep breath, and pressed a red button. A millisecond later the antenna, floating at the surface, picked up the electronic detonation signal and transmitted it to the mine. Notchka had just turned toward Kalid intending to bump him again, jar the round object loose and claim her reward. A huge underwater explosion erupted, sending a foamy geyser 50 feet into the air. The powerful shock wave stunned her. Confused, dazed, and in pain, she tried to understand what had happened. The only past experience to which her dolphin frame of reference could compare the sensation, was being pounded by a very strong wave. Terry had already surfaced 200 feet away. She still felt the impact, as if she had been punched in the stomach. She saw a dorsal fin swaying uncertainly at the surface. "Notchka!" She shouted, swimming toward the injured dolphin as fast as she could. Notchka, semi-conscious, was barely afloat, Terry reached her and cradled her head, keeping her blowhole above the surface preventing her from drowning. A police diver swimming from the opposite side of the QM2 was partially shielded from the full force of the shock wave by the ship's hull and was momentarily knocked unconscious. Another police diver approaching from the stern was not as lucky. His teammates pulled him from the water seriously injured, blood pouring from his eyes and ears.

Chapter 39

June 30ᵗʰ

The pilot of a network news helicopter flying north over the Hudson between New York and New Jersey pointed out the QM2 to his cameraman. "Hey, Al, we're about to pass the Queen Mary 2 down there on our right. Why don't you shoot some video? Might make good stock footage if we ever run a future story about her." Just as Al was focusing his Sony-Cam on the ship, the pilot saw a red flair arc through the night sky, then descend toward the water. "That's an emergency flare, Al! Let's take a closer look. Keep your tape rolling!" He swooped lower and closer to investigate. His curiosity was rewarded when his cameraman caught the explosive geyser erupting alongside the ship. An NYPD copter intercepted them and quickly ushered the news helicopter away from the ship but not before Al's video camera captured the chaotic action below. The pilot immediately radioed his newsroom he had dramatic video of a possible terrorist attack on the QM2. Other news media organizations routinely monitoring the unsecured radio channel, intercepted his report. Within minutes they converged on the site, by land, sea and air, as close as the police would allow. During the confusion the *Crescent Moon* slowly cruised back to the marina, unnoticed.

Returning to their van, Ahmed noticed a piece of paper stuck under the windshield wiper. Pulling it from under the wiper blade, he saw it was a parking ticket. He glanced at the undecipherable parking sign 20 feet behind them. He spit an epithet and tore the ticket, tossing the pieces into the gutter. Then they got into the van and returned to Brooklyn. Ashur was shocked hearing about Kalid's death. Speechless at first, Ashur finally asked, "Why, Ahmed?" Ahmed looked at his two surviving team members and his eyes met Ashur's.

"Because his death was part of my larger plan. Allah may require martyrdom in completing this holy mission. Kalid's reward was just earlier than ours."

Terry swam with Notchka, guiding her to her pen, and Hans quickly arranged to transport the injured dolphin to the aquarium. The police dive boat rescued their injured diver and dispatched a new dive team to search for additional enemy divers and examine the QM2's hull for more mines. Joe and Sergeant Barone noticed floating body parts surrounding their Zodiac. Joe reached into the water and retrieved two severed arms, a leg severed at the knee, and a second leg still attached to its thigh. Missing were the diver's feet and fins, which had been blown off at the ankle. A short distance away Joe spotted a floating scuba tank attached to a torso. "Over there!" he pointed, and Barone maneuvered the Zodiac closer. "Give me a hand, Phil, I can't get a good grip," said Joe trying to pull the limbless form into the Zodiac. Together they hauled it aboard like a side of beef. The head, covered by a black neoprene dive hood but minus the mask, was barely attached and rolled from side to side as the small craft bobbed in small waves. The dead diver was recognizable as male only by the remains of a singed moustache. The blast had smashed the faceplate, lacerating and shredding the diver's face. Joe grimaced as the water in the zodiac's bottom turned pink, then red.

"Lucky his BC didn't get blown off," commented Barone. "We may be able to match the serial number to a buyer. From that hole in his chest, looks like that's where he caught the full force of the blast."

"What's attached to his BC?" asked Joe. Barone opened a zippered nylon case containing a square waterproof box. Wires protruded from the box and a red LED light continued blinking on and off.

"Beats me. Some kind of electronic gizmo. Hey, look at this." He noticed a long wire leading from the box into the water. He began pulling in the wire until all 50 feet were in the boat. "Looks like a long antenna. I guess we'll turn this stuff over to the wiz kids back at the lab. See anything else?"

"Nope. Let's bring this in." Just as they turned the Zodiac toward the dock they heard a voice behind them.

"Hey guys! Take these, too." They turned and saw an NYPD diver bobbing in the water behind them holding up a pair of fins he had retrieved from the muddy bottom. Barone maneuvered the Zodiac next to the diver, who tossed the fins over the side. They landed at Joe's feet with a wet thud. Dive booties were still strapped to the fins. Inside each bootie was a human foot.

"Well, looks like we collected all of Humpty Dumpty's parts," said Joe, surveying the surface, now lit by floodlights. "Now let's see if we can put him back together again."

Chapter 40

June 30th

Terry comforted Notchka during the truck ride to the aquarium, speaking softly and stroking her skin. The injured dolphin, supported in her fleece-lined sling, faded in and out of consciousness. Terry knew she must keep Notchka awake because Cetaceans lack the breathing reflex, which humans possess. For dolphins and whales, breathing is a conscious act. Consequently, they can never be totally asleep and still breathe. Terry noticed the wet fleece turning crimson and shouted. "Hans, she's bleeding but I can't tell from where! Tell the driver to hurry!" She heard the police escort's sirens ushering the truck onto the Belt Parkway. Commercial vehicles were prohibited from that highway, but it was the shortest route to the aquarium. "Let's hope my truck will clear these low pedestrian overpasses," the driver shouted back. "We're not really supposed to take this route." They arrived thirty minutes later, and Notchka was lowered into the pool's shallow end, still inside her sling. Terry jumped in and stood next to the sling, stroking Notchka's skin as the vet on call, Alison Carey, quickly examined her. She listened to her breathing using a stethoscope, looked into her blowhole and checked for cuts and lacerations. "Is she alright? Is she badly hurt?" asked Terry in the desperate tone of a mother quizzing an emergency room doctor examining her injured child.

"Let's move her inside. I'll take X-rays and order other tests. What exactly happened?" Alison asked Terry.

The police had transformed a small warehouse on the dock near Pier 92 into an emergency command center. In one corner, two tables had been moved together. On one table they laid out Kalid's body parts as if they were going to stitch them back together. On another table they spread out his equipment. In another corner of the building technicians were hastily assembling video conferencing equipment. Outside, sirens wailed sporadically as an endless parade of official vehicles carrying police brass, laboratory and CSI technicians, and detectives continued arriving.

Bill Ryan and Commissioner Jackson arrived first, asking questions as they walked in. "Okay, Barone, what've we got?" Jackson asked impatiently.

Sergeant Barone cleared his throat, then began. "Sir, my divers were performing routine surveillance in the area around the QM2, constantly checking her hull with our LIMIS scanner." He paused as Ryan whispered into Jackson's ear.

"Limpet Mine Imaging Sonar."

"At 0200 hours four NYPD divers, Mrs. Manetta and the dolphin were in the water. Suddenly the dolphin leaped clear of the water, next to the QM2, about 200 feet from the stern, indicating an unknown diver was directly beneath her. I fired a signal flare alerting the team there was a probable threat. Then Mr. Manetta and I jumped into the Zodiac and headed for the location where the dolphin had jumped. Officer Perez brought our dive boat into the immediate area. We were still several hundred feet away when there was an underwater explosion, about twenty feet from the QM2's hull. The blast injured two police divers. The dolphin was also injured and was taken to the aquarium for treatment. We recovered the body of the diver who we suspect carried the mine. He's over there," he pointed to the table across the room. "We also recovered his communications equipment. The lab boys are examining it now."

"Any damage to the ship?" Asked Jackson.

"We don't know yet. A visual observation indicated sections of the hull near the blast buckled slightly from the force. Ship personnel informed us there are no leaks, but tomorrow they'll inspect the hull electronically looking for damage like hairline cracks. Cunard told us the QM2's hull is extra thick, reinforced steel to withstand stormy transatlantic crossings. Even if the mine had been magnetically attached it would have blown a small hole in her but never sunk her. The damage would have been very localized."

"So the mine wasn't actually attached to the ship when it exploded?"

"No sir. The dolphin was trained to keep bumping the diver until he dropped the mine. That may have delayed him from attaching it, but we don't know for sure exactly what happened."

"Let's examine what you recovered." They stepped over to the tables as Barone continued.

"As you can see, the explosion's force ripped the diver apart. The fact that he wore a thick wet suit help keep the separate pieces intact." Jackson and Ryan looked at the exposed body parts laid out like a solved jigsaw puzzle. They were visibly relieved when Barone directed them to the table with the equipment. Ryan noticed the commissioner swallow hard. *Hope his dinner's not coming up,* he thought, as Barone resumed his presentation. "Steel 120-cubic feet capacity scuba tank, painted black for reduced visibility, buoyancy vest, fins, and wet suit. But this item is interesting. The partial remains of a full-face mask, a communications pack and this long antenna."

"Excuse me, sir," interrupted an officer carrying a loop of antenna wire. "A diver found this floating in the river just behind the ship." He handed it to Barone, who examined it and compared it to the antenna on the table.

"Looks identical to the other one, except one end is frayed, maybe charred, too. I guess the sci-fi boys from the lab can explain what it all means."

"Okay, I have enough information for now. Let's video conference Homeland Security, the Secret Service, our FBI buddies,

CIA Headquarters, and Cunard Line Officials and tell them what we know so far," said Jackson.

"Excuse me, sir," interjected Lieutenant Marie Wilcox, whose official title was Chief of Media Communications and Public Relations. "What will you tell the media? Hundreds of reporters are outside and our phone's been ringing off the hook at headquarters."

Jackson thought for a second, staring into space, visualizing possible newspaper headline images running through his mind. Then he smiled, selecting one that appealed to him. "Marie, write this headline: 'NYPD dive team prevents underwater terrorist attack against the Queen Mary 2.' Also mention two police divers were injured, and we recovered the body of the suspected terrorist. Finally, inform them we'll hold a news conference at One Police Plaza nine o'clock tomorrow morning." Joe and Sergeant Barone saw Bill Ryan whisper into Jackson's ear again and saw him nod. "Oh Marie, also work into this your story: 'Hero dolphin injured protecting the famous ocean liner.'" She looked up, surprised, as Jackson nodded again, confirming what he had said, then continued writing.

Joe rolled his eyes and shook his head at a grinning Bill Ryan. Turning to Barone he quietly said, "Oh God, I can see the tabloid headlines now: *Flipper Foils Fanatical Frogman!*"

Chapter 41

June 30th

erry spent the night at the aquarium comforting Notchka. The injured dolphin refused food, so the vet inserted a stomach tube, force-feeding her a special diet high in fat and protein. "It's critical we maintain her weight until she's strong enough to eat on her own. I don't see any broken bones on the X-rays, but she's passing blood in her urine, so I suspect kidney damage." She pressed a cloth against the tiny ear opening, a small hole just behind her eye, and showed Terry a small crimson stain. "You can see there's also slight external bleeding from her ears. I also noticed traces of blood in her blowhole when she exhales, so her respiratory system probably suffered internal hemorrhaging from the explosion's concussive force. I gave her a strong antibiotic, just in case there's any infection."

"Will she live?" Terry asked, apprehensively.

"Too early to tell. I want to study the X-rays more thoroughly and see what her blood tests show. One thing in her favor is that she was a very healthy animal before this happened. Do you have any idea how old she is?"

"Not really. I've known Notchka for over 10 years and she already had at least one calf by that time. Recently she had another. How long do dolphins live?"

"Females have a life expectancy of about 30 years, sometimes more. Males have a shorter life span, around 20 to 25, since they lead more active lifestyles, competing for mates, that sort of thing. From what you've told me, Notchka's probably at least 15 years old. I'll examine her more closely and try to determine her age more accurately after the test results come back."

"I just want to take her home to Mexico as soon as possible."

"Well, I'm afraid she can't travel for a while, a couple of weeks at least, perhaps a month. With her injuries she'd never survive the flight right now. Changes in air pressure and stress could prove fatal." As Alison spoke Terry patted and stroked Notchka's smooth skin. "I'm going to turn in. I can drop you somewhere if you like."

"I'll stay here for the night. I don't want her to be alone," Terry said.

"I'm sure that'll help. They're very social animals so your company will do her good. I'll be back early tomorrow morning, but here's my cell number. If anything changes call me right away, okay?"

"Yes, thanks. I will. Good night, Alison." Just as the vet left, Terry's cell phone rang. She saw Joe's number pop up on caller ID. "Hello, Joe."

"Hi, Terry. You sound tired. Are you okay? How's Notchka?"

"One question at a time. I'm tired. I'm okay but . . . well, no I'm not okay, Joe. Notchka's hurt. We don't know how seriously yet, but she suffered internal injuries. She can't fly home right now."

Joe heard, and felt, the pain in her voice. "Terry, I'm sorry. I feel . . ."

"I wish I hadn't let you and Bill talk me into this damn fiasco. If she dies . . ."

"Terry, Notchka helped prevent an attack. It wasn't like what she did wasn't important. She . . ."

"Joe, please spare me the hero speech. I don't want to discuss it now."

"Are you returning to the hotel tonight?"

"No. I'm staying here.

"Okay, I'll take a cab and be right . . ."

"No, Joe. I just want to be alone with Notchka tonight. I'll call you tomorrow," she replied coldly. Notchka floated at the pool edge and Terry heard her wheeze with each breath. She bit her lip, worrying about her friend.

"All right, Terry, I understand. I'm attending the Mayor's press conference at police headquarters tomorrow morning. I'll call you after it's over and give you an update . . . hello? Are you there?" Joe stared at the phone, realizing Terry had already broken the connection moments earlier.

Chapter 42

The press conference at One Police Plaza, NYPD Headquarters, was a three-ring circus, with Commissioner Jackson skillfully playing ringmaster. First, he introduced the Mayor, who read a prepared statement summarizing the previous night's events and confirming details already disclosed: A single unidentified diver had carried out an attack against the Queen Mary 2. The method had been an underwater mine, known in the trade as a limpet mine. An explosion killed the mysterious lone diver and injured two police divers. Damage to the ship was minimal. Queen Elizabeth had held a reception on the ship and departed less than four hours before the attack, but whether she had been a target was just speculation at this time. The investigation would continue, and the police would update the news media accordingly.

Then Commissioner Jackson fielded questions from television and press reporters. As Joe expected, and feared, media attention soon focused on the role of the mysterious dolphin, whom Commissioner Jackson had termed a "hero" during last night's press conference. Answering questions as rapidly as reporters' hands went up, he said, "Yes, the dolphin alerted us to the threat by leaping from the water over the diver's position . . .No, she was not trained as a killer dolphin, but she had probably bumped the diver, preventing him from securing the mine to the ship's hull . . . No, the dolphin was not part of the

Navy's dolphin team." He faltered when questions centered around Mrs. Manetta, the civilian diver mentioned in the press release.

Bill Ryan, standing next to Jackson, stepped forward. "For security reasons we are not disclosing details regarding specific people involved in the case. However, we did secure the assistance of two divers from Mexico who have experience with dolphins." *Too much info for these land sharks, Bill,* Joe thought, shaking his head. Predictably, the press' focus shifted to Bill, and they bombarded him with new questions: Who are these two divers? Where are they from? What role did the Mexican government play in sending the dolphin? Did the U.S. State Department specifically request assistance from Mexico? Was the dolphin injured? Where is it now? Bill, untrained in media relations, realized he had blundered into a minefield and had the classic, 'deer caught in the headlights' look. Jackson rescued him, cutting off the questions.

"That will be all for today, ladies and gentlemen. We will update you as the investigation proceeds. Thank you for coming." Jackson quickly left the podium with the mayor, Bill, Joe and the rest of the team in tow. They convened in an adjoining conference room to discuss the latest results of the crime scene analysis.

Ahmed, the remainder of his team, and Ashur and his men were glued to the 42-inch plasma television in the general meeting room. They were fascinated watching the news conference. CNN kept replaying the news helicopter's aerial footage, showing the arcing flare and then the subsequent geyser erupting twenty feet from the QM2's hull. Individually, the men approached Ahmed, expressing condolences. "I'm so sorry your friend was killed and your mission defeated, by a stupid fish of all things!" Assuming a humble facade, he graciously accepted their sympathy. Only Ashur and Ahmed's surviving team members, Salen and Waleed, knew Kalid's true fate. There was no need for the others to know the real story or details about Ahmed's real mission.

Secretly, Ahmed was thrilled events were playing out as he had planned. While suppressing his joy he boosted the group's mood with a short speech. "Do not be discouraged, my brothers. In several days you will see Allah triumph in glory over these miserable infidels. Until then my team and I have much work to do. Keep your spirits up and do not lose your faith."

Chapter 43

July 1ˢᵗ

Notchka swam to the pool edge and squirted a stream of water into Terry's face. She woke with a start and blinked. "Well, good morning," she said, laughing.

"How's our patient doing?" asked vet Alison Carey.

"As you can see, her sense of humor is intact," replied Terry, drying her face with a towel "Any further results yet?"

"Not yet. Notchka seems stable. Why don't you return to your hotel, get some rest and return this afternoon. I should have more definitive answers for you by then."

"Sounds like a plan. I didn't sleep very well last night. I kept waking up to check on Notchka. I could use several solid hours of shut-eye. I'd really appreciate it if you would call a taxi."

"Sure thing. Follow me. I'll call a cab from my office."

Several minutes later a taxi arrived at the aquarium. Terry gave the driver directions and settled into the rear seat for the ride back to Manhattan. Exhausted from her nightlong poolside vigil, her eyelids fluttered. As she began to doze, the Mayor's situational update meeting convened.

"Anything new?" asked New York City Mayor Ron Williamson, as the team members settled into their seats around the large oval table.

"Yes, but I want to conference in Langley and DC first," said Police Commissioner Jackson. "Is the video feed up, Marie?"

"Working on it. Let me see, I push this button, then this one and . . . yes, there we are!" CIA officer Jeff Becker and his boss, Deputy Director of Intelligence Tom Walsh, appeared on one monitor, and FBI agent Tom McHale with New York State Director of Homeland Security Mike Bilboa appeared together on the other monitor.

"Good morning, gentlemen," said Commissioner Jackson. "I'm here with Mayor Williamson, Lieutenant Bill Ryan, Sergeant Phil Barone, senior lab technician Jill Kramer, and Joe Manetta, Mrs. Manetta's husband, who is also assisting us. Can you see and hear us?"

"Yes we can," said Tom Walsh.

"Okay here," replied Tom McHale.

"Good. Here's what we've learned since last night. There were no further attempts to sink the QM2. No additional mines have been found, no other enemy divers. Of course, we'll keep our NYPD divers in the water around the clock until she departs for England on July Fourth. Unfortunately, we won't have the dolphin's services. She's being treated at the New York Aquarium for concussive injuries sustained from the explosion. I don't suppose we could get a Navy dolphin here on short notice?" he asked, looking at DDI Tom Walsh in Virginia.

"Negative, Commissioner. I made several calls, but all their dolphins are busy in the Middle East right now. Best they could commit is possibly two weeks."

"Well, by that time the QM2 should be back in Southampton. Okay, Phil, you and your dive team will continue with the resources you've already got. I'm turning the meeting over to Jill Kramer, senior crime scene lab analyst. Ms. Kramer."

Jill Kramer was 39, but appeared ten years younger. While that was advantageous in social situations, she preferred appearing her age when making important presentations. So she tied back her long blonde hair in a twist, and substituted tinted black-frame glasses for her usual contact lenses. Flats temporarily replaced her usual heels. Her final accoutrement, a white lab smock, hung loosely over her stylish silk blouse and slim-tailored skirt, transformed Jill from an attractive woman exuding subtle sexuality to a serious professional projecting competence and credibility.

She stood and walked to a laptop set up at the end of the conference table beside a large cardboard box. Reaching into the box, she carefully held up the charred, bent frame of a dive mask. The faceplate was missing, though a few shards of tempered glass remained in the frame's edge. "An NYPD diver recovered this dive mask early this morning. This type of full-face mask is used for communicating with other divers or someone at the surface. It's consistent with this communications pack and antenna," she said lifting the components from the box and placing them on the table. "This type of antenna is similar to ones used by submarines running deep when they have to communicate with their base. They extend the antenna, which floats to the surface, perhaps three or four hundred feet above, so the sub can send and receive messages." She pushed the "enter" button on her laptop and a diagram of a submarine appeared, showing an antenna floating at the surface.

"Does anyone suggest the diver came from a submarine?" asked FBI Agent McHale. After several seconds of silence, Deputy Director of Intelligence Walsh spoke.

"Highly doubtful these terrorists would have a submarine at their disposal to penetrate New York Harbor and the Hudson River."

"Sorry, I didn't mean to imply they did," replied Jill. "I used the submarine reference just to illustrate their probable communication method." She paused for additional questions and then continued. "Divers also recovered parts of a limpet mine housing." She held up four curved pieces of gray fiberglass, then laid them on the table in a circular pattern. "Many pieces are missing, but you can visualize its shape and size by mentally filling in the gaps. We also found several other components." She placed several deformed pieces of metal in the middle of the ring.

"Were you able to identify the type of mine?" asked Agent Jeff Becker.

"Yes. It's called a Maindeka mine."

"That's the most advanced underwater mine available on international markets," interjected Becker's boss, DDI Walsh.

"That's my understanding," replied Jill. "It contains about one kilogram of explosive, about two point two pounds. The mine weighs about six kilograms, a little more than thirteen pounds. Here's a picture of a complete Maindeka mine." She pressed "enter" on her laptop and a cutaway diagram appeared, showing the mine and its components. "Now here's something else we found, and it really puzzles us." She held up another antenna. "You can see it's identical to the other one. But one end is frayed and charred. We think this one was attached to the mine so it could be fired by remote control."

"Why does that puzzle you?" asked Police Commissioner Jackson.

"Well, this mine utilizes the most advanced electronic and mechanical timers available, and also the latest safety devices. No way this mine explodes accidentally. Furthermore, why explode it remotely? You can just set it and forget it. No need to overcomplicate the issue by manually overriding the automatic firing system and risk exposure if someone spotted the antenna floating on the surface."

"This reminds me what's going on in Iraq with all these IEDs," said DDI Walsh.

"Excuse me?" asked Bill Ryan.

"IED's. Improvised explosive devices," explained Walsh. "The advantage is you can put the explosive in place, then transmit an electronic signal exploding the damn thing when a tank, Humvee or another attractive target passes. After the smoke clears, no more tank or Humvee."

"Well, in this case, they could have been waiting for a target of opportunity," replied Jackson. "You know we've been protecting Queen Elizabeth against the assassination attempt your operative uncovered. What was his name?"

"Delgado. Navy SEAL Anthony Delgado."

"Right. The agent who was killed gathering the information. Perhaps that was their plan. A timing device wouldn't be appropriate unless you knew the queen's schedule to the minute, which we didn't publicize. So using a remote detonator makes more sense in that scenario. I think we've solved that mystery."

"Except for the fact that she had already left the ship," disagreed Becker, "and also the jewelry reference to hanging her with her necklace."

"Well, as far as the timing maybe they just blew it, pardon the pun," replied Bill Ryan. "Perhaps they didn't know she had already left. And, if they did know, maybe they thought she would return. These guys aren't supermen. They can screw up, too."

"Yeah, sometimes we forget that," said, Walsh.

Jackson noticed Jill Kramer shifting uncomfortably on her feet. "Ms. Kramer, I'm sorry. Anything else?"

Good thing I didn't wear heels today, she thought. "Yes, sir. We tried obtaining the serial numbers on the recovered equipment so we could compare them with what was bought from the scuba shop in Long Island, but the numbers were either filed off or the explosion damaged them too much. I understand the owner couldn't recognize the diver from a photo since his face was mangled. But she said our description of the recovered equipment sounded like what was purchased in her store. We're sending it to the various manufacturers to determine if it was shipped to that dive shop. We feel there's enough evidence to petition the court again for a search warrant."

"Bullshit!" whispered the mayor, leaning toward his police commissioner. "I'm not going to sit here and wait until these assholes blow up my city. Get a couple of your best breaking and entering guys right after this meeting. Guys you can really trust to keep their mouths shut. I don't want to know their names. Get into that Sackett Street building and find out what the hell's inside. They report back only to you, and you report your findings only to me. Understand?"

Commissioner Jackson took a deep breath, trying not to appear shocked that his boss had given him an order that could land them both in federal prison for violating the U.S. Constitution. He looked at the Mayor, nodded, and then turned toward Jill. "Thank you, Ms. Kramer. Anything else?"

"No, sir. That covers everything we came up with," Jill replied, returning to her seat.

"Well, I think we can chalk up one for the good guys!" exclaimed Mayor Williamson. "I'd like to thank the CIA team for their excellent advance information about the attack, and the FBI for coordinating so closely with the NYPD. The Queen is well protected and we'll focus our resources on her for the remaining four days until she leaves on July Fifth. I think we're almost home free. We'll keep our guard up until she's in the air, and finally home safe in Windsor Castle."

The monitors went dark and Jackson breathed a sigh of relief. "Let's break for lunch and then review any last thoughts. By the way, Joe, any word about your dolphin?"

"I'm calling Terry now, Commissioner," said Joe, punching in her speed dial number on his cell phone.

Chapter 44

July 1ˢᵗ

Terry's cell phone rang. She looked at the screen and saw Joe's number appear in caller ID. She briefly considered not answering but then pressed the connection button. "Hello Joe. How was your meeting?" she asked coolly. Terry's icy tone upset Joe, but he took a deep breath and pointedly ignored it.

"Fine, but we're having a follow-up meeting after lunch just to discuss where we stand. Then I think we can all go home. How's Notchka?" Several seconds of silence worried Joe. "Terry? Are you okay? How's . . . ."

"I heard you," Terry replied. Joe heard the strain in her voice. "The vet said we can't leave New York until she can fly, probably not for at least two weeks, maybe three. She's hurt worse than we thought, Joe. She has internal injuries to her lungs and kidneys, and her hearing may have been damaged. On top of that, the vet said she's older than we thought. She examined her teeth more closely and looked for other signs of aging. She said Notchka's at least 20 years old, maybe more. I had estimated only about 15."

"Did she say how long dolphins live?"

"Females around 30, males about 25. But I can't leave here without her, Joe."

"I agree. And I'm not leaving without you, so we're both staying. I'll call you as soon as we're through, okay? Bye. Love you." Joe listened for Terry's reply. *CLICK*. It was the first time he could ever recall Terry not reciprocating by replying, "Love you too." He sighed and returned to the follow-up meeting.

"The mayor had other meetings to attend so he asked me to apologize for his absence and express his thanks to all of you for a job well done," Commissioner Jackson began. "Okay. Your reactions to this morning's meeting?" Silence. "Anyone? Yes, Phil."

"Based on what I heard, I don't think the QM2's in further danger. We'll keep our divers in the water until she leaves, but I think the bad guys shot their wad."

"Okay. Let's go 'round the table. I want everyone's input. Bill?"

"I agree with Phil. We'll transfer more assets to cover today's celebrations, protect the Queen during her rest day tomorrow, during her General Assembly presentation the following day, attendance at July Fourth celebrations, and finally her motorcade to JFK on the Fifth. But I don't see anyone getting near her for an assassination attempt, using a necklace or anything else."

"Jill?"

"Commissioner, we were called in after everything hit the fan. Our department just analyzes hard data. We have no expertise interpreting anyone's intentions. Personally, however, I agree the terrorists took their best shot to kill the Queen and missed. I don't expext they'll try again, but who knows?"

"I agree with all of you. I don't see any further . . . Oh hello, Joe. Didn't realize you were among the missing. We were just exchanging opinions as to where things stand. Any final comments?"

Joe was silent for a moment, collecting his thoughts. He took a deep breath and then spoke. "Well Commissioner, several things have been bothering me. May I?" he asked, stepping up to a white board.

"By all means," said Jackson, handing him a blue marker.

"Okay. Point one. Jill's analysis on their remote firing plan using that antenna bothers me. It bothered her, too," he said, looking at Jill. "There's a reason for that. If you want to blow up the QM2, just do what she said. Remember? 'Set it and forget it.' Even DDI Walsh said the method reminded him of how Iraqi insurgents wait for an attractive target to drive past and then explode their bombs, or IEDs, or whatever the hell he called them. That tells me they may still be after Queen Elizabeth. Maybe they just messed up their timing.

"Point two. Why did the bomb blow up anyway? Jill said the way that thing's designed an accidental explosion is impossible.

"Three. Why only one bomb? They must have known two pounds of explosive wouldn't sink that baby. She's built with a reinforced steel hull and watertight compartments. She'd never go down from one bomb. They'd need several limpet mines to finish the job.

"Four. Up until now our intelligence has been right on the mark. So I don't think we should ignore all this information we heard about 'great loss of life,' 'large economic loss' 'the Queen never leaving New York' and this assassination attempt using her necklace, jewels or whatever. I don't believe these guys are finished." Joe looked around the room and saw four sets of eyes boring into him. He realized he may have overstepped his bounds and decided to temper his remarks. "But hey, I'm just an ex-detective," he said, glancing at his former partner, Bill Ryan. "What the hell do I know?"

Bill spoke first. "Well, *ex*-partner, before you became an *ex*-detective you always had an uncanny knack for turning a tough case on-end and coming up with the right answer."

The room fell silent as the group studied the white board Joe had filled with his analysis. After several seconds Commissioner Jackson broke the silence. "Your points are well taken, Joe. I'll discuss them off-line with our friends at CIA, FBI and Homeland Security. We'll get back to you. When are you and Terry leaving?"

"Oh yes, I've been meaning to talk to you about that. Looks like we're stuck in New York for a couple of weeks. Notchka can't fly because of her injuries. Terry won't leave without her, and I won't leave without my wife."

"I'll talk to the mayor about upgrading your accommodations," Jackson said. "Bill, why don't you drive Joe to the aquarium so he can check on the dolphin and visit his wife."

Chapter 45

Bill and Joe drove across the Brooklyn Bridge in silence. Turning off the bridge onto the Brooklyn Queens Expressway, Bill finally spoke. Smiling, he said, "Well, ex-partner, just as we were all looking forward to regular schedules and enjoying the end of the holiday, you had to muck things up with your analysis."

"Sorry, old buddy," Joe teased back. "But I really don't think these guys are finished. And in any case, don't we, I mean you, still have to apprehend the guys who pulled off this attack?"

"Yeah, good point. We, not including you, have to locate them. But, with everything we've recovered we have some good leads." The BQE led into the Gowanus Expressway, the elevated highway running above the neighborhoods of Park Slope, Sunset Park and Bay Ridge. Then the roadway became the Belt Parkway, running alongside New York Harbor, passing under the Verrazano Bridge and out toward Coney Island. They took the New York Aquarium exit and pulled into the parking lot. Bill displayed his police credentials and breezed past security. Inside, they navigated the holiday crowd as inconspicuously as possible and met Terry next to Notchka's tank.

"Hi, hon," said Joe, kissing Terry, trying to ignore her indifferent response. She also ignored Bill's formal greeting. "How's the patient today?" asked Joe.

"A little better, I suppose. The vet said she's coming along. She's eating better, which is a good sign, but she's still listless. Here comes Alison now."

"Hello, everyone," said Alison. "I suppose you're anxious for an update. Notchka's stable, eating live fish on her own. But she's still exhibiting signs of internal bleeding, resulting in her lack of energy, which I know Terry has noticed. The other concern is her hearing. We saw some blood oozing from her ear holes the first day, but that seems to have stopped. Dolphins don't have the same external ear structure as most mammals, and their hearing works differently, too. They also pick up sounds through their jawbones and other organs in their head. We did some tests, and she isn't reacting to sounds in the usual frequencies that dolphins use for communication. That's troublesome because dolphins are social animals. Without hearing her pod's calls she'll lose contact, won't know where food sources are located, and, well, she wouldn't last very long."

"Is her hearing loss permanent?" asked Terry, concerned.

"We don't know. It may return completely, or it may not. Time will tell. If you don't have any other questions I have to tend to a sick harbor seal. I'll be keeping a close eye on Notchka, and I'll call you if there are any changes. For now she's doing as well as you can expect." Alison left, and Terry buried her face in Joe's chest, sobbing softly as he embraced her. Bill was about to speak, but a glance from Joe told him silence was best for now.

They left the aquarium and walked toward Bill's dark blue, unmarked police Crown Victoria. Just as they got in, Bill's cell phone rang. He answered, and as he listened a large smile formed on his face. Finally he said, "Hey, that's great news. I'll tell them right away."

"Tell us what?" asked Joe as Bill navigated through the parking lot traffic and retraced his route back to Manhattan.

"Well, you're now official guests of New York City. Since you'll be staying with us longer than you planned, the mayor has upgraded your hotel accommodations to the Waldorf Astoria." Bill looked into the rearview mirror and saw Joe's raised eyebrows. "We may have a few other small surprises for you as well."

"Hey, hear that, hon? We'll be rubbing elbows with society's upper crust," Joe said, laughing, trying unsuccessfully to buoy Terry's spirits. Forty minutes later they arrived at the entrance of the fabled Waldorf Astoria Hotel on Fifth Avenue. Bill noticed a crowd outside and Joe heard him quietly utter, "Uh oh."

"What's the problem, Bill?"

"Get your running shoes on, folks. Looks like someone leaked your arrival to the media. As soon as I pull up to the curb jump out and bolt for the entrance."

Bill had barely stopped the car when Joe flung the door open and pulled Terry from the car. The media hounds closed in. "There they are!" someone in the crowd shouted. TV camera lights glaring, reporters shoved microphones in their faces and screamed questions.

"Let's go, hon." The action snapped Terry out of her lethargy, and she ran close on Joe's heels, bewildered by the chaotic scene.

"Tell us how the dolphin is doing!"

"How do you like New York City?"

"What are your plans now?"

"How did you capture the dolphin?"

"Were you hurt in the explosion?"

"What the hell was that all about, Bill?" gasped Terry as the concierge guided them to a private check-in area.

"Well, I'm afraid someone must have tipped them off. Someone as in, Marie Wilcox, remember her? NYPD's Chief of Media relations and Communications? You two really do deserve the City's best hospitality for all you've done. But the mayor is running for re-election this year, and someone probably applied some pressure to ensure your limelight rubs off on him," explained Bill.

Joe shook his head but Terry's ire was stirred. "Son-of-a-bitch! Next time I see him I'll . . . ."

"Hey, my advice is to relax and enjoy being wined and dined in style. As I said, you deserve it, and this was a small price to pay."

After checking in, they were ushered into a private elevator for a ride to their suite. The bellhop opened the door and Terry stepped inside. She did a double take and screamed, "Oh my God!"

Chapter 46

July 1ˢᵗ

Jaime Rameriz was sitting on the sofa facing the door. On either side of Jaime sat Jackie and Peter. "What are you . . . I mean, how did you get . . ." Before Terry could formulate her question the children ran into her open arms as she knelt, hugging them. Joe stepped into the room and peeked over Terry's shoulder at the children. He reached over and tousled Peter's hair, then hoisted him up with a kiss.

"How're ya doin', tiger." Then he picked Jackie up and twirled her around. "You really surprised us, princess."

"Did we daddy? Did we?" Jackie squealed.

"You sure did," answered Terry. "Jaime, what's going on?"

"Well Terry, late last night I got a call from the mayor's office in New York inviting us to visit because your stay had been extended. The kids had no school, and it seemed like a good idea. I know I should have asked you first, but there was no time, and we thought surprising you would be fun."

"It's a shock, but a happy one. I'm glad you all came," she said, hugging both children and then Jaime.

"We have some fun stuff planned for you," said Bill. They spun around, forgetting he was in the room. "You'll be the mayor's special guest tonight at the fireworks display over the East River. Then, for the next couple of days, guided city tours and free museum passes so you can explore New York on your own."

"Can you shield us from those obnoxious media people?" asked Terry. "Being the focus of the New York paparazzi isn't my idea of fun. And from a security perspective I'd just as soon keep a low profile."

"I'll see what I can do," replied Bill. "For now just unpack and relax. We transferred your luggage from your other hotel."

"Mom, how's Notchka?" asked Jackie.

"Yeah, can we go see her?" asked Peter.

"Sure, kids. We'll visit her before the fireworks show. She's doing okay. After we unpack we'll take a ride and go."

In downtown Brooklyn Ahmed and his team were preparing for the next phase of their mission. They were huddled studying street and highway maps, blueprints and making notes. The wide-screen television was on constantly, as Ashur's men channel- surfed for additional news about the recovery of Kalid's body and the QM2's status. "And here are the heroes who helped stymie the terrorist attack on the Queen Mary 2," said the news announcer.

Ahmed and his men looked up as the channel surfer paused. All were fixated on the TV screen. "Shown here getting out of their car and running through a gauntlet of reporters into the Waldorf Astoria are Terry and Joe Manetta, the husband and wife divers who brought Notchka the dolphin from Cozumel, Mexico." The cameras caught the chaotic scene as Joe pushed through a phalanx of reporters and cameramen, waving away microphones and pulling Terry behind him. One camera angle caught her turning around, bewildered by the scene. Ahmed studied her face as the news reporter continued. "The couple chose not to make a statement at this time. We understand the mayor has moved them to a private luxury suite at the Waldorf as a token of New York City's appreciation for their assistance in foiling the attack, in which one terrorist was killed. Now back to Jim and Lynn in the newsroom."

Several men cursed watching the segment. "American whore bitch!" swore one, shaking his fist at the flat-panel screen.

"Spineless dog of a husband," spat another.

"Waleed, please get me the address of that hotel and a street map," said Ahmed, quietly.

"Ahmed, surely you are not going there," asked Ashur. "They will have mountains of security. It may even be a trap!"

"No, not now. But information is a powerful tool, Ashur," he replied. "You can never have too much because you never know when it will become useful."

Chapter 47

July 2ⁿᵈ

The Queen rested for a second day, enjoying the hospitality of Mayor Williamson and his wife, who hosted a modest reception at their home in her honor. Gracie Mansion occupies a small area bordered by the East River on one side, York Avenue on the other, and wooded grounds on the north and south sides. NYPD patrol boats guarded the nearby riverfront. Police blocked York Avenue from pedestrian and vehicular traffic for two blocks on either side. They also patrolled the adjacent grounds, and helicopters made frequent flyovers scanning the area from above. Security personnel had been fully briefed on the CIA-gathered intelligence and were determined to prevent a personal attack against the Queen during their watch. Inside, the Queen's entourage, Mayor Williamson and his wife and invited guests shared afternoon tea. "I could have used some of this security last year. Those transit union negotiations got a little heated at times," the Mayor quipped. The Queen received frequent compliments on the diamond and sapphire necklace she wore, openly defying the terrorists' threat.

In downtown Brooklyn, the safe house occupants filed into the large room carrying their prayer blankets. Walking past the television, Ahmed and his team paused as CNN showed a picture of Gracie Mansion. They listened to the announcer's voice-over. "And here in Gracie Mansion the Mayor of New York hosted a reception for Queen Elizabeth, one of the most heavily guarded events in New York City history. Hundreds of police, combined with boats, helicopters and other undisclosed security arrangements, provided impenetrable security. Now back to you, Richard."

"It appears their security forces will be focused on the British Queen, following her wherever she goes, Ahmed," said Ashur.

"Yes, it does seem so. You know, Ashur, sometimes coincidence can be welcomed like a good friend who visits unexpectedly," he replied, smiling. Ashur was puzzled to see his friend in such good spirits watching these developments. "Let us go inside and pray to Allah for success," Ahmed said, turning off the television and walking into the large meeting room. Ashur followed him inside, spread his prayer blanket on the bare wood floor and began praying, unaware that two NYPD undercover officers were carefully analyzing the contents of his home.

Earlier that morning, Ashur had left his Sackett Street building, got into his car and started the engine, giving little thought to the Verizon telephone repair truck parked across the street. Inside, two detectives compared the photograph they carried to the old gentleman driving away. "That's him," confirmed Pete Donaldson to his partner, Harold Walker.

"Let's give him ten minutes in case he forgot something," cautioned Walker. Ten minutes later, Donaldson made a U-turn and parked in front of Ashur's building. They unloaded a ladder and leaned it against a telephone pole, conveniently near the building. Donaldson scaled the ladder and pretended to splice a wire, while Walker pressed the doorbell, holding a clipboard. As expected, no one answered the door. "Okay, no one's home, Pete. Come on." Donaldson walked up the front steps and stood behind Walker, shielding him from the view of any curious passersby. Walker selected the appropriate lock pick and skillfully worked it into the keyhole. In several seconds he sprung the lock. He opened the door a crack, pretending he was speaking to someone behind it, just out of sight. Then the two men walked in and shut the door.

"Hello. Verizon," shouted Walker, in the event someone was in the house but had not heard the doorbell. After seconds of silence he said, "Okay, we have a basement, a ground floor and a second floor. Let's be quick, thorough, and leave no trace we were here. Samples first." The two detectives slipped on rubber gloves and moved from room to room, wiping all surfaces and countertops with chemically treated swabs. Minutes later they inserted the swabs into small plastic bags and sealed them. "Those should keep the bomb squad analysts busy," said Walker. "Got your camera ready?"

"Yep, let's go," replied Donaldson. They took pictures of every room, then carefully opened all drawers and closets, examining, photographing and then carefully re-arranging the contents. "Not too much here, Harry. Just normal stuff, if you consider all this anti-American hate literature normal," Donaldson said, glancing at an open desk and coffee table covered with militant Islamic pamphlets and books.

"Well, Pete, normal or not, it's not illegal. Let's look for dive equipment, receipts for purchases, anything tying this guy to the attack on the QM2." Thirty minutes later the detectives had thoroughly searched Ashur's house but found nothing incriminating. "We're done. Give a last look around and make sure everything's as it was. We don't want to tip this guy that anyone was here. I didn't see anything suspicious, but maybe someone will spot something in a photo, or these swab samples will test positive for explosives."

"Let's get out of Dodge," replied Donaldson, satisfied they had left no evidence of their visit. Exiting the building, he looked back inside as he closed the door. "Thanks very much, sorry to bother you," he said to no one, for the benefit of a young man eyeballing them suspiciously as he walked past the building.

Chapter 48

July 3rd

Queen Elizabeth's motorcade left Gracie Mansion the next morning. The four-car caravan turned off York Avenue and headed south on the FDR Drive for the five-minute drive to the United Nations. Terry, Joe and specially invited guests were already seated in the gallery when she arrived. The General Assembly President spoke first. His welcoming remarks were followed by a short speech from the President of the United States, who had just flown in. Finally, Queen Elizabeth rose and strode purposefully toward the podium. She had exchanged the diamond and sapphire necklace for a subtler gold necklace with an emerald pendant. But the fact that she wore a necklace at all was a deliberate, bold statement, impressing those aware of the threat.

While the Queen spoke, a single car left downtown Brooklyn. Ahmed, Salen and Waleed rehearsed details of their upcoming attack while he drove. Delayed by traffic, they reached the scene in an hour. Ahmed's plan required them splitting up. Waleed and Salen would be stationed at one location, Ahmed at another. Either could initiate the attack, functioning as a backup in the event one was prevented from carrying out his assignment. Today's exercise was reconnoitering locations from which to initiate tomorrow's attack. The requirements were simple. They needed unobstructed sight lines in a place where they could mingle, appearing as typical American citizens relaxing and enjoying a holiday. Driving slowly through the area where Waleed and Salen would be stationed, Ahmed stopped the car and pointed.

"Over there. I see a good spot. Let's take a walk."

He parked the car, and they walked through a wooded area to a grassy clearing where several families gathered around picnic tables preparing barbecues. The park contained small portable volleyball nets and sections marked off for soccer and softball. The three men stopped near a row of benches where sun worshippers were reclining, using silver reflectors to magnify the sun's tanning rays on their faces. Ahmed watched them and shook his head. "By midnight tomorrow these vain infidels will have more to worry about than their appearance."

"If they are still alive after midnight," said Salen, laughing.

"I think this location will make an excellent place to carry out the attack. I'll drop you off several hours earlier. You can relax and then move into position at the appropriate time. Let's go. I need to find a spot for myself." They returned to the car and drove for about thirty minutes. Ahmed slowly passed several potential locations until he found one he liked. "Ah, this is perfect. From here I can sit peacefully and watch everything unfold. Okay, let's review everything again, from the beginning."

After the Queen's address, she met privately with the U.S. President. They spoke briefly, and the Queen asked him to convey her deepest sympathy to the Navy SEAL's family for sacrificing his life to uncover the threat against her and the QM2. The president promised and bid her farewell. Then, his motorcade sped along the FDR Drive to the mid-town heliport where he boarded one of three identical helicopters for the short flight to Washington D.C. The United Nations General Assembly President hosted a reception for the Queen and General Assembly dignitaries, after which she would return to Gracie Mansion and rest until tomorrow's July Fourth celebrations.

Terry left the U.N. with Joe and Bill Ryan to pick up Jackie, Peter and Jaime for a trip to the aquarium. In addition to visiting Notchka, their plans included a private behind-the-scenes tour.

Arriving at the aquarium they went directly to Notchka's tank. The dolphin recognized them, swam to the tank edge and squirted water on Jackie and Peter, who squealed in delight. The aquarium director took the children and Jaime on their tour. Terry watched them walk toward the shark exhibit, and then she and Joe met with the vet. "How is she, Alison?" Terry asked.

"Well, the bleeding has ceased, but she's developed a lung infection, similar to pneumonia. Come over here, I'll show you." Alison stepped to the tank's edge and slapped the water. Notchka swam over and she said, "lean over her blow hole and smell her breath when she exhales." Terry did as Alison instructed and her eyes flew wide open, tearing as if she had inhaled smelling salts. Joe followed suit, with a similar reaction.

"Phew! That's a pretty mean odor. Smells like rotten eggs," he said.

"Yes. I've upped her antibiotic dosage and supplemented it with a stronger antibiotic. That should suppress the infection in several days."

Terry watched the children run to the beluga whale exhibit, then she turned to Alison. "When do you think we can return to Cozumel, Alison?"

"If she improves, I'd say in a week. If not, difficult to say."

"I understand. Thank you. Excuse us, but we have to see what trouble our troops are in. I'll be in touch." She found the children with a trainer, feeding the walrus.

"Mom, this is so cool," said Peter, throwing a fish as Terry and Joe laughed.

"Way to go, tiger," he said. "Okay, Jackie's turn."

An hour later they bid the aquarium staff farewell. As Bill drove from the parking lot, he said, "Well, how about a ride on the Staten Island Ferry and a tour of lower Manhattan before dinner?"

"Sounds like a plan," said Terry. "You look pretty relaxed compared to this morning."

Bill glanced at his watch. "Well, by now the president should be at the White House and the Queen should be sipping sherry with the mayor, so the heat's off. The bad guys took their best shot at the QM2 and the Queen and missed, so that threat's over. Of course, we're still keeping our security level up. We'll be diverting security assets from the QM2 to cover the Queen during tomorrow's festivities. And we'll maintain Code Red status for the remainder of the week. We'll follow up our leads and track down Humpty Dumpty's friends, but I expect they've probably left the country by now."

"Yeah, having those guys still running around is a loose thread that really needs tying up," said Joe.

"Well, at least you folks can all relax, enjoy the rest of your New York visit and focus on getting Notchka home," said Bill.

Chapter 49

July 4ᵗʰ ... 7am

The next morning Joe dressed while Terry, the children and Jaime slept. His buzzing Norelco electric shaver woke Terry. She rolled over, stretched and rubbed her eyes. "Hey, where're you bound for, it's only seven," she said, checking the alarm clock.

"Bill asked me to attend a final meeting downtown early this morning. It's a recap on where everything stands. I shouldn't be long. What's your agenda today?"

"I'm taking Jaime and the children to the Hayden Planetarium and Museum of Natural History. We can have lunch there and spend the day. They've never been to such a large museum. Then I thought we'd all eat dinner at the Marriott Marquis Hotel. They have a revolving restaurant. The kids will get a kick out of that. Afterwards, I planned on using the special comp tickets Bill got us for the Empire State Building's observation deck. He said from up there we'd see fireworks displays over both the East and Hudson Rivers, and even at the tip of Manhattan, near the Statue of Liberty. The kids and Jaime would love that. Me too! It'll be a clear night, so New York should look fabulous all lit up."

"Sounds good. After my meeting, Bill and I are having lunch in mid-town with some old buddies. We'll probably spend the afternoon catching up on cop gossip. You know, who got promoted, who's still married and who's not, who's retiring soon, all that interesting stuff.

I'll scoot over to the Marriott and meet you guys for dinner. Then we can all visit the Empire State."

"That's the plan," agreed Terry.

"Okay, see you later," Joe said, leaning over and kissing Terry before leaving for the meeting.

Exiting the elevator, Joe found Bill waiting in the hotel lobby. "Okay, Joe-boy. The car's right outside. We'll be at the meeting in a few minutes. Afterwards I'm sure we can officially cut you two loose."

"Sounds great. Let's go."

Twenty-five minutes later they arrived at One Police Plaza. Commissioner Jackson was already conducting a three-way video conference call with Deputy Director Of Intelligence Tom Walsh and FBI Special Agent Tom McHale. Jackson turned around when they entered the conference room. "Bill Ryan and Joe Manetta just joined us, gentlemen. Have a seat, guys." Bill and Joe had just settled into their seats when the Mayor and New York State Director of Homeland Security Bilboa walked in a moment later, flanked by crime scene analyst Jill Kramer and NYPD dive team leader Officer Phil Barone. "I think we're all present now," said Jackson as Mayor Williamson nodded. "I'll throw out some thoughts, and you all can react as you see fit. Basically I think we're home free. The Queen is well protected at Gracie Mansion, and she'll have full security covering her during today's events. The president is back in the White House. The Queen Mary 2 sails this evening. There are no high-value political figures aboard. She's just headed on a typical cruise. I believe Phil Barone's scuba team has her covered until she leaves her berth," he looked at Barone, who nodded affirmatively, "and the Coast Guard will accompany her leaving the harbor. Frankly, I don't see any other risks. Does anyone else here in New York have any other conclusions?" He scanned the room.

"Excuse me," interjected Jill Kramer. "We expect confirmation any day that the recovered dive equipment was the same equipment purchased in that Long Island scuba shop. I'm confident we'll get our search warrant for the Sackett Street premises. Something may . . ."

The Police Commissioner politely cut Jill off. He had already learned that his illegal break-in had yielded no additional evidence. "We'll pursue that investigation of course, Ms. Kramer, but it's doubtful that anything will turn up before the ship leaves New York tonight and the Queen leaves tomorrow. Does anyone else have anything to add?" No one spoke. "Washington and Virginia?"

"We concur," replied Tom McHale in Washington.

"I feel the same way," said DDI Walsh, in Virginia. "As you know, the CIA thought both queens together, the real queen and the ship, fit the information profile we had gathered. Joe Manetta, Commissioner Jackson shared your points with me. I was very impressed with your analysis. Any chance you'd like to join our team?"

"Thank you, sir, but I'm having too much fun living out every guy's Caribbean fantasy," replied Joe as everyone laughed.

"I was afraid you'd say that," replied DDI Walsh, chuckling. "Well, we concur that this case is closed, except for some mopping up on your end."

"Yes, and we're helping out with some federal manpower," interjected Special Agent Tom McHale.

Mayor Williamson stood. "It sounds like we're all in agreement. I'd like to personally thank everyone here for your assistance. It is gratifying to see major departments, the NYPD, FBI, CIA and Homeland Security working so well together. And Joe, you and Terry provided invaluable assistance as private citizens. I believe we can terminate these proceedings. Thank you all once again."

The video screen went blank, and everyone in New York stood and shook hands. Joe made a quick circuit around the room accepting congratulations and then left with Bill to meet their NYPD friends for lunch, laughs and drinks at Clancy's, a bar and grill on Second Avenue in the 50s.

1pm

In Brooklyn, Ahmed and his men ate lunch quietly. Each man reflected on his assignment. Ahmed handed Salen and Waleed envelopes. "Inside is cash, a reservation at a Holiday Inn near Newark Airport and a reservation for your plane ride home tomorrow morning. You will travel west to Los Angeles and then to Pakistan. I will travel east from JFK and meet you there."

"I thought we were going to become martyrs, like Kalid," said Salen.

Ahmed smiled. "Do not be disappointed. I am pleased you are willing to offer Allah your lives. But it is not necessary. Regretfully, my plan required Kalid's early death. But there is no need to sacrifice more brave fighters like you. We'll need you again. Speaking of fighting, I almost forgot. Take these." He reached into a canvas bag and pulled out two Glock nine-millimeter automatic pistols. He passed them across the table. "This is just in case anyone attempts to interfere with your mission. Only use them as a last resort. Hopefully you won't need them. Remember, discard them before you arrive at the airport." He looked at his watch. *By midnight, my year of planning will explode into glory.* "It is time. Let's go."

5:45pm

Bill dropped Joe off at the Waldorf. "Well, Joe-boy, thanks again for everything. I'll be in touch before you leave for Cozumel."

"My pleasure, Bill. But let's never do it again," Joe said, smiling. "I'm going to change and meet Terry at the Marriott Marquis for dinner. I'll call you before we leave."

Chapter 50

Joe hailed a cab for a ride across town. After weaving through rush hour traffic, he arrived at the Marriott Marquis Hotel and took an elevator up to the dining room. He spotted Terry, Jaime, Jackie and Peter at a table reading menus. He waved and walked over. "We expected you an hour ago. How'd your meeting and lunch with the boys go?" asked Terry.

"Sorry about that, hon. We were reminiscing about the good old days and then they filled me in on recent events. I guess time just flew. Then I got caught in rush hour traffic. A twenty-minute cab ride took over an hour. But everything else is fine, I guess. All's well with the world, peace reigns, and the country's safe."

"Do I detect your usual sarcasm, dear?"

"Well, I raised some pretty good points the other day and thought I poked some holes in their rosy balloon. They claim they considered my analysis, but I think they just dismissed me as a raving, frustrated pessimist."

"Oh don't be so glum. They're probably right. I mean, not about my hubby being a raving pessimist, but that's what they do for a living, isn't it? Evaluate disparate facts and make conclusions?"

"I suppose. They did offer me a job in Langley, though."

"You didn't accept, I hope!" replied Terry, feigning anxiety.

"Well, I thought you'd like the idea of me as a secret agent, like an American James Bond," said Joe, playing along.

"If I wanted James Bond I could have always lured him to Cozumel. But I chose you instead, shaken, not stirred."

Joe laughed and glanced at Jaime, who looked puzzled. "You have to see the movies to get the joke, Jaime." He turned to Terry. "No, honey, I turned 'em down."

"Aw Dad, you could've been so cool," said Peter. "Fast cars, secret weapons, all that stuff."

"Now Peter, I think your dad's very cool just the way he is," replied Terry.

"Yeah, Peter," chided Jackie. "Dad had guns and a badge and all that stuff. And he saved Mom's life, too."

"I still think secret agents are cool," retorted Peter, defensively.

"I feel dizzy," said Jaime, holding his head. "I think the room is moving!"

"Of course it's moving, Jaime. That's the attraction here. You stay in one place and your panoramic view changes. Isn't it fun?" asked Terry.

"Perhaps I'll feel better after I eat something," remarked Jaime. "Can we order?"

"Sure. I'm hungry too. Waiter?" Joe beckoned, gaining the nearest server's attention. Waiting for dinner, Joe and the children stepped over to the restaurant's curved floor-to-ceiling window-wall and enjoyed the slowly changing views of New York City and its outer boroughs.

Eventually the revolving dining room faced west, toward the Hudson River.

"Hey dad, is that the Queen Mary down there?" asked Peter.

"Sure is. Looks like a pretty big ship, even from up here, doesn't it?"

"Even bigger than the cruise ships that come to Cozumel?" asked Jackie.

"Yep. That ship's a giant. Later tonight from the Empire State Building we'll watch her sail."

"Wow!" exclaimed Peter.

"That's right," said Terry, showing Peter the observation deck tickets. "And we'll get a great view of all the fireworks tonight, too."

"I can't wait!" exclaimed Jackie.

Twenty minutes later, two waiters approached their table with steaming, hot trays. "Oh, food's here. Let's eat." Terry said.

7:50pm

Ahmed parked the car near the park they had visited yesterday. The three men got out and embraced but briefly to avoid unwanted attention. Then Salen and Waleed turned and walked to their positions. Ahmed returned to his car and drove to the location he had selected. He felt his heart racing and his breathing becoming rapid. *Calm yourself, Ahmed*, he thought. *Midnight will come soon enough. Don't let exciting thoughts of impending destruction and killing thousands of infidels interfere with your mission.*

Chapter 51

July 4th . . . 8:30pm

After dinner, Terry, Joe, Jaime and the children descended into the subway for a short ride to the Empire State Building. It was Jaime's and the children's first exposure to the New York City subway system. Terry and Joe pulled Jackie and Peter back from the platform edge as the Number 1 Local barreled into the station. Jaime and the children squeezed their palms against their ears as the train screeched to a halt. Emerging at 34th Street and 7th Avenue, they took a quick detour through Macy's Department Store. Exiting Macy's, they strolled east toward Fifth Avenue and saw the Empire State Building looming over them. "Wow! That building sure is tall!" exclaimed Peter, craning his neck to see the spire, which appeared to "scrape" the sky.

9:15pm

Entering the famous art deco lobby, Terry said, "Oh Joe, it looks just like the scene in *Sleepless In Seattle*. How romantic!" They presented their special complimentary passes and the guard ushered them past a long waiting line into an elevator. Peter charged ahead.

"C'mon! Uncle Bill said the fireworks start at 9:30," he shouted over his shoulder. After changing elevators at the 80th floor, they rode to the 86th floor observation deck and stepped outside to the building's north side.

"Dios mio! What a view!" exclaimed Jaime. The sun had set, but there was sufficient dusky twilight to see the city and beyond. "What is that big patch of green?"

"That's Central Park. Farther north is Harlem and the Bronx. It's so clear this evening you can even see Westchester County and Connecticut," said Joe. They walked around to the observation deck's east side. Joe pointed. "That's the East River. On the other side is a borough called Queens, and farther out is Long Island, where I used to live."

"Hey look at those three bridges down there!" said Peter.

"That first one on the right is the famous Brooklyn Bridge and next to it is the Manhattan Bridge. Just up from that is the Williamsburg Bridge."

"The lights on the bridge are so pretty, Dad," said Jackie.

"Yes, they are, princess. All the city's bridges are lit at night. It's very beautiful."

Walking around the deck to the south side they saw the skyscrapers of New York's financial district several miles in the distance. Peter grabbed the handles on a swiveling binocular, mounted on a stand. "Hey Mom, how does this thing work?"

"It says 50 cents. I think we need quarters," she said, fumbling in her purse for two coins, then dropping them into the slot.

"Oh cool!" exclaimed Peter. "I can see the Statue of Liberty, and the harbor, and all the ships!"

"Lemme see, lemme see!" pleaded Jackie.

Peter reluctantly stepped down and let his sister assume his post. Jackie stepped up and peered into the binocular-type eyepiece. "Oh wow! Peter's right. This is so cool! I can see everything like it's up close!" she exclaimed. "Dad, what's the name of that very long bridge way in the distance?"

"That's the Verrazano Bridge, at the entrance to New York Harbor. It joins Brooklyn, on your left, to Staten Island on your right side."

"Oh, with all the lights it's so pretty. It looks like a string of pearls stretching over the water."

"I suppose you could say that," replied Joe looking at the bridge without using the binoculars.

"I think you're right, Jackie," said Terry. "That's very poetic. Maybe you should be a writer when you grow up. Where's Peter?" she asked, spinning around.

"Over there!" pointed Jaime, watching Peter running to the deck's west side.

They followed Peter and watched the sky turn deep purple as the sun dipped farther below the horizon. In the fading twilight Joe pointed out the dim mountainous outline of the New Jersey – Pennsylvania border. In the foreground they looked down at Manhattan's west side and the piers extending into the Hudson River.

9:30pm

A hint of dark blue was the only fading color remaining in the evening sky, just before it slipped into black. Their eyes were drawn to a silvery trail, rising vertically over the middle of the Hudson. Just as the skyrocket spent the last bit of fuel, it seemed to hang in the sky, then erupted into a red fireball followed by a golden starburst. "Wow!" exclaimed Peter.

"How pretty!" chimed in Jackie, as the Macy's fireworks display commenced. Then, heads turned as a red-white and blue starburst illuminated the Eastern sky, as another fireworks display started over the East River.

"Look!" exclaimed Jaime, pointing south toward lower Manhattan, as the world famous Grucci fireworks bathed the Statue of Liberty in silver and gold.

"Oh Joe, isn't this amazing?" remarked Terry. "I've never seen anything like it. I don't know where to turn next!"

"Hey, there's the Queen Mary again!" Peter shouted, pointing toward the Hudson..

"Right you are, tiger," said Joe.

"From way up here it looks even smaller than before. Hey Dad, what are those tiny boats next to it?"

"Those are tugboats. They're small but very strong. They can push and pull her if she needs help moving from the berth and turning in the right direction. She also has special propellers near the bow, called thrusters, so she might not need the tugboats' help. Looks like she's getting underway. Want to watch?"

"Sure. This is great."

They watched the huge ship, bathed in flood lights, slowly edging away from the pier. Flash bulbs sparkled as passengers and well-wishers on shore snapped photos. The tugs waited, like bridesmaids eager to assist their bride, but the ship backed away without help. Aboard an NYPD dive launch, Sergeant Phil Barone and his dive team watched the huge luxury liner back into the river. Backslapping and exchanging high-fives, they celebrated their security mission's successful end. Clearing the pier, the ship stopped, motionless in the middle of the Hudson. The water around the bow churned foamy as her forward thrusters powered up and the ship pivoted within her own length. A Coast Guard cutter escort waited farther out in the river. Overhead, an NYPD helicopter hovered protectively.

"That's some operation, isn't it kids?" asked Joe. He watched Jaime, who appeared fascinated by the mid-river ballet. Then he glanced at Terry, who seemed lost in thought. "Hey, you'll need a botox injection if you keep your pretty brow furrowed much longer. What's up?"

"I'm not sure. Something's nagging me, I . . ."

"Where does it go now, Dad?" asked Jackie.

"Well, she'll head south, that way," said Joe pointing left. "She'll steam down the Hudson, then enter the Lower Bay, cruise past the Statue of Liberty, and several miles later slip under the Verazzano Bridge and head into the Atlantic. I don't know where she's headed, but if it's Europe she'll head east across the Atlantic. If she's sailing to the Caribbean, where we live, she'll turn south and . . ." Terry tugged Joe's sleeve and he turned. "What's up hon?"

"Joe that's it!"

"Huh? What's it?"

"What Jackie said. About the string of pearls. Remember? The bridge all lit up, looking like someone hung a string of pearls across the water. Get it? A pearl *necklace*! They're going to blow up the Verrazano bridge when the Queen Mary passes beneath."

Joe stared at her, dumbfounded. "Joe, it all fits! I can't recall exactly, but what was all that stuff in the message? It said, *the Queen will never leave New York*, and something about, *hanging a necklace*. Everyone's focused protecting the wrong queen! Suddenly Joe's eyes looked as if a veil had just parted. He turned and watched the QM2 complete her pivoting maneuver, now facing south. Then he ran to the observation deck's southwest corner and saw the Verrazano, eleven miles distant. The bridge's support towers, almost 700 feet tall, were floodlit. Between the towers, shining through the dark, a 4,000 foot pearl necklace was suspended 230 feet above the choppy Narrows.

Chapter 52

July 4th . . . 9:50pm

"Holy shit!"

"Dad!" admonished Jackie, shocked by her father's expletive.

"Sorry, princess. Forget you heard what I just said." Joe patted his pocket, hoping his cell phone was there. It wasn't. "Terry, do you have your cell phone?"

"Sure. What are we going to do?" she asked, the anxiety thinning her voice.

"I gotta contact Bill!" he said, frantically pressing the unfamiliar cell's buttons. "Damn!" he said, after redialing a wrong number. "C'mon, c'mon, Bill, answer your damn phone!"

"Ryan here!"

"Bill, we figured out what this plot's all about!"

"What plot?"

"They're gonna blow the Verrazano when the QM2 passes underneath. You have to stop that ship and check out the bridge!"

"Joe, we've been through all this. You made some solid points in the meeting the other day. The CIA evaluated them but . . ."

"Bill it all fits. It's the *only* thing that makes sense. The bridge lit up at night looks like a string of pearls. Get it? Like a *necklace*."

"I didn't realize Al Qaeda was such a literary outfit," Bill replied, sarcastically.

"How the hell do I know? Maybe whoever did their mission recon was a foreign exchange student taking creative writing 101." Joe pressed his case. "And just like the message said, *the Queen will never leave New York*. With thousands of tons of steel and concrete falling on her she'll sink right in the middle of the Narrows. What else did the CIA boys say? *Major loss of life*, right? As in, several thousand passengers and crew, not to mention hundreds, maybe thousands of motorists on the bridge. What else? Oh yeah, *economic chaos*. Were you ever curious why that bridge wasn't built until the 1960s?"

"Not until now. Enlighten me, partner."

"My dad was a kid when they were building the bridge, and he learned all about it. He told me all kinds of facts whenever we'd cross it or drive under it on the Belt Parkway. There were plans to build a bridge across the Narrows as far back as the 1920s, but it never happened. The military was afraid a saboteur could blow the bridge and block New York Harbor for months. The Brooklyn Navy Yard, where they built the battleship Missouri, was in full operation during World War II, requiring open access to the Atlantic. But by the 1950s the thinking had changed. Everyone figured if the Cold War heated up it would go nuclear and be over in a few hours. Sabotage was the last thing anyone worried about. But now, we've come full circle. Think about it. No ships in or out or New York Harbor for weeks or months. Oil tankers, container ships, freighters, . . ."

"Okay, okay, Joe, I get the picture."

"That half-assed June 30th attack on the QM2 was just a diversion. They wanted us to think they failed so we'd take off the heat, relax security.

"But what about all that intel about Queen Elizabeth?"

"I don't know. But evidently she wasn't the real target." Joe thought for a second. "By the way, when did the CIA obtain their information?"

"They said around early May."

"And when was the Queen's trip to the USA made public?

"I'm not certain, but I think they kept it quiet until June."

"So when Al Qaeda planned this operation there's no way they even knew she would be in New York City. Not even when Delgado intercepted the information. The fact she was here was just a very convenient coincidence."

"Joe, this'll take some time. I'll have to call . . ."

10:00pm

"Hey Dad, the ship's moving!" exclaimed Jackie. They saw the water behind the ship's stern churn white as the Queen's four main propellers came alive. Slowly, imperceptibly, the huge vessel edged forward and her raked bow began cutting the water.

"Bill, you don't have much time! The Queen Mary's just leaving port. She's proceeding slowly but she'll probably reach the bridge in an hour, maybe two at most."

"I'll notify the police commissioner and the mayor's office."

"Bill you better hurry! I'm watching the ship through binoculars and . . ."

"Where the hell are you calling from, Joe?"

"I'm on the Empire State Building observation deck. Remember, you gave Terry the comp tickets? And while you're at it, contact the CIA and FBI. They may have some ideas and we don't have much time. Patch me in if you think you'll need me to convince them."

"You didn't think I was going to stick my neck out alone, did you, *partner*?"

Chapter 53

July 4ᵗʰ . . . 10:20pm

Ahmed sat on a bench in Bay Ridge, Brooklyn, along Shore Road, a tree-lined boulevard of expensive homes with million-dollar views of New York Bay and the Narrows. He glanced up at the Verrazano's elevated entrance and exit ramps, filled with cars crossing between Brooklyn and Staten Island. Ahmed smiled, playing a mental game estimating how many motorists he would soon send to watery graves. He hoped most cars would be filled with families rather than just single drivers. He saw a bus heading over the bridge. *I didn't think about buses.* He smiled, calculating the math. *Each bus carries thirty or forty people; probably ten buses on the bridge at any one time. So, that means . . .* He watched a steady stream of cars on the Belt Parkway passing beneath the bridge . . . *more Americans will die than I had dreamed,* he thought. Then he looked north, to his right, toward Manhattan, anxiously waiting for the Queen Mary's approach, carrying 3,000 additional victims. He watched the Grucci pyrotechnics display illuminate lower Manhattan's night sky in a multi-colored blaze of rocket trails and starbursts. He smiled again. *My fireworks will dwarf anything these infidels have ever seen,* he mused.

The ship was not yet in sight, and he glanced at his watch. *I hope it left on time.* His gaze returned to the bridge, particularly the two massive anchorages, located 1,400 feet behind each tower. The concrete structures were a 130 feet high, 160 feet wide and almost

300 feet long. Each anchorage supported the bridge's 36-inch-thick suspension cables. Each cable was fastened to rolling saddles resting on steel posts, transferring the weight of the Verrazano's towers and center span to a system of eye-bars and steel girders. Also inside each anchorage was more than a ton of high explosives Ahmed and his team had strategically placed for maximum destruction. He still couldn't believe the anchorage entrances had been unprotected. Ahmed was impatient as an expectant father, visualizing the upcoming scenario, only one hour away. He visualized detonating the explosives, destroying the anchorages and shredding the Bridge's three-foot thick steel cables. Lacking support cables, the towers could not hold the center span's load and would collapse inward toward each other. The Queen Mary 2 would never leave New York, strangled by the combined weight of 264,000 tons of steel towers and suspended double-deck concrete roadway collapsing onto her superstructure. Ahmed looked across the Narrows toward Staten Island, where Salen and Waleed waited. He dialed Salen's cell phone. Salen jumped, startled when the phone rang. "Are you and Waleed in place?"

"Yes, Ahmed. I can feel my heart pounding, ready to leap from my chest."

"I felt the same way earlier, but I am calm now. You must remain calm. How is Waleed?"

"Waleed is fine. He's right here next to me." Salen handed Waleed the phone.

"I feel wonderful, Ahmed. I am ready to finally complete our mission. I'm growing more excited as the time grows near."

"Let's review our backup plan one last time. I will detonate all the explosives in both bridge anchorages when the ship is within 50 meters of the bridge. That will allow time for the ship to be directly underneath when the bridge collapses. But if only one side explodes, you detonate immediately. Understood?"

"Yes, Ahmed."

"Now, if there is no explosion when the ship has reached the bridge that means my detonator has failed and you must fire your detonator immediately. Do you understand?"

"Yes, Ahmed."

"Good. Can you see the ship yet?

"No, not yet," said Waleed, looking at the bay toward Manhattan and checking his remote controlled radio transmitter anxiously.

"Okay. Whoever sees the ship first will call the other. Good luck." As soon as Ahmed hung up Salen and Waleed were bathed in headlights. A voice spoke through a loudspeaker.

"Turn around and don't move!" ordered an officially unfriendly voice. Salen and Waleed turned toward the light, shielding their eyes from the glare.

Chapter 54

Bill Ryan's cell phone rang for the third time in five minutes. "Yeah, Joe?"

"Anything yet, Bill?"

"Joe it's almost eleven o'clock on a holiday night. We're trying to contact everyone."

"Bill, I told you we don't have much time. I can see the ship's already approaching the tip of Manhattan."

"Okay Joe. Wait. I just got a beep." He read the caller ID information. "It's the mayor's office. Hang up and I'll call you right back and patch you through." Joe hung up and stared at the cell phone, willing it to ring. He looked at Terry and took a deep breath.

"Jaime, would you please take Jackie and Peter back to the hotel and wait for us?" she asked.

"Aw Mom," groused Peter. Jaime saw Terry was in no mood to argue. Before she responded to Peter he waved his Metro Card ticket.

"Come, children. We can ride the subway again!" Jaime led the children toward the elevator and turned to say goodbye. "Adios, Terry. We'll meet you at the hotel later." She nodded, but Joe was glued to the observation deck binoculars watching the QM2 steam toward its destiny. He saw the Coast Guard cutter several hundred yards ahead of the ship. Finally, his cell phone rang.

"Yes Bill?" he shouted into the handset.

"Joe, I have Mayor Williamson, Commissioner Jackson, New York Homeland Security Director Bilboa and DDI Tom Walsh in Virginia. I haven't been able to raise Agent McHale."

"What's this new theory of yours Mr. Manetta?" the mayor asked, snarling into the phone. Joe took a deep breath and recounted the analysis he had told Bill Ryan. The several seconds of silence that followed seemed an eternity. Finally the Mayor spoke.

"Does any of this make sense to anyone?"

"Unfortunately, yes," said DDI Walsh. Relieved, Joe let out an audible sigh. "We should have analyzed the time-line more thoroughly. We would have realized these terrorists probably had no idea Queen Elizabeth was coming to New York when Delgado intercepted their planning session."

"Joe, do you have any theories about how they could blow the bridge?" asked Bilboa.

"Well, no, Mike. I'm no explosives expert. But based on their earlier attack, they obviously have expertise exploding bombs using remote control detonators. My guess is they're stationed somewhere where they can see the ship pass under the bridge. At the right moment they'll detonate whatever they have. No more bridge, and no more Queen Mary."

"Deputy Director Walsh, any recommendations?" asked Commissioner Jackson. There was no reply. "Hello, Tom? Are you still on the line?" The steady electronic hiss indicated that DDI Tom Walsh had already terminated his call. "Well, he's gone. I guess we're on our own," he said, puzzled by Walsh's sudden departure. "How the hell could they pack that much firepower on the bridge? We inspect all bridge towers and cables continuously, and we stop any truck or van that looks suspicious," said Jackson.

Joe lost his patience. "Excuse me, guys. We need to act, not analyze. We have less than an hour before the ship reaches the bridge. I'm watching her, and she's passing the Statue of Liberty. Who's doing what?"

Joe's sharp comment jolted the Commissioner into action. He took charge and delegated assignments. "Ryan, contact the 63rd

Precinct and Highway Patrol. Shut the Belt Parkway between 65th Street and Bay Parkway, and close all ramps leading to the bridge. Get SWAT and Bomb Squad teams onto the bridge and find those bombs. Bilboa contact the Coast Guard and Cunard Line officials and have them stop the QM2. Don't let her pass under the bridge. Okay, let's go!"

Joe resumed tracking the QM2 through the binoculars. He noticed she had made a slight course correction and was heading directly toward the center span of the Verrazano Bridge.

Chapter 55

The 24-year-old rookie patrolman, only a year out of the police academy, approached Salen and Waleed cautiously. He kept his police cruiser's headlights trained on them and aimed his flashlight into their eyes as he approached. *Probably another couple of queers*, he thought.

"Is there a problem officer?" asked Salen, as respectfully as he could pretend.

"The sign says the park closes at dusk. Didn't you see it?"

"Sorry, I guess we didn't."

"You'll have to leave now. We've had several incidents of gay-bashing in the park and we're trying to protect you people by keeping you out of dangerous areas."

So he thinks we're homosexuals, thought Waleed, sickened by the insult, which offended his Islamic morality.

"But it's such a nice cool evening," replied Salen. "Our apartment down the block is so hot and stuffy we just thought we'd get some fresh air."

The young officer, already annoyed having to roust homosexuals from the park, an assignment conferred because of his rookie status, was impatient. His tone turned brusque. "Show me your identification, please."

Salen reached into his pocket slowly, pulling out his wallet. He handed the officer his phony driver's license. Waleed's had draped his sweater over his left arm. As the officer examined Salen's identification he slowly removed the Glock from his waistband, concealing it under the sweater. The officer studied Salen's license as Waleed edged closer. "This says you live in Brooklyn, not Staten Island. What stuffy apartment down the block were you referring to?" When neither Salen nor Waleed answered, the officer became more suspicious and shone the light directly into Salen's eyes. Originally he assumed the men were probably Italian. But now he thought, *perhaps Middle Eastern*? Waleed took another step closer. He was profiling too. The young policeman was tall, just over six-foot, with blue eyes, short blond hair, and freckled cheeks. *So fucking American!* thought Waleed, seething with hatred. When Salen failed to answer his question, the officer decided to act. "Please step over to the car."

Waleed lunged, jamming the sweater against the officer's chest. Before he could react Waleed pulled the trigger. With the Glock's barrel pressed against the policeman's uniform and wrapped inside the sweater, the gunfire was muffled. They looked around to see if anyone heard the shot. The park was almost deserted, except for a few stragglers strolling toward their cars. The officer winced in pain, then looked shocked, as the Teflon-coated, "cop-killer" bullet pierced his supposedly bullet-proof vest. He opened his mouth, but no sound came out. A red stain blossomed around his silver shield. He fell silently, the only noise his flashlight clattering to the ground. The light winked out. They dragged the dead policeman away from his car headlights' glare, into a thicket of bushes. Waleed ran to the police cruiser, shut the engine and turned off the headlights. He ran back to Salen, who was already covering the body with branches and leaves. "You didn't have to risk everything by shooting him!" Salen scolded.

"Yes I did," replied Waleed. "Look!"   Salen turned and saw the Queen Mary's lights, barely three miles away. His cell phone rang.

"The ship's coming! Do you see it?" shouted Ahmed into the phone.

"Yes, yes! We're in position!" exclaimed Waleed.

Chapter 56

Commodore, we've just received this urgent communication from the Home Office." Stephen Wilson, the QM2's First Officer, handed Smyth a sealed envelope stamped *Confidential*. Wilson watched Smyth's eyebrows arch as he read the message. "Sir?"

"Cunard just received an emergency call from New York State Homeland Security warning of a possible terrorist attack on the Verrazano Bridge."

"What do they want us to do?"

"They've advised, but haven't ordered, that we not pass under the bridge. They'releaving it to my discretion as the ship's captain. But as far as I'm concerned stopping the QM2 makes her a nice big target, sitting dead in the water. I don't like that strategy one bloody bit. Furthermore, this warning they received could be a ruse just to stop us so terrorists could easily attack."

"What are you going to do?"

"I'll request additional details about their information source and press on.

For all I know it could also be just a crank threat." Looking ahead from the ship's bridge they saw the Verrazano's center span looming ahead, now less than three miles away.

The radio crackled. "Sir, it's our Coast Guard escort. They heard the same information and they're asking our intentions."

The harbor pilot on the bridge looked at Smyth. "Commodore, you've got to make a decision quickly. You can't stop a ship this size on a dime." Smyth turned to the harbor pilot and bristled. His eyes flashed and his clipped British accent became even more British.

"After serving at the helm as a First Officer for Cunard Lines for ten years and then commanding ocean liners on the high seas for the past twenty years, don't you think I know how to handle a ship like the QM2?"

"Sorry, sir, no offence intended. I just thought . . ."

Cutting the pilot off, he ordered, "Mister Wilson, advise the Coast Guard cutter we're proceeding ahead unless we receive hard evidence confirming a terrorist plot."

"Aye, sir."

11:30pm

Atop the Empire State Building Joe watched the QM2 through the observation deck binoculars. "What's going on, Bill?" he asked. "She's still moving."

"I was just informed the QM2's Commodore wants more information before he stops the ship."

"What? Is he crazy? We don't have time to give him a formal presentation! Just have the Coast Guard order him to stop the damn ship!"

11:35pm

Ahmed watched the QM2's lights approaching, now only two miles away, ten minutes from the bridge and destruction. He opened a knapsack and removed the radio transmitter he would use to send an electronic signal, detonating the explosives in both bridge tower anchorages. The sky rumbled, and he glanced up. *Strange. I hear thunder, but I can still see stars.* He ignored the sound and activated the transmitter. It beeped and a series of red LED lights began flickering in a deadly sequence.

On the Staten Island side of the Narrows, Waleed and Salen also heard distant thunder but focused on preparing their transmitter. When the rumbling became constant, Waleed looked skyward, expecting rain.

11:37

"Bill, looks like the ship's still moving. What the hell's going on?"

"I called Homeland Security and had them order the Coast Guard to stop the QM2. It's out of our hands now, Joe."

"Shit!"

Aboard the QM2, Commodore Smyth gazed ahead, admiring the picturesque Verrazano, spanning the Narrows, a mile distant.

"Any word from the Home Office or the Coast Guard, Mr. Wilson?"

"No, Commodore. Their Cutter is trying to contact us again but now I'm just getting static."

11:40pm

Ahmed saw the Queen Mary clearly now, less than a mile from the Verrazano. He stepped over to a black wrought-iron fence for a better view. He noticed traffic on the Belt Parkway, just in front and below him, had ceased. The roadway was clear. Then he turned, looking up at the bridge's entrance ramps. He saw flashing red lights of police vehicles. Behind the red lights traffic was blocked, at a standstill. He glanced at the center span of the bridge and saw it also was clear of traffic. His stomach tightened into a knot, as if powerful unseen hands had a vice-like grip on his mid-section. *Something is wrong! And that damn thunder won't stop.* The Queen was closer, a half-mile away, only three minutes from destruction. Ahmed checked the detonator one last time. The LED readout indicated it was functioning properly, just waiting for him to push the red button. He took a deep breath. The rumble above became a loud roar, and as Ahmed looked up he saw the flashing lights of a jet plane turning in a tight radius, and then a second jet. He looked at the Queen. *Just two or three more minutes!*

Atop the Empire State, Joe was frantic. "Bill, she's almost at the bridge! But from here I can't tell how close."

Commodore Smyth stepped outside on the wing of the QM2's bridge and looked up at the Verrazano's twin towers.

"Commodore, we cannot stop the ship now. We'll have to pass under the bridge."

"Proceed, Mr. Wilson," Smyth shouted, over the annoying roar he heard above his ship.

"Aye sir."

11:42pm

Ahmed watched the ship finally reach the kill zone he had calculated under the collapsing bridge. His eyes became wide as saucers. He felt his heart race. This was the moment he had dreamed about for a year. He knew this was why Allah had placed him on Earth. He breathed deeply. "Allah Ackbar!" he screamed, pressing the red firing button. Ahmed flinched, anticipating the tremendous explosion. But all he heard was a *CLICK* and the incessant roar above. "Oh no!" he shouted, pressing the button repeatedly, looking at the detonator, willing it to work. *CLICK . . .CLICK . . . CLICK.* He bit his lip, frustrated, watching the ship steaming closer to the bridge. But all was not lost. According to his backup plan Waleed and Salen still had time to destroy the Queen Mary.

From the Staten Island side of the Narrows, Waleed and Salen saw the ocean liner pass the point where Ahmed should have exploded the bombs. They heard another loud roar above their heads. Confused, they looked at each other. "Something happened to Ahmed. It's up to us now," said Salen. The ship had almost reached the bridge. Waleed pushed the button on his detonator. "Press the firing button! Press it!" exclaimed Salen.

"I did! I did! Nothing happened. Look!" shouted Waleed, repeatedly pressing the button. *CLICK . . .CLICK . . .CLICK.*

"We're near the anchorage," said Salen. "We can explode the bombs manually. Come!" They raced past the empty police cruiser. From the car's radio speaker they heard a dispatcher's voice vainly attempting to contact the dead officer, who should have checked in already. They ran past another police cruiser entering the park searching for the missing police officer. The officer jammed the brakes and jumped out.

"Halt!" He chased Waleed and Salen up an embankment as they raced toward the bridge anchorage, as police converged onto the bridge deck from helicopters, searching for explosives. A SWAT team saw a uniformed officer, gun drawn, racing after two men running toward the bridge anchorage and joined the chase. Salen and Waleed reached the bridge anchorage's steel doors. A wire antenna extended beneath the door. Salen aimed his weapon at the lock and blew it apart. They ran inside the dark interior, the only light reflected from nearby streetlights. Waleed felt his way along a wall until he found the antenna and confirmed it was still attached to the plastique explosive.

"Come out with your hands up!"

"Salen, I need more time! Only a few seconds! Stop them!"

Salen ran to the open door, crouched and began firing. A salvo of automatic weapons fire shredded his body. Waleed, splattered by Salen's blood, saw him propelled backward by the hail of police lead. Then, Waleed saw a small grenade bounce through the doorway. He rolled himself into a ball. The stun-grenade exploded in a flash of blinding light and thunder. Waleed recovered and attached the end of the antenna directly into his detonator. Suddenly bright lights and screaming voices filled the room. He turned into the glare, a frozen tableau, holding the detonator, his thumb just above the firing button. "He screamed, "ALLAH ACK . . ." But Waleed never finished his unholy exclamation. A volley of bullets tore through his body. He dropped the detonator and fell to his knees. He reached for the device, inches from his hand, just as more rounds slammed into his torso. He was dead before he landed on his back.

The SWAT team rushed in. One officer reached for the detonator. "STOP! Let the bomb squad boys mess with that!" ordered the team leader. He played his flashlight around the anchorage's cavernous perimeter, then onto the Verrazano's massive suspension cables. "Holy shit! Look at all this stuff!"

11:45pm

From the Brooklyn side of the harbor, Ahmed watched the Queen Mary 2 pass beneath the Verrazano's string of pearls, unscathed. *Why didn't Salen and Waleed blow the bridge?* He wondered, panicked. He pulled out his phone, frantically dialing their cell. But all he heard was static. He looked at the phone. The network icon on the small screen displayed no bars, indicating no carrier signal. He was unaware that no cell phones or radios in Staten Island and Bay Ridge were working at that moment. He cursed, smashing the transmitter on the pavement. Ahmed buried his head in his hands. *A year of planning, all for nothing!* He wept in despair. The roar above continued unabated. Then he heard helicopters and watched uniformed men rappelling down ropes onto the bridge, searching for explosives. He saw other heavily armed men racing up the ramps past stopped automobiles. Helpless, Ahmed watched the QM2's lights recede in the distance, heading toward the open Atlantic. He realized there was nothing else to do. He slowly walked to his car and drove away.

July 4th . . . 11:50pm

Wilson and the harbor pilot joined Smyth on the outer wing of the QM2's bridge and looked back at the Verrazano, receding in the distance.

"Just as I suspected. Nothing! Those bloody fools wanted me to stop my ship for a crank threat." Growled Smyth. The Commodore shook his head as they stepped inside the bridge. Smyth glanced at the harbor pilot. "Your pilot boat is approaching. I believe we can navigate from here. You may return to your boat when you're ready."

July 5th... 12:06am

The Queen Mary 2's four electric turbine motors accelerated as the ship headed northeast across the Atlantic, toward Great Britain.

Chapter 57

July 5th . . . 12:15am

Joe's cell phone rang. "Yeah. Bill?" asked Joe anxiously, pressing the phone's speaker button so Terry and he could hear.

"Joe, you won't believe this! There was a vicious firefight on Staten Island. A SWAT team killed two bad guys inside the bridge anchorage. They found hundreds, maybe thousands of pounds of ammonium nitrate in barrels and plastique explosive wrapped around the cables and bridge supports, wired to explode by radio control. The same detonating method they used on the QM2, just like you thought. They didn't find any bombs on the bridge itself but they're searching the Brooklyn anchorage now."

"Any good guys get hurt?"

"Yeah, unfortunately. They found one cop, a rookie, dead. He was shot in the chest at point blank range in a Staten Island park, overlooking the bay. The bastards used cop-killer bullets. Went right through his vest. He probably came across the scum-bag terrorists preparing to detonate their bomb."

"And where's the ship now?"

"Past the Verrazano, out in the Atlantic, on her way to England. I don't think that captain realizes he's the luckiest son-of-a-bitch in the world tonight. Hey, I'm getting a beep. Probably more updates. I'll call you back."

Joe looked at Terry. She just shook her head.

"This is surreal. I can't believe it all really happened. Let's hurry back to the hotel and check on Jaime and the children." They took the elevator down from the observation deck hailed a cab and returned to their hotel. Exiting the Empire State on 34th Street they hailed one of many cabs in a sea of yellow. Halfway to the Waldorf, Joe's phone rang again. He glanced briefly at the caller ID information. "Hi Bill, anything new?" He put the phone on speaker so Terry could hear Bill's report.

"Plenty. They found another stash of explosives inside the Brooklyn anchorage, just like the Staten Island side. Also set to explode by remote control. If they had, the towers and center span would have collapsed, right on top of the ship."

"So why didn't they blow?" They heard Bill laugh.

"Oh man, you two wouldn't believe what happened. Remember when DDI Walsh left the conference call early? Just after you mentioned your theory about how they might blow the bridge?"

"Yeah. I thought it was weird that he left so suddenly."

"Well, your theory clicked with him. He got on the horn and contacted some very senior Navy brass. Walsh's son is serving on the aircraft carrier Ronald Reagan. The ship had just left New York for the Mediterranean this afternoon. They were only a hundred miles out. His kid's a squadron commander for the VAQ-139 Cougars."

"You're losing me, Bill."

"The Reagan has several different squadrons. They use different planes for different type of missions. The Cougars fly EA-6B Prowlers."

"Bill, in English, please. Enough with the alphabet soup."

"As I understand it, they use Prowlers for electronic warfare. Specifically, they interrupt enemy electronic activity and communications." After a brief silence, Bill continued. "Joe, they jam communications, radar, and electronic signals. Get it?"

"The picture's getting clearer. I think. Continue."

"Walsh has been plugged into the roadside bomb problems in Iraq. The army's been preventing insurgents from blowing up convoys by jamming entire areas. But the problem is, when they do they jam their own communication signals, too. Walsh and his spook geniuses have been working to solve the problem, but they haven't been successful. So he used that problem to solve this situation. He has direct access to very senior Navy brass. So, he requested his admiral buddies to authorize several Prowlers from the Reagan to patrol over the bridge and jam the hell out of the airspace around Brooklyn and Staten Island so these bozos couldn't detonate their remote control bombs. Homeland Security ordered the FAA to clear airspace for the operation."

"Amazing how fast bureaucracy works when you push the right buttons."

"Yeah. We were lucky in more ways than one. The Prowlers were already on the flight deck because the Reagan was preparing a night training exercise. Otherwise they probably couldn't have launched in time. I heard Walsh's son even led the mission. Looks like it worked."

"Must be a lot of angry drivers stuck in traffic who can't phone home to keep their dinners warm," said Joe.

"Well, you can't please all the people all the time," Bill replied. "Listen, we have another meeting at eight o'clock tomorrow morning at Police Plaza. The mayor wants you and Terry to attend, okay?"

"Sure. This should be interesting. And I hope it's the last meeting." Turning to Terry, Joe said, "Well, hon, tomorrow morning we have one last command performance."

She reached her hand around behind Joe's head and pulled his face close. "All right. But tonight I want you all to myself," she said, kissing his lips lightly. "And then take me home to Cozumel as soon as possible."

"Will do," Joe replied, wrapping his arms tightly around Terry. *It feels damn good to have my wife back*, he thought. *I hope it's for good.*

Chapter 58

July 5ᵗʰ...1:05am

Gloom gradually evolved into blind fury as Ahmed drove through deserted streets. Arriving back at the safe house, he pulled into the underground garage and jammed the brakes, screeching to a halt inches from the back wall. He slammed the car door then kicked in the door leading to the common area. Twenty heads turned in his direction. He looked past them and saw they were watching a CNN broadcast detailing his abortive attack. The news anchor had termed it *The Battle of Brooklyn*, even though all the shooting actually occurred on Staten Island. Ahmed's red-rimmed eyes locked with Ashur's.

Ashur spoke first. "Both Waleed and Salen are dead?"

"I don't know. If that's what the television says it must be true. If they died as martyrs then they are in Paradise now with Allah and 72 virgins each. I wish I were with them instead of standing here, a failure before your eyes."

"Ahmed, your plan was brilliant, truly amazing. Success would have brought joy and happiness to our people. You must not blame . . ."

"All that matters is I failed," Ahmed spit, through clenched teeth. He collapsed into a chair, resting his head on the table. He spoke without looking up. "There was this terrible sound the entire time. Loud thunder. My head was pounding." His shoulders shook as he sobbed. Then he fell silent, breathing deeply. Ashur and the other men watched him, stunned by Ahmed's physical transformation. His adrenalin had finally stopped pumping, and he seemed to shrink before their eyes. The attack had been his focus for a year. After months of planning and preparation, carrying out last week's diversionary attack on the QM2, and finally the rush from last night's futile attack, it appeared his life force was draining from his body. Ashur directed several men to help Ahmed upstairs and let him sleep.

"But first please remove his weapons," he said with concern, before they carried him to bed.

Later that morning Ahmed awoke and stumbled into the common room. He found everyone still watching news programs, as more details were revealed. "How are you feeling, Ahmed?" asked one man.

"I feel a little better than last night," he shrugged.

"But you still look like shit!" Ashur said, smiling, trying to lift his spirits.

Ahmed watched the television through glazed, bloodshot eyes. "They knew we were going to attack. They were prepared. Perhaps we have a spy among us. Perhaps even Salen or Waleed was a spy. Maybe that's why they didn't blow up the bridge after my transmitter failed."

"No, Ahmed. There was no spy. And your transmitters did not fail. The loud sound you heard? Like thunder? It was American jets jamming your electronic signals. You had no chance. Salen and Waleed had no chance either."

"But how did they know ahead of . . . ."

"Watch," Ashur said, changing channels until he found a station providing further details.

The FOX News anchor stated, "And so, a young couple visiting New York, not professional intelligence analysts in Washington, correctly deciphered the hidden meaning in a cryptic message a CIA operative intercepted months earlier during a secret Al Qaeda meeting in Pakistan. As a result, counter-terrorism forces prevented a deadly attack on the world famous Verrazano-Narrows Bridge and Queen Mary 2, the jewel of Britain's Cunard Line. The couple, shown here on tape . . ."

Ahmed watched the broadcast, dumbfounded, as the news anchor essentially verified Ahsur's version of events. He slammed his fist on the table, recognizing Terry's face as FOX News rebroadcast their chaotic arrival at the Waldorf several days earlier. Conflicting emotions had tormented Ahmed for the past 24 hours: Hate, despair, anger, self-pity, rage. But now, one emotion dominated all others: Revenge. He resolved to extract the ultimate toll from Mr. and Mrs. Manetta. Ahmed swore they would pay dearly for dashing his plans and reducing his glorious dreams to dust.

Chapter 59

July 5th. . .8am

Across the East river in Lower Manhattan, Commissioner Jackson was concluding the meeting at Police Plaza. "Well, there you have it, ladies and gentlemen," he said, summing up the events. Before we adjourn I'm sure I speak for us all in saying thank you to Terry and Joe Manetta for their assistance, which proved more vital than we ever could have imagined." Jackson continued after the applause subsided. "And thank you for bringing Notchka. She interrupted their diversionary attack against the QM2."

Terry nodded, forcing a smile. She still worried about Notchka's health and hoped she would recover sufficiently to travel home soon. "There is one loose thread, however. We believe there are still more terrorists still running free. Our investigators found the shattered remains of another transmitter on Shore Road, a street in Bay Ridge with an unobstructed view of the Narrows and the Verrazano Bridge. It's identical to the transmitter recovered from the terrorists killed inside the Staten Island anchorage. It was a perfect spot from which to carry out this attack. Our theory is that when the device didn't work, the Al Qaeda operative lost his cool and smashed it. We'd really like to find him. Looks like they had a pretty good plan. Our electronic wizards told me both transmitters were programmed to broadcast on identical frequencies. And both tower anchorages were within the range of each transmitter. So their attack plan had built-in redundancy. If one transmitter failed, or if one team was captured, the other team could still blow the bridge and sink the ship."

"But our plan was better," Bill Ryan shouted, to a chorus of cheers from attendees in person and those video conferencing from Washington and Langley.

"Go Navy!" DDI Walsh in Langley exclaimed, to more cheers. After Jackson terminated the videoconference everyone in the New York meeting shook hands and congratulated each other again. Terry sat quietly, lost in thought, her eyes staring at swirling patterns on the tile floor.

"Hey, penny for your thoughts," said Bill Ryan.

She looked at him. "I was just thinking. Since their underwater attack on the QM2 at the pier was only a ruse, we brought Notchka here for nothing. We risked her life and injured her, all for nothing."

Joe sat next to Terry and held her hand. "But hon, no one had any idea what they had planned. We all acted on the best information available and made the most logical assumptions. If we had . . ." She cut him off.

"Logic aside, we probably endangered Notchka's life for nothing. I just hope she pulls through and we get her home to Cozumel safely."

"That's what we all hope for," interjected Bill Ryan, as Terry threw him a withering stare. Bill took a deep breath and pressed on. "Terry, whatever their plan was Notchka helped disrupt it. She's a hero in my book." Terry remained mute, so Bill changed tack. "Listen, it's almost lunch time. Why don't we grab a bite, and I'll drive you both to the Aquarium so you can check on Notchka."

After lunch in Chinatown they drove to Brooklyn and the aquarium. Their route took them along the Belt Parkway, passing under the Verrazano. Looking up at the bridge, Joe said, "You know, when I lived here I passed that bridge almost every day without giving it much thought. My father talked about it all the time. Now I realize why. Look at it. It's the first thing people see arriving by ship, and sometimes even by plane, depending on the route they fly. They see it even before the Statue of Liberty. It's the gateway to New York

and America. And we saved it. The thought gives me goose bumps."
Terry squeezed his hand and smiled.

"I think I understand how you feel now."

They arrived at the aquarium twenty minutes later and were
ushered inside. Notchka saw them enter the pool area and greeted
them with a back flip. "Hey, our girl looks pretty healthy today!"
exclaimed Joe. Aquarium vet Alison Carey was already waiting.

"Hi folks," she said, greeting them and shaking hands.

"How is Notchka?" asked Terry anxiously.

"She's doing fine. Her injuries have healed, and her lung infection
is under control. We'll discontinue the antibiotics in several days.
Then we'll watch her carefully for another week. If she doesn't
relapse she can return to Cozumel."

"Oh, that's wonderful!" said Terry. She hugged Alison and then
stepped to the pool, slapping the water. Notchka swam over and
playfully squirted her. Terry held her hand out and Notchka swam
over, letting Terry stroke her. After a half-hour visit they drove back
to Manhattan and Bill dropped Joe and Terry at their hotel.

"What are your plans for the rest of the day?" he asked.

"Well, I thought I'd take the kids and Jaime to a Yankee game,"
said Joe. They love baseball but they've never seen a major league
game in person. Terry just wants to chill at the hotel and catch up on
some reading."

"Sound's like a good plan. I'll see you before you return
home."

In downtown Brooklyn, Ahmed was making his own plans. He
prepared several items, and then carefully placed them in a canvas
bag. When he was finished he met with Ashur.

"I have one last mission. I may see you later this evening. But if
I do not return, please accept my gratitude for all you have done."

"We were happy to assist you, my brother. I only wish . . ."
Ashur stepped forward. They embraced and Ahmed left quickly.

Outside he hailed a taxi. Ahmed stepped in and sat heavily,
directing the driver to a specific address. Along the way, Ahmed
noticed they were passing a florist. "Stop! Wait here," he ordered.

He got out and returned several minutes later carrying a flower arrangement.

"A gift for a friend?" the cabby asked, attempting to make conversation.

"No. Not a gift for a friend. It's for the funeral of an acquaintance."

The cab driver drove across the Brooklyn Bridge, north along the FDR Drive and then across town to Park Avenue. Finally, the cab pulled over to the curb and the cabby turned to Ahmed. "Here you are." Ahmed paid the taxi driver, opened the door and stood on the curb. He stared at the bold, block gold lettering on the building's façade and sneered. To him, the name symbolized Western decadence: **Waldorf Astoria**.

Chapter 60

Ahmed scanned the front desk personnel and selected a young customer service agent who appeared distracted, entering information into the hotel reservation system while also answering phones. He hoped she would be too busy to follow proper security procedures. He noticed her name tag: *Lydia*. "Excuse me, Lydia," he said, trying to sound charming, or as charming as a cold-blooded killer could sound. She looked up and saw a young man with dark, intense, almost piercing eyes holding a large flower basket.

"May I help you?" she asked.

"I have a flower delivery for Mrs. Terry Manetta." He maintained eye contact with Lydia and smiled, trying not to appear anxious. He waited while Lydia scanned the reservation system.

"Hmm, I don't see that name . . ." Ahmed skipped a breath. "Oh here it is, under Mr. and Mrs. Joseph Manetta." His pulse quickened, like a predator closing on its prey. "Just leave the flowers with the concierge, please. He will bring them up to her room."

"Oh, I can bring them up, Lydia. What room are the Manettas in?"

"I'm sorry sir. Security rules don't permit me to release that information or let you go to their room," she replied, her tone now less friendly, more formal. "Please leave the flowers with the concierge, like I asked you. Right over there," she pointed. *Clearly*

I picked the wrong damn clerk, Ahmed thought, his mind racing. Making a scene in the hotel lobby was the last thing he wanted.

"Thank you, Lydia," he replied, forcing a smile. He walked toward the concierge desk and by the time he had crossed the 30-foot lobby he formulated an alternate plan. It would require a little bluffing, but this was low risk compared to other daring exploits in his terrorist career. When the concierge finished helping another hotel guest Ahmed spoke quickly, feigning urgency. "Excuse me, but Lydia over there," he pointed, "directed me to you. I have a flower delivery for Mr. and Mrs. Manetta. I also have a message I must deliver personally. Lydia said I cannot go to her room without an escort, but she said you can arrange that." He placed the flowers on the concierge's desk. The concierge looked at Lydia just as she glanced toward him. They made eye contact and the concierge pointed to Ahmed. *If they speak, my plan is finished!* thought Ahmed. Lydia just nodded her head, assuming Ahmed was following her directions, unaware of the actual conversation between him and the concierge.

The concierge assumed Ahmed had relayed Lydia's instructions accurately. "Fine." He turned to a bellboy standing just behind him. "Please take these flowers and bring this man to the Manettas' suite." As the concierge wrote the number on a note pad and handed the paper to the bellboy, Ahmed casually strolled toward an elevator bank, out of view from the front desk. Lydia glanced up again and saw only the bellboy walking alone carrying the flowers toward the elevators. She assumed Ahmed had already left the lobby, but her incorrect assumption would soon have dire consequences.

Just as the elevator's doors closed on Ahmed and the bellboy, the adjacent elevator's doors opened. Joe, Jaime, Jackie and Peter exited. They walked past the front desk and Lydia recognized Joe. She was about to call out and tell him a flower delivery had been sent to his room when Jackie and Peter bounded through the lobby, giggling as they ran out the door onto Fifth Avenue.

"Hey, slow down you two," shouted Joe running after them. Lydia decided the information wasn't critical. Mr. Manetta would see the flowers when he returned.

Ahmed and the bellboy rode up silently. Ahmed read his nametag: *William*. He had only a few seconds to establish a rapport. He studied him. Young, most likely a teenager; perhaps he attends school; probably still lives with his parents. "So William, how long have you worked at the Waldorf?" William was startled that the flower messenger knew his name, then realized he had read his nametag. He smiled at Ahmed.

"Oh only since last month, sir. My uncle works here and got me a summer job to help pay my college expenses."

"That's nice. Do you like it?"

"Yes, very much. I enjoy speaking to people. My mom says I'm a people-person. Here we are." As they walked down the hall William asked, "Would you like to hold the flowers, sir?"

"Oh no. You hand them to whoever answers the door. Perhaps you'll get a better tip," Ahmed replied. "And then I'll deliver my personal message."

"Gee, thanks! I really appreciate that," gushed William.

Stupid, gullible, greedy American, thought Ahmed. *Having two free hands will make this easier.*

They arrived at the Manettas' room and the bellboy knocked. "Who's there?" a female voice asked, through the locked door.

"Flower delivery and a special message," said the bellboy smiling at Ahmed. He noticed the flower messenger now had a strange, intense look in his eyes.

"Just a minute, I'm on the phone," replied the woman. Terry spoke into the phone. "Joe, it's room service or something. We have a special delivery. Just hold on a minute." Ahmed moved directly behind the bellboy, placing his left hand gently in the middle of his back, so lightly William did not feel his touch. Ahmed's other hand was in his pocket, gripping the handle of his Glock automatic. Terry squinted through the peephole and saw only a smiling bellboy holding a flower bouquet. The lock clicked open.

Chapter 61

Terry opened the door a crack. Ahmed lunged into William, shoving him as hard as he could. The bellboy's face smashed into the slightly ajar door, breaking his nose. The force of both bodies propelled the door edge into Terry's forehead. She fell hard, onto her back, the breath knocked from her lungs. William fell heavily on top of her. Their eyes locked in shock and confusion. Terry was stunned watching blood pour from William's shattered nose onto her blouse. They heard a loud bang as Ahmed slammed the door shut. Then a second, louder bang, and William's handsome face disappeared into a formless, pulpy red mass. Terry blinked and found herself covered in warm, sticky blood. She recoiled, pushing William's limp body off her chest. She glanced into the hateful eyes of a young Arab man standing over her, aiming a pistol at her forehead. Terry opened her mouth but emitted no sound. She froze, and watched her assailant walk over to the desk telephone, confirming the handset had been hung up. But he was unaware Terry had been speaking on her cell phone. Alertly, she rolled on top of her cell phone, hiding it from view and muffling Joe's voice coming through the speaker.

"Get up, American whore!" Ahmed commanded.

As Terry slowly rose to her knees she palmed the phone as skillfully as a magician performing a magic trick, slipping it into her pocket, leaving the connection open.

"What do you want?" Who are you?" she asked, collecting her thoughts.

"Who am I? I have been sent by Allah to send you and your family to Jahannam!"

Terry blinked, confused by the unfamiliar term. "To where?"

"To hell!" clarified Ahmed. With a flourish he unbuttoned his trench coat, revealing his explosive vest. He enjoyed Terry's shocked expression. "Where are they? Call your family out here. I want to see the look on your husband's face when I blow you all up!"

Terry, stunned by the blow to her forehead, looked at William's bloody, faceless body and tried to avoid sliding into shock. She stared at Ahmed, trying to make sense of the last thirty seconds. "My husband? How do you know my husband?"

"I don't. I feel as though I know you better."

"Me? How do you know . . ."

"I saw you twice on the television. First after we attacked the Queen Mary and again after you denied me the glory of destroying both that damn British ship and the bridge."

Suddenly her fog lifted. "You're the terrorist who escaped!"

"Call them out here! Now!" Ahmed shouted. "Are they hiding like scared dogs under their beds?"

"They're not here. They won't be back until much later," Terry said, trying to buy time, trying to think of a plan.

"Lying American bitch! I should shoot you right . . ." Ahmed raised the Glock and aimed at Terry's face.

"I'm telling you the truth! They went to a baseball game but it won't be over until ten or eleven."

Ahmed looked at his watch. It read seven o'clock. He knew little about baseball, or how long a game could last. Terry hoped Joe could hear the conversation. She was trying to save her family. Convincing Ahmed they wouldn't be back until after someone started looking for the missing bellboy might force him to detonate his bomb now. She would die, but at least she would save her husband and children.

"What's wrong, Joe?" asked Jaime.

"I don't know. Terry was on the phone, then she stopped talking and I heard a loud bang. Now I just hear muffled conversation." Joe turned to the taxi driver. "Drive back to the Waldorf. Now!" They had just entered the northbound FDR Drive toward Yankee Stadium. But it was jammed with slow moving traffic and they were trapped between exits. "Damn!" Joe exclaimed. He dialed Bill Ryan.

"Hello?"

"Bill it's me. Don't talk, just listen. We're stuck on the FDR. I was just talking to Terry back at the Waldorf. She mentioned something about a special delivery, then there was a loud bang, like gunfire. Now all I hear is muffled talk. Can you get someone over there?"

"Will do, Joe-boy! I'll call you back."

Terry watched Ahmed. She clearly understood he intended blowing up himself and her family in a blaze of twisted Islamic glory. His wild eyes darted about the room like a bird seeking prey. His mind raced, planning his next step. *I'm not sacrificing myself to kill one American bitch. But if I just stay here some lowly clerk or dumb hotel cop might catch me. I need a new plan. Think, think!* Finally she saw a serene look come over his face. Ahmed had made a decision. *She will die, but in a way that will chill every American's heart and send fear into their souls.*

Chapter 62

"Come with me," ordered Ahmed. "But first wash your face and change that bloody shirt." Terry stood and paused. She had to step over William's body to reach the bathroom. Ahmed followed her. Terry was shocked when she saw herself in the mirror. Her hair, tied back, was free of blood. But her face was splattered with dark, sticky clots. There was an angry vertical black-and-blue bruise on her forehead, from her hairline to her eyebrow, where the door edge had slammed into her. Her white blouse was soaked, a shiny crimson. She slowly removed it, peeling the sticky wet garment from her body. Then she washed her hands and face with warm soapy water.

Terry had a swimmer's body: well-developed arms and shoulders, narrowing into a slim waist, firm thighs and toned calfs. She removed her bloodstained bra and saw Ahmed watching her in the mirror. Terry thought his eyes would explode from his skull when he saw her firm, rounded breasts. She heard his breath catch in his throat. Ahmed saw her looking at his eyes and he averted his gaze, embarrassed. Terry noticed a bulge in his crotch, and he saw that she noticed. Enraged, Ahmed grabbed her arm and dragged her into the bedroom. The strength of his grip surprised Terry. She felt as if her arm were in a vice. He flung her across the bed. *This infidel whore has tempted me and my body has responded*, he thought. Ahmed was torn by the intense inner conflict between his sexual urge and his deeply ingrained conservative Islamic moral training.

His eyes glazed as he recalled the night, 21 years ago, when his father had discovered his teenage son masturbating onto an old *Playboy* magazine centerfold he had stolen from a local trader. He blinked, remembering the pain of his father's leather belt, lashing his bare back. His father was more furious by his son's sin of impurity than his thievery. Ahmed heard his father's harsh voice screaming 'Janabat' (unclean state because of seaman discharge), between sharp belt cracks as he beat him, scolding him for his weakness, for submitting to a Western infidel whore's temptation. The unwanted flashback angered him further as he stared at Terry, sprawled on the bed. He felt shamed by his weakness again. "Dress yourself quickly!" he shouted. "I promise you will die slowly and painfully," he said coldly. Terry believed him.

Terry quickly changed her blouse. She stood facing him. Ahmed noticed Terry's full red lips and had another idea. "Get me the lipstick you use to paint your lips," he ordered. Then he grabbed her wraparound sunglasses from the dresser and handed them to her. "Paint the inside with your lipstick."

"But I won't be able to see."

"I don't want you to see. I'll lead you, every step of the way." Terry did as he ordered. Before she slipped on the sunglasses he said, "Wait." She watched him pull a plastic handle from his pocket. He plugged a wire from the handle into his explosive vest. "Now it is armed. One word, one false move, I squeeze this handle and blow us up, killing everyone within a hundred feet. Now put those glasses on." Terry complied. The opaque lenses disoriented her and she held the dresser for support. Then Ahmed grabbed her arm. "Come!" Just before leaving the room Ahmed roughly pulled off Terry's hair clip, letting her hair fall, partially obscuring her face. They walked to the elevator. Another couple was already waiting. They nodded and Ahmed nodded back. Exiting at the lobby Ahmed walked as quickly as he could, trying not to seem as though he was dragging Terry along. "Keep moving! The lobby is full of people. Do you want to be responsible for their deaths?"

"No," was all Terry could say. Ahmed smiled, realizing he controlled a captive who would never endanger anyone around her. They walked through the lobby onto Park Avenue. Some people turned momentarily but just assumed the lady wearing the dark sunglasses walking somewhat strangely was slightly stoned or perhaps visually impaired. In any case, like typical New Yorkers, they just kept walking as if she were invisible. Ahmed let the doorman hail a taxi. He pushed Terry into the backseat, and slid in next to her. He told the cabby a Brooklyn address. Before the cab left the curb a police cruiser pulled up behind them and two officers exited. One glanced toward the cab. Ahmed watched and tensed, applying pressure to the bomb's trigger. He relaxed when the officers turned and walked into the hotel lobby.

Several minutes later Joe's taxi pulled up. He saw the parked police cruiser and a chill ran up his spine. He asked Jaime to stay with Jackie and Peter in the lobby and headed for the elevator bank. Exiting at his floor he ran to his room. An officer stopped him at the door. "It's my room. Is my wife okay?" The cop recognized Joe from newspaper photos and let him inside. He stopped cold, stunned, seeing the blood-covered carpet, then the bellboy's body, spread-eagled on its back, lacking a recognizable face. "Terry! Are you in here?" he shouted. He ran through the three bedrooms in the suite, relieved not to find Terry inside.

"In here!" he heard an officer call. Joe took a deep breath, steeled himself for the worst and stepped into the bathroom. His eyes froze on a bloodstained washcloth crumpled on the floor, focused on red flecks on the sink edge, and then locked onto a blood-soaked blouse and bra in the sink. He skipped a breath and turned, expecting to see his wife's body on the floor. "Sir, without touching anything can you identify this clothing?" asked a crime scene officer.

Joe leaned closer to the bloody clothing, examined the labels, checked the bra size and recognized the blouse as one of Terry's *Victoria Secret* favorites. "Those are my wife's clothes. My God, what happened in here?" Just then Bill Ryan, flanked by crime scene technicians, entered and secured the crime scene. Joe told Bill and another investigating officer about the mysterious cell phone call.

"Okay, let's think this through," said Bill. "Terry says, 'Wait a minute, someone's at the door with flowers.' Then, you heard a gunshot, then muffled voices like the cell phone's still on, but she doesn't get back on the line?"

"Right. That's about it."

"We found this, sir," said an officer, handing Bill the card contained in the floral arrangement."

"Interesting. A downtown Brooklyn address" he said, pocketing the card. "Well, here's my theory, Joe. Whoever did this really planned it out. He figures he'll pose as a deliveryman, so he buys flowers. He gets here and finds out he can't go upstairs unescorted, so he cons that poor kid into bringing him up here. Terry opens the door and he pushes in. He kills the kid but not Terry."

"But the blood all over her clothes," interjected Joe. "She's probably . . ."

"We don't know whose blood it is yet. Let's assume it's not hers. It's probably the kid's. Somehow she keeps the phone on. Your lady's pretty cool, Joe. She's figuring we'll trace the cell signal with GPS as long as it's on. And if she keeps the line open it's even easier to trace as they move from one cell area to another. Which is what we'll start doing, right now."

"How's he controlling her, Bill? I know Terry. She'd either fight or make a break."

"Hey Joe-boy, how many theories can I come up with at one time? Give me a break, buddy," he said, trying to lighten the somber mood. Switching gears again, Bill said, "Give me her cell number and we'll start a trace."

Chapter 63

Terry sat motionless as the cab bounced along Manhattan's potholed streets. Ahmed noticed she was angling her head, trying to view passing street signs through the sides of her darkened wraparounds. He yanked her arm. "Keep your head straight. Remember what I told you in the hotel, about this handle I'm holding." He noticed the cab driver eyeing him in the rearview mirror. "You should keep your eyes on the road, my friend. You can never tell what might happen in this crazy New York traffic, you know?" The cabby nodded, forced a smile and averted his eyes, focusing on the traffic. *This is a strange couple*, he thought.

Bill Ryan's cell phone rang. "We got a GPS report that your cell phone just turned off the FDR Drive onto the Brooklyn Bridge. C'mon, I'll drive." They ran from the hotel lobby and pulled away from the curb, tires squealing. Navigating through the streets Bill contacted his dispatcher. "Keep me and the other units constantly updated on the GPS coordinates. It's all we have."

Ahmed looked at Terry. He noticed how her long auburn hair fell to her shoulders. She stared straight ahead, and he admired her profile, her smooth soft skin. Against his will his eyes fell to the outline of her breasts through her tight blouse, rising and falling with each breath. The vision of her naked breasts reflected in the hotel bathroom mirror earlier was seared into his brain. Once again he felt his body reacting, and he hated her for it. His mind danced, rationalizing, trying to reconcile his desire with his moral training. *Allah would not punish me for raping an infidel. Perhaps before killing her I will* . . . BEEP. The sound startled him, interrupting his developing fantasy. *Oh shit, the phone battery's dying!* Terry realized. She moved her hand over her pocket muffling the sound, trying to buy some time, a few seconds, anything. BEEP. "What's that sound?" asked Ahmed, his eyes searching the cab, his senses heightened.

Terry replied, "I didn't hear any . . ." BEEP. Ahmed realized the sound emanated from Terry's clothing. He patted her jeans pocket closest to him. Then he reached across her body to pat her other pocket, but Terry turned slightly, so he couldn't reach the pocket. Frustrated, he reached behind her and pulled her across his lap, pushing her face into the seat. Holding her head down with one hand, he reached around her hip with his other hand and pulled the cell phone from her pocket. He blinked, seeing it was flipped in the open position. BEEP. He turned the power off and snapped the phone shut. Then he grabbed Terry's hair and pulled her upright. "Remain still and shut up!" he hissed. He looked ahead and saw the cabby's eyes looking at him in the rearview mirror again. Instinctively, Ahmed knew he would inform police about his two strange passengers and where he had taken them. *Now I'll have to kill him, too*, decided Ahmed, spontaneously improvising once again.

Bill answered his phone. Joe saw him listening, then shaking his head, pursing his lips. Joe held his breath. "Not good news. They lost Terry's cell phone signal somewhere on Atlantic Avenue, not far off the expressway."

"Shit!" Joe exclaimed.

"Well, at least we have a general idea of her location," Bill said, trying to maintain a positive outlook for Joe's sake.

"Yeah, but I remember this part of Brooklyn is called Little Arabia," said Joe. "It's a very dense area. She could be anywhere in a hundred square blocks, in one of hundreds of small buildings or apartments."

The cab driver arrived at the address Ahmed had given him. "I'm afraid I made a slight mistake," Ahmed told him. "Drive around the block until I see the house I'm looking for." Several minutes later Ahmed saw what he was really searching for: a deserted street with no traffic. "That way," he pointed, leaning over the front seat where the protective plastic partition between the passenger and driver should have been but was missing. The cabby drove slowly down the quiet street, until Ahmed spotted a parking spot. "Pull in right there," he ordered. As the taxi slowed to a stop, Ahmed glanced over his shoulder, then in front. The street was deserted.

"Is this okay?" asked the driver.

"This will do fine," replied Ahmed. The cabby flipped off the meter.

"Thirty-seven-fifty, please," he said, turning to face Ahmed and collect his fare. His eyes froze, seeing the business end of Ahmed's Glock, aimed at his forehead. Ahmed had all he could do to keep from laughing, watching the young man staring cross-eyed at the gun barrel, less than three inches from his face. "Please . . . ." he implored. Terry turned toward his voice, sensing something terrible was about to happen. BOOM! She jumped, startled by the gun's loud report, fired in close quarters with the windows closed. There was no one outside to hear the explosion.

"Don't move, or I'll kill you right now!" Ahmed ordered. "I must attend to my overly curious friend." Terry froze, then sneezed as the pungent cordite odor stung her nose. Ahmed jumped out of the cab, ran around the front and pulled the driver's door open. The bullet's impact had knocked the cabby against the door and he fell backward spilling onto the pavement. Ahmed looked at him, amused by his victim's wide-eyed, open-mouthed startled expression. A perfect, small round hole marred the handsome young man's smooth forehead. The bullet had not exited the back of his skull, but spent its force turning his brain to jelly. Ahmed reached into the dead man's pants pocket and removed a thick wad of bills. *This will make it appear as just an armed robbery*, he calculated. He pulled the rear driver-side door open and Terry flinched, not sure if Ahmed's next bullet was meant for her. He glanced up and down the deserted street. "Out!"

he commanded. When she hesitated he grabbed her hand and pulled her from the cab. "I said get out!" He spun Terry around and led her down the block toward the corner. "Walk quickly." He ordered. "And don't forget. One false move and I'll blow you up along with a hundred innocent people around us." At the corner he pulled her arm and she almost lost her balance. "This way!" he said, changing direction. Several pedestrians glanced at the rough way the young man treated his female companion. Watching Terry stumble along, one elderly lady shook her head disapprovingly, and whispered to her friend.

"The poor man must be frustrated having to drag his drunk wife around like that in the middle of the day." Noticing Terry's auburn hair and facial features, her friend replied, "He should have married a nice Arab girl, not some unruly American woman. Serves him right." They both laughed.

Several minutes later they arrived at the safe house. "Stop." Ahmed glanced around, checking to see if they were being followed. Satisfied no one was tailing them, he pushed Terry toward the front door and into the house.

Chapter 64

Bill and Joe repeatedly crisscrossed Brooklyn's downtown streets, searching for anything that didn't fit, for anyone who seemed out of place in the homogeneous population. Such as a tall athletic woman, with long auburn hair and striking features accompanied by a man described by the hotel staff as young, poorly dressed, slim, 5-5 to 5-7, dark curly hair, olive-complexioned. Joe looked around, noticing over twenty young men matching that description. But they were either alone, with male friends, or accompanied by women who did not match Terry's description. He was anxious, frustrated, worried, and felt pangs of despair. He feared losing a woman he loved for the second time in his life. A female dispatcher's voice crackled through the car's radio. "Attention all units. Cab driver found murdered at . . ."

"Jot down the address! That's near here!" exclaimed Bill. "We'll be there in five minutes." He pulled the magnetic cherry from under the dashboard and slammed it against the roof. His unmarked car roared down the street, turned the corner of a busy intersection tires squealing and headed toward the address the dispatcher reported.

Ashur and his men stared at Ahmed and his female companion, dumbfounded.

"Ahmed, why have you brought this woman here? What are you doing?"

"I'm completing my new mission, and you will help me." His long trench coat opened and the men gasped, seeing his explosive vest. Reading their thoughts, Ahmed was disappointed seeing how they feared death and lacked his commitment. But he needed their cooperation so he reassured them. "You have nothing to worry about. She is the only one who will die. But in such a way that will make these weak Americans sick with fear. But we must act quickly. They're searching for her as we speak. Ashur, come with me." He led Terry down a long flight of stairs to the same basement rooms where he had prepared the bombs for his original mission only several short days ago.

Ashur saw Terry stumbling. "What's wrong with her? Did you drug her?"

"No," Ahmed said, laughing. "She just cannot see. I couldn't very well walk out of the hotel with her blindfolded, so I used the whore's cheap, red lipstick to black out her sunglasses." Terry stood motionless, listening but not understanding as the men conversed in their native Arabic. Then, Ashur watched Ahmed spread a plastic drop cloth on the floor in the middle of the room, and position a wooden chair on the cloth. He dragged Terry to the chair. "Sit!" he ordered, pushing her down. "Give me those ropes," he said to Ashur. He bound Terry's wrists and ankles to the chair. He stepped to the table where Waleed had assembled his remote detonators and grabbed a pen and paper. He scribbled a list and handed it to Ashur. "I need these things immediately. Hurry." Ashur looked at the list, then at Ahmed.

"But why do you need . . ."

"Don't question me! Just hurry!" Ahmed screamed. "I don't know how much time we have!"

Bill saw a police cruiser's red and blue flashers two blocks ahead. The cruiser turned down the next block and Bill followed. Four other precinct cars were already at the scene. Bill screeched to a halt and they jumped from their car, running to the parked cab. The cops standing around the taxi parted, letting them through. Joe saw a body on the pavement, half out of the driver's door, covered by a sheet. He noticed the rear driver-side door was also open. They scanned the officers' faces. "Well?" asked Bill.

The first officer on the scene spoke. "Except for covering the body and searching his pockets nothing was touched." Joe stepped next to the body, pulled back the sheet and studied the bullet wound.

"The other door was already open?" asked Joe. The officer nodded. Joe's police training kicked in, helping him visualize the events. He talked his way through his recreation of the murder. "Okay, the killer would have pushed Terry into the cab at the hotel, so she would have been sitting next to that door, behind the driver. The kidnapper would have sat next to her in the back seat." Joe looked up and down the street, now crowded with curious residents. "This street was probably empty, so he makes the driver stop here. The cabby turns to collect his fare, and he shoots him through the open partition. From the powder burns on the poor kid's forehead he gets shot inches away from the gun barrel. The killer looked into his victim's terrified eyes and just blew him away. This guy's a pro. A real cold-blooded pro. The shot knocked the victim back against the driver's door. The door wouldn't have opened by itself, so for some reason the killer walks around and opens the door so the kid's body spills out onto the pavement." Joe shook his head. "I don't get it. Why didn't Terry make a break? Maybe she did. That would explain the open door. But she would have called someone by now. I don't . . ."

"Joe," interrupted Bill. Joe looked up. "We don't even know if Terry was in this cab. It could have been a simple robbery." Joe blinked, then looked at the officer in charge.

"We checked his log, sir. I believe your wife was abducted at the Waldorf, correct?" Joe nodded. "Well, his log puts him in that vicinity, but he didn't make an entry when he picked up his fare. Sometimes they save time by writing the pick-up and drop-off points at the completion of the trip. And we checked his pockets. They were empty. No cash. Looks like a robbery. Nothing here indicates a kidnapping." Bill watched Joe deflate like a pricked balloon. But then he rebounded, shaking his head.

"Bill, a simple robbery just feels wrong to me. Call it instinct, intuition, whatever. But I know this is it. Damn it! I can feel Terry was in this cab."

"Well, let's get back in my car and continue cruising, see what we can find. Maybe we'll see something." He turned and walked toward his car. Joe looked at the cab again, then turned to follow Bill. But as he turned, something inside the cab glinted, catching his eye. He blinked, and then stared inside. He stepped to the cab, his eyes riveted on the back seat.

Chapter 65

Terry sat nearly motionless, working her wrists and ankles, trying to slip her binds. She felt, and heard, the plastic drop cloth rustle under her feet. The crinkling sound unnerved her. She knew Ahmed put it there to prevent blood from staining the floor. Her blood! Questions flooded her mind. *How will this madman kill me? Will it hurt? What will it feel like to die? What will happen to my children? Will my husband ever know what happened to me?*

"For a celebrity you are very quiet," remarked Ahmed.

"I'm no celebrity," Terry replied. "I'm an ordinary person. You won't gain anything by killing me. Why don't you just let me . . ."

"Wrong!" Ahmed interjected. He walked over and removed her sunglasses. A bright overhead bulb made her blink. Then Terry focused and looked into the eyes from hell. "That is exactly why your death will have the impact I want. Not as much as I could have had if you and you husband didn't ruin my original plans, but good enough."

"But I don't underst . . ."

"Because now, ordinary Americans will see how Allah's holy warriors can slaughter them even in their own country. They will realize they are not safe anywhere. Millions will see you die and shiver in fear every night when they go to bed. They will wonder . . ."

As Ahmed droned on Terry thought, *he really is crazy. But he's right. No one can stop him!*

Bill looked back and realized Joe wasn't following him. He saw Joe bend down, kneel on the cab's back seat and reach inside. Bill stopped and walked back to the cab. When Joe stood he was holding something in his hand. The object glinted in the afternoon sun. "Find something?" asked Bill. Joe turned and faced him.

"Terry's wedding ring! It was in the fold of the seat. She must have slipped it off hoping someone would find it. This guy staged the robbery to throw us off the track."

"And it almost worked," agreed Bill, calling the other police officers over. "Okay, gentlemen, this changes everything," he said, holding up Terry's ring, glinting gold catching the sunlight. "Mrs. Manetta and her abductor can't be very far away. They must be on foot. I want all units to look for a man and woman fitting their description walking or running through these streets." He turned to Joe and handed him Terry's wedding band. "Put it in your pocket buddy. You'll need it soon." But Joe appeared even more worried than minutes earlier. "Hey, great job spotting her ring. I thought you'd be relieved we're closing in. What's wrong?"

Joe looked at Bill, then glanced up and down the street. "We're not going to spot them now. Think about it. He dumped the cab here for a reason. Two reasons actually. Obviously, one because it's a quiet street. And two, because it's gotta be near the building he and his support troops, or whatever they are, are using. He wouldn't risk being spotted. I'd bet my life it's somewhere in a two or three block radius from here."

"You could be right. But that means they could be in any one of several hundred buildings," said Bill looking around.

Ashur handed the Radio Shack clerk Ahmed's list, and followed him around the store while he selected the items. Ten minutes later the clerk prepared to ring up the sale. "Anything else? Batteries for the remote? Extra DVDs?" Ashur shook his head.

"No thank you, this is all I need."

"Okay, that'll be $948.45, please." Ashur handed the clerk his Chase MasterCard. Leaving the store, he noticed unusual police presence in the neighborhood. Many more patrol cars than usual, cruising more slowly than usual, the cops inside eyeballing the pedestrians very closely. He began perspiring and breathing more rapidly. He averted his gaze, stared straight ahead and walked briskly. Like most guilty people, he assumed every cop was looking at him, searching for him, closing in on him. He heard someone shout. "Excuse me, sir! Please stop!"

Ashur froze. His breath caught in his throat. He thought his heart would leap from his chest. *Should I turn around? Drop the packages and run?* A cop in a patrol car waiting for a red light stared at him. Panicked, he decided to run. But a hand gripped his arm. He spun. "Wha . . ."

"Sir, you forgot your credit card." Ashur's wild-eyed expression startled the store clerk, who had followed him from the store. "Sir, are you all right?"

"Oh. Yes. Thank you very much," he whispered hoarsely. He took the credit card and slipped it into his pocket. The light changed to green and the patrol car continued through the intersection. He resumed walking toward his building. Five minutes later he leaned against the door and slipped the key into the lock. He almost collapsed into the vestibule when the door swung open. He closed the door and steadied himself, taking several deep ragged breaths. Then he carried the packages downstairs to Ahmed's workroom. When he opened the door he was startled by the changes in the room. On one wall hung a large cloth banner, red with black lettering. It proclaimed Allah as the one and only God, and threatened death to all infidels who defied Allah's will. Terry was seated, securely tied to a chair just below the message, several feet in front of the banner.

"Did you get everything on my list?" asked Ahmed.

Ashur simply nodded and handed him the packages. He took them to the table and opened them with the joy of a child opening Christmas presents. He called out each item on his list as he placed them on the table. "Sony DVD camcorder, blank DVDs, tripod, small floodlight with stand, nine-inch TV monitor. Wonderful! Everything's here." He saw Terry watching him. Her terrified expression amused him. She was recalling the horrifying execution videos she had seen broadcast by Al Jazeera television on the internet. Terry thought, *But bloody executions only occur in Iraq. Not here in the United States. This could not happen to me, not inside the United States!* She moved her feet and felt the plastic drop cloth rustle under her feet. *Could it?* Ahmed knew Terry now realized how her life would end.

Chapter 66

Bill unfolded a Brooklyn street map across the hood of his car. "Let's see. Here's our location," he said, pointing to a short one-block long street called Denton Place, paralleling Third and Fourth Avenues east and west, and dead-ending on Carroll Street to the north and First Street to the south. "Now if your assumption is correct, they're holding Terry somewhere in this area," he said, penciling a circle around several blocks in each direction. He scanned the street names he had circled, and shook his head.

"What's wrong?" asked Joe.

"Something's familiar about one of these names. This one," he said pointing to Sackett Street, located at the edge of the circle. "Wait a minute! Remember the guys who bought the scuba equipment? I think the car was registered to some guy on Sackett Street. I have an idea." He viewed the contact list in his cell phone, and then dialed the number he wanted.

"Parking Violations Bureau. Ms. Walker speaking. How may I . . ."

"Susie? It's Bill."

"Hi Bill. Haven't heard from you in a long time. What's up?"

"I need some fast research. Fast as in like right now!"

"Really? Is it a matter of life and death?" she laughed casually.

"As a matter of fact Susie, it is. It really is." Her tone changed as she snapped to attention. She adjusted her headset.

"Okay Bill. What do you need?"

"I need you to check on parking tickets issues in Manhattan on June 30th."

He glanced at Joe, who had a questioning look in his eyes. "The night the QM2 was attacked," he whispered.

"Bill, I thought you were in a hurry. There are a hell of a lot of tickets in the system for that night. This may take a while."

"Okay, let's narrow it down. Just tickets issued in these two precincts on the West Side." He provided Susie with two precinct numbers and waited while her computer system churned through its massive database.

"That helps. Still got 97." Bill thought for several seconds.

"Just search for tickets issued on that date that are still unpaid."

"Okay, we'll try that. You chasing down scofflaws these days?" Susie asked, waiting for the numbers to appear on her screen.

"I wish," Bill replied, trying unsuccessfully to force a laugh. There was a pause. *Please, don't tell me the system is down. Not now!* Joe noticed veins standing out at Bill's temple. He thought he saw one vein pulsate as Bill massaged his forehead.

"Got it!"

Thank God!

"Hmm. Not much help. That's only several days ago, including a holiday. Nobody pays their tickets that fast. The system shows 89 parking tickets still unpaid for June 30th, issued in the two precincts you specified."

"Can you just read me ones issued on streets near the Hudson River?"

"Sure. That's better. Looks like only four. One on 12th Avenue and 58th Street, another on West-end Avenue and 63rd, one on Riverside Drive and 79th Street, and the last one downtown, on Vescey Street, near the Wall Street Marina."

"What time were the tickets issued on Riverside Drive and Vescey Street, Susie?"

"The one issued on Vescey Street was at 9:38am and the one on Riverside Drive was issued at 11:55pm." Bill thought for a moment.

"The QM2 was attacked soon after midnight. Isn't Riverside Drive and 79th Street near the upper-west side marina, the Boat Basin?"

"Uh, yes, I think so."

"I think we got it, Joe! There was a ticket issued at the 79th Street Boat Basin, the same night the Queen Mary was attacked. Okay, Susie. Give me that plate number and the owner's name and address." He copied the plate as Susie continued to read.

"It's a van, registered to a Mister Ashur Sharib, at 225 Nevins Street."

"Nevis Street? Are you sure?"

"That's what it says in the computer, Bill."

Okay, thanks, Susie." He hung up and looked at Joe, puzzled. "Damn! I was sure she'd give me a Sackett Street address. One more call to make." He speed-dialed his FBI contact, John McHale.

"Special Agent McHale."

"John, Bill Ryan. NYPD, remember me?"

"Sure, Bill. What can I do you for?"

"Remember the license plates you ran on the car those guys who bought the scuba equipment drove?"

"Yeah. Unfortunately it was a dead end. If you recall, some pain in the ass stickler of a judge cited lack of probable cause, and wouldn't give us a search warrant. So, we staked out the location on our own for a few days. I think it was in downtown Brooklyn, on Sackett Street. Unfortunately we came up dry. Nothing suspicious. We only observed some old guy leaving early in the morning and coming back late every evening. By the way, Bill, you didn't hear this from me, but rumor has it that a couple of your NYPD boys visited the premises. Shall we say, unofficially on their own?" John paused, hoping Bill would fill in the pregnant silence with a confirmation.

"Interesting scuttlebutt, John, I hadn't heard that," said Bill, truthfully.

"Well, we even took some photos of the guy, but we got no hits from our database. We also showed the photos to the dive shop owner, but she definitely said he wasn't one of the men who purchased the equipment."

"Remember the guy's name and address?"

"No, sorry. When nothing panned out I didn't keep the information, but I did jot down the plate number somewhere. Just a minute. It might be under this pile on my desk."

Bill held his breath, waiting, listening to the crinkly sound of McHale shuffling through papers. *Please find it, John. Please!*

"Yeah, here it is."

Bill exhaled.

"But I only have the plate number the scuba shop owner gave me. Got a pen?"

"Shoot!" McHale read the New York State plate number twice. But it did not match the number Susie had given Bill. "Okay, got it. Thanks, John." Bill grimaced and sagged against his police cruiser.

"Well?" asked Joe, concerned by Bill's negative body language.

"It's not the same plate number. Damn, I don't get it. I was sure we'd get a match." He looked into Joe's eyes. The despair he saw frightened him. "Wait! I have another idea." He pulled out this cell phone again.

"Parking Violations Bureau. Ms. Walker speaking. How may I . . ."

"Susie, it's Bill again. Listen if I give you a plate number can you work your magic and give me a name and address?"

"Sure, I'll just run a reverse search. Hit me." Bill read the plate number that Agent McHale provided, and held his breath. Several seconds later, Susie replied, "This one's a car, registered to a Mister Ashur Sharib, at 325 Sackett Street."

"Got it! Thanks a million, Susie! I owe you big time. At least a dinner."

"I'll hold you to it," Susie laughed. "Bye. And good luck, Bill."

"What'd you get?" asked Joe, anxious.

"It's the same guy, but with two different vehicles registered at different addresses, within a few blocks of each other. We know from what McHale just told me that Sackett Street's a dud. I'll bet my pension this is where Terry is," he said, tapping his finger on 225 Nevins Street, located in his penciled circle on the map. "We have more than enough probable cause."

"Let's roll!" exclaimed Joe.

Chapter 67

Ahmed left Terry and went upstairs to find writing material. While he was searching for a pen and paper Terry noticed a razor blade on the table edge, several feet away. *If I can get my fingers on that blade I can cut these damn ropes*, she thought. She pushed herself up with her feet and shifted her weight. The chair slid an inch. She pushed and shifted again. Another inch closer to the table. *I just need a few more hops.* Terry pushed and shifted but instead of sliding the chair leg snagged on a plastic ripple. She felt the chair tip past its balance point. *Oh Shit!* she thought as the chair fell over. Ahmed heard a crash and raced downstairs. He saw Terry still tied to the chair, lying on her side. He laughed as Terry looked over her shoulder, glaring at him. Ahmed bent down and righted the chair, then dragged it back to the center of the room. "Why don't you stop fighting and just accept your fate?" he asked.

"Why don't you go to hell!" Terry replied coldly, mustering all of her self-control.

"Fine. Have it your way. Just follow my instructions." Ahmed talked while he set up the video equipment. He placed the camcorder on a tripod ten feet in front of Terry. "First, say your name, where you were born, and where you live." Then he set the floodlight behind and to the side of the camera, lighting Terry and the banner on the wall behind her. "Next, tell your audience why you should live, how much your children and your husband would miss you. Beg for your life." He set up the small television monitor so he could watch the video as it was recording. "Finally, tell all Americans this will be their fate if they oppose Allah's will, and if they continue subjugating the Palestinian people and supporting Israel." Satisfied with his makeshift recording studio, he turned around looked at Terry. "Understand?"

"Go to hell, you sick bastard!" Terry shouted at the top of her lungs. Ahmed was embarrassed knowing the men upstairs must have heard her. No woman had ever challenged him, and none used profanity. He felt rage rise like bile in his throat. Terry decided she had nothing to lose and continues to rail at him. "If you think I'll help you with your propaganda you're out of your fucking mi. . . ."

"Silence!" He slammed the door shut, stepped in front of her and slapped her hard across her mouth. Terry was stunned. She looked down and shook her head, clearing it. She noticed flecks of blood on her jeans, then bright red drops trickled from her bleeding lip. "American men have never taught their women respect. But you will learn respect from me before you die. The world will see how brave you really are when you feel cold steel slicing your throat." Terry didn't raise her head, thinking of her children. She didn't want Ahmed to see the tears welling up in her eyes. He sat at the table with a paper and pen and began writing. "I will prepare my words before we begin."

Ashur and his men met in the large common room, engrossed in a lively and noisy discussion about what was happening in the basement and what they should do about Ahmed and his failed plans. Should they halt him? Or let this situation play out his way?

While the debate raged behind closed windows and drawn shades, they did not know a large force of heavily armed men had blocked adjoining streets, isolating their building. SWAT teams were stationed at front and rear entrances and beneath every ground floor window. A small armored vehicle was poised to crash through the metal garage door. A dozen men had clambered across adjoining rooftops and were prepared to break into the building from above. Bill and Joe huddled behind a police car in front of the building.

"Okay, buddy," said Bill. He reached down and pulled his back-up weapon, a snub-nose .38 revolver, from his ankle holster. He handed it to Joe. "Here. You may need this. We won't be conducting a loudspeaker session where negotiators bond with these assholes, like you see in the movies. When that battering ram smashes the door it's gonna be slam-bam-thank-you-ma'am. Ready?"

Joe checked the revolver's action and nodded.

Chapter 68

Finished!" proclaimed Ahmed. "And this is what I want you to say," he said, showing Terry a paper filled with his jumbled scribble. He watched Terry, but she refused to read his morbid script. She kept her eyes glued to the floor thinking about her family and how her life would soon end. Ahmed waited for her to look up but soon realized she would never cooperate. "I suppose I'll have to read your lines for you too," he sneered. He stood and strapped on the explosive vest, letting the cord and detonating handle dangle by his ankles. Terry turned and watched it swaying by his feet wishing she could reach the handle and squeeze it, ending her life quickly without pain and suffering. She wiggled her wrists trying to slip her binds Ahmed noticed and read her intentions. He stepped further away from her.

"Don't get any heroic ideas. I'm wearing this vest to inspire future suicide bombers, who will turn America's so-called amber waves of grain into soggy fields of red blood. I can't personally deliver my video to Al Jazeera television if I let you blow me into little pieces, can I?" He laughed at his joke and turned on the camcorder and television monitor. Then he flipped a switch and a floodlight illuminated the room. He passed the table, picked up his speech and a long knife with a sharply curved blade and stepped behind Terry. He stared into the camcorder lens, pushed the remote and waited several seconds until a bizarre tableau of Terry, himself and the slogan-filled wall behind them appeared on the screen. Satisfied everything was working properly, he held the knife and his script in one hand, then grabbed Terry's hair with the other and pulled her head up with the other so her face was visible to the camera. He began reading his insane monologue.

Bill looked at Joe, and nodded to the SWAT commander, who shouted into his radio. "Go! Go! Go!" Like a well-choreographed Broadway production, everyone moved as one. Four heavily muscled officers stationed at the front and rear entrances swung thick metal battering rams. The reinforced doors buckled on their first try and caved in on their second attempt. Police on the roof hacked through another access door with fire axes. The armored vehicle surged forward, crushing the metal garage door like an eggshell. At each ground floor window one officer smashed the glass pane with a club and a second officer hurled concussion grenades inside. Loud flashes accompanied by deafening roars stunned everyone inside. Bill, Joe and a team of helmeted police stormed unopposed into the building, shouting, "Down! Down! Down! Hands on your heads!" The dazed occupants were too shocked to resist, but Joe tackled one man attempting to flee. Landing on top, he grabbed a handful of hair, smashed the man's face into the floor and quickly pulled the man's head up. Joe pointed the revolver at his saucer-wide eyes. The .38's snub-nose barrel looked like a howitzer to the terrified man.

"Where's the woman? Where's the woman?" Joe shouted in his face.

"Downstairs. There!" the man screamed through broken teeth, and heavily accented English, pointing with his eyes as blood poured from his shattered nose. He winced in pain as Joe jumped on his back and ran toward the basement stairs.

Ahmed looked at the ceiling when he heard explosions, men shouting and footsteps. Fearing the worst, he spoke faster, determined to finish reading his message to the world and then killing his victim. Suddenly the basement door burst open.

"Freeze! Police!" Joe shouted. Ahmed stopped reading, turned and saw Joe standing in the doorway poised to shoot. He dropped his script, released Terry's head and slowly transferred the knife to his right hand. For an eternity-filled moment no one moved, each paralyzed trying to comprehend the scene from unique individual perspectives. Terry didn't believe the visual message her eyes were sending her brain. She blinked and simply said, "Joe?" Ahmed couldn't believe his plans had been thwarted once again. Joe, relieved to hear Terry's voice, focused his attention, and his weapon, on Ahmed.

"I'll make you an offer you can't refuse, pal. Drop the knife and live, or enjoy fucking your 72 virgins immediately and for all eternity. I just want this life with my wife!"

Ahmed locked onto Joe's eyes and slowly lowered his knife. Suddenly he grabbed Terry's hair. In one motion he pulled her head back and pressed the razor-sharp blade against her throat. Joe saw a trickle of blood run down her neck and immediately squeezed the trigger, aiming for Ahmed's torso, not risking a headshot he might miss. The first bullet struck Ahmed's arm, the impact sending the knife wheeling across the room. Joe rapidly squeezed the trigger four more times. Three torso hits and a leg-shot spun Ahmed across the room spurting blood from his thigh. Joe's body shots had struck Ahmed's vest but did not detonate the explosives. The bullets' impact knocked Ahmed against the cinder block wall, where he struck his head, falling unconscious in a pool of his blood.

Joe picked up Ahmed's knife, ran to Terry, cut off her ropes, and pulled her to her feet. They embraced without speaking. Holding Joe tightly, Terry finally whispered in his ear, "Take me home, Joe. I want to see Jackie and Peter."

A few seconds later, Ahmed regained consciousness. He looked around, dazed, and realized he was sitting in a sticky, warm, red pool. He lifted his left hand and stared at his bloody palm. With a bemused, detached expression Ahmed watched his blood spurting like a pulsating fountain from the femoral artery in his thigh. His shattered right arm was numb, useless. He knew the police would come downstairs soon and arrest him. Perhaps they might even save his life. But the prospect of rotting away in a Guantanamo jail cell did not appeal to Ahmed's terrorist spirit. He took a deep breath, sighed, and then reached across his body with his good arm. His fingers groped through the sticky blood until he found what he was looking for. Across the room Joe saw Ahmed smile, his eyes turned toward the ceiling, glazed as if enjoying some insane vision. Joe knew what fantasy Ahmed was visualizing. He pushed Terry toward the door.

"Get out of here! Now!" Still in shock, she hesitated. He grabbed Terry's hand and pulled her up the stairs, colliding with Bill and several officers coming downstairs. "Get back!" Joe shouted. They just reached the top step when an explosion shook the entire building.

Joe, Bill and several SWAT officers froze, waiting for the weakened floor to collapse. It held. Several minutes later they carefully made their way downstairs, through a dusty haze, picking through the debris and rubble of Ahmed's ersatz recording studio and operations center. They saw Ahmed's upper torso, arms and head lying upright against the wall on one side of the room. His lower torso and legs were on the floor, near the opposite wall. Joe looked at Ahmed's face, puzzled. He could not decide if Ahmed's expression was a smile or a grimace. Looking into Ahmed's sightless eyes, he wondered if his final earthly emotion had been the frustration of defeat or the pleasurable anticipation of a sexually fulfilling afterlife.

Bill Ryan touched Joe's shoulder, breaking his concentration. "Hey buddy, let's get the hell out of here. This ceiling might cave in any minute." Joe looked at him and nodded.

Exiting the building, Joe embraced Terry, and squeezed her hand. Then he took a tissue from his pocket and blotted the bloody scratch on Terry's neck. He blinked back a tear, thinking about what would have happened if he had arrived several minutes later. He looked into her eyes. "I got what I wanted. Perhaps he did, too. Let's go home," he said.

They walked toward an officer opening the door of a police cruiser, when Joe stopped and put his hand in his pocket. "Oops!

Wait a minute. I almost forgot something," he said, smiling. He opened Terry's hand and slipped her wedding band onto the third finger of her left hand, covering a pale ring of skin. She stared at the gold ring, and gently caressed it with a finger. She looked into Joe's eyes and smiled.

"I'll never take it off again, Joe."

"Well, Ter, I'm glad you did this one time. It saved your life."

Chapter 69

July 15th

Ten days later, Joe and Terry stood on the tarmac at a remote section of JFK airport, waiting to board a Navy C-130 Hercules to Cozumel. Jackie, Peter and Jaime were already seated, and Notchka was also aboard, floating in her specially designed travel tank. Bill and aquarium vet Alison Carey accompanied them to the airport. "I hope Notchka will be all right," said Terry. "She's been through so much."

"Well," replied Alison, "she's beaten the respiratory infection. And she's recovered from her internal injuries, at least as far as we can determine. But she doesn't seem quite the same dolphin that arrived only a short time ago."

"What do you mean!" asked Terry, nervously.

"Well, as you said she's endured significant trauma and stress. Just the travel must have been stressful. She's had to adapt to different environmental conditions, colder water and also a different diet. Then there are the injuries from the explosion, anxiety from being separated from her pod and her age. Those are all important factors. Even humans don't handle disruptive situations as well when they age. She seems okay now, but I'm concerned her resistance has been compromised. It's a good thing she's not staying here any longer."

"I think we can all agree about that," said Terry, looking at Joe, then at Bill.

'Terry, Joe, I don't know how can we thank you two for everything you did for New York City," said Bill Ryan. "Besides saving the Queen Mary we broke up a large, well-organized terrorist cell. Ashur and his group could have done a lot more damage."

"Well, sleep on it partner. I'm sure you'll think of something appropriate," Joe, said, slapping Bill's back. "And by the way, old buddy, my compliments to you. Figuring out where Terry was being held was a hell of a detective job on your part."

Bill smiled. "A little luck and a good memory. I remembered when my dad was on the force talking about how they took down some guy shooting young adults with a 44 magnum in a series of lover's lane attacks back in the late '70s during the summer. Remember the Son of Sam killings?"

"I remember reading about them," Joe nodded. "I think the newspapers dubbed him 'the .44 caliber killer.'"

"Yeah, that's right. Well, the cops couldn't find this guy for anything. Couldn't figure where he'd strike next. The entire city was terrorized. Then, after a shooting in the Bath Beach section of Brooklyn, a middle-class Italian neighborhood, they checked parking tickets issued in the area that night. It seems an old VW was ticketed for being parked near a fire hydrant. They traced the plates to a guy who didn't live anywhere near there. They were suspicious why a guy whose age and ethnic background didn't fit with the local population would be in that particular location so late at night. Several nights later on a stakeout they nabbed the guy heading out his front door carrying automatic weapons on a mission to kill people at a nightclub. They got lucky."

"I'm glad we were as lucky," said Joe, smiling at Terry. Bill shrugged.

"Yeah, plus I played a hunch. I figured terrorists focused on blowing up an ocean liner and a bridge wouldn't be very concerned about violating our parking laws, and even less so about paying any tickets promptly. You remember about hunches, right, old buddy?" he said, looking at Joe. Joe smiled.

"Oh yeah, partner. I recall us breaking more than a few cases by following a good hunch."

"Well, good thing for me your memory still works. And the next time you're planning a Cozumel trip please let us know," said Terry.

"Hey, thanks for the invite!" replied Bill.

"What invite? We just want advance warning so we can get out of Dodge!" Terry shot back, with a smile.

"Excuse me, folks, but we've just been cleared for an immediate takeoff," interrupted the plane's first officer."

"Well, that's it. You two better get aboard." said Bill. Terry and Joe ran up the stairs and waved to Bill as they stepped inside. Terry and Joe went back to visit Notchka. The dolphin rolled slightly, looked up and squirted a jet of water into Terry's face, then squawked playfully. Terry stroked her smooth skin.

"Looks like she's in good spirits," said Joe.

"Yes that's a good sign," replied Terry. "We should take our seats."

They arrived in Cozumel six hours later, after a refueling stop and a thunderstorm delayed them in Texas. They accompanied Notchka to a holding tank at Chankanaab's dolphin exhibit, where she would remain until her pod was sighted.

After she was settled, Joe and Terry offered Jaime a ride home with them and the children. "Gracias," he replied. "But I would like to sleep in my own bed for the first time in many days."

"Okay, Jaime. We'll drop you off and see you when you wake up," said Joe.

"Si, in about a week," replied Jaime, laughing.

Two days later Terry received a phone call from Chankanaab Marine Park. "Senora Manetta, we just received a radio call from Jaime Ramirez. He's out with a bunch of tourists near French Reef and he spotted a dolphin pod."

"We'll be right there. Gracias." Hanging up the phone she called Joe. "Let's go! Jaime spotted dolphins off French Reef. Good bet it's Notchka's pod."

Twenty minutes later Terry and Joe and the children arrived at Chankanaab Park. They boarded the dolphin-catcher boat, *Santa*

Rosa. But today the boat would be returning a dolphin to the wild, not taking one into captivity. Notchka floated in her special tank. Terry saw she was excited, perhaps sensing her release into her home waters was imminent. Forty minutes later they were cruising Cozumel's southern-most reefs. Terry pointed to a boat off the starboard bow. "Look, it's the *Jolly Mon*. I can see Jaime." They passed Jaime's boat heading north, toward the marina. Terry waved and Jaime smiled, waving his hat in return, pointing south, pantomiming dolphins swimming. "They must still be around," she exclaimed. "Put out all the speed you've got," she yelled to the *Santa Rosa's* captain.

"Mom! Over there!" shouted Peter, ten minutes later. Terry scanned the area where Peter was pointing. Then she saw several curved dorsal fins breaking the surface.

"I see them! Turn to port, 45 degrees," she yelled.

The boat swung into position to intercept the pod, and was soon surrounded by a dozen dolphins. The captain cut the motors and let the boat drift. Terry and Joe jumped into the water while the crew lifted Notchka in her sling and swung her over the side of the boat. As soon as they let her down she wiggled out of her sling and swam into the middle of her pod. Terry and Joe watched the dolphins swim circles around Notchka, taking turns swimming along side and brushing against her. After reacquainting with her pod, Notchka led them south toward Punta Sur and the open Caribbean. Terry watched them swim away and Joe swam up to her, putting his arm around her.

"You okay?"

"Yeah. Well, no, maybe not. I feel as though I lost my best friend. She just swam away without looking back, no gesture of any kind."

"She's where she needs to be, where she belongs," said Joe.

"I know. It's not that. I'm upset about the way she left. Like she was angry about what we did. We took her away from her home and family, and she got hurt. We abused her trust in us. It was as if she doesn't know how much she means to me."

"You and Notchka have a special bond," Joe said. "I'm sure you'll see her again."

Chapter 70

Terry and Joe resumed operating their dive business. After almost a month in New York, they had to address a myriad of details. They met with dive operators to whom they had referred customers and called their customers confirming they had received satisfactory service. They contacted new customers, reconfirming future bookings. They serviced their equipment, ensuring regulators and BCs were working perfectly. Finally, they visited Manuel at the marina and made sure the *Dorado II* was fit for diving. During their absence he had creatively made his personal financial ends meet by working with other dive operators, taking customers on snorkel trips, and even running an impromptu water taxi service between the resorts at the island's south-end and downtown Cozumel.

Two weeks passed with no sign of Notchka. Late one afternoon, after a full day of diving, Terry and Joe rested on their top-floor veranda, reclining on padded lounge chairs. They sipped margaritas, on the rocks with salt, feeling the sun's warmth decrease as it dipped behind a row of puffy cumulous clouds in the western sky. "Here's to another great Mexican sunset," said Joe as they clinked frosted glasses, watching the sun's rays explode from behind the clouds like a giant multi-colored pinwheel.

"Mom, Dad, come quick! Dolphins!" yelled Jackie, who was collecting tiny shells on the beach with Peter. Terry and Joe ran to the porch railing and scanned the water, squinting into the sun, which had just peaked out under a cloud. The sea was calm as a mirror, but they didn't see anything.

"Where?" Terry shouted to Jackie.

"Right out there, in the shiny water," she pointed.

The setting sun reflected a silvery path on the calm sea, like a shimmering road extending from the beach toward the horizon. Joe grabbed his binoculars and panned the area. "Oh yes! I see them. Look, Terry! Three dorsal fins breaking the surface. In the middle of that shiny patch of water."

"Got'em," she replied, excitedly. "They're definitely approaching. They're coming to visit, just like they used to!" she exclaimed. They ran down to the beach, anticipating a happy reunion, wading knee-deep in the water. The three dorsal fins were slowly heading toward the beach. "They're swimming strangely, aren't they?" Terry commented, a trace of apprehension sharpening her voice.

Terry watched the three fins coming closer. They were abreast, with the middle fin taller than the two outside fins. "Yes," said Terry. "The middle dolphin is swimming higher in the water. I think the other two are supporting it with their pectoral fins."

"Teacher told us dolphins will do that to help carry one that's injured or sick," said Peter. Terry broke her gaze and looked at him. She felt a chill run up her spine.

"Yes. Peter, that's right. I've seen them do that." She became unsettled, anxious, worried. The dolphins were closer now and Terry saw the middle dolphin, larger than the other two, was not swimming but was carried by the other two. Then the large dolphin feebly raised its fluke, disclosing a signature feature. "It's Notchka!" shouted Terry, wading deeper. They heard the dolphins clicking and whistling among themselves. They accelerated toward the beach, building momentum, and two stopped. Notchka glided in alone, coming to rest, barely brushing the sand near Terry's feet. Joe, Jackie and Peter slowly waded in and stood next to Notchka, stroking her skin. She rolled to one side and made eye contact with Terry, who saw a different look than she had ever seen before. Notchka's mischievous sparkle and playful expression was missing. She looked tired, old.

"Oh Notchka, what's wrong?" She bent to hug her, just as Notchka exhaled. The odor emanating from her blowhole struck Terry like a hammer. "Ugh!" she coughed, repelled by the foul smell, waving her hand to disperse the odor. Joe bent over and smelled it.

"Phew! Her respiratory infection's back. Worse than before."

"She needs help! I'll call a vet and order more antibiotics!" Terry exclaimed.

"No Terry. She . . ."

"What do you mean, 'No'? She's sick, Joe! We have to . . ."

"Terry, Notchka's dying. Look at her."

Terry stared at Joe, stunned, as if he had slapped her. She blinked, trying to comprehend words she heard but would not accept. Then Terry took a deep breath, looked at Notchka, and stroked her skin. No longer smooth and supple, it felt brittle. And Terry saw she'd lost weight and looked gaunt. She squeezed her eyes and tears trickled down her cheeks.

"No!" she cried. She looked at the other two dolphins. They had retreated a short distance to deeper water, waiting. She recognized Gemini, Notchka's calf, but not the other dolphin. Perhaps a blood relative, or Notchka's mate, or another pod member? Terry reached down, embracing the dying dolphin. "I'm so sorry, Notchka. After all you did for me, for us, we betrayed you. You trusted us but we took you away from your home, we . . ." Joe leaned over and placed his hand on Terry's shoulder.

"Terry, I think she came to say goodbye and also to let you know it's all right. Whatever she feels it's not anger or betrayal, nothing like that. Otherwise she wouldn't have come back to see you." Jackie and Peter leaned forward and gently patted Notchka's head.

"Good bye, Notchka. We'll miss you," said Jackie, barely above a whisper. Peter said nothing, but Joe observed his Adam's apple jump as he suppressed the lump in his throat. Joe leaned over and stroked Notchka's skin. She rolled and glanced at him. She squirted a thin stream of water at him and he smiled.

"Thanks for everything, old girl," he said, recalling when Notchka, had saved Terry's life ten years ago, giving her and Joe a life together. He reflected how she had saved his children's lives only two months earlier. "I owe you a lot. An awful lot," he whispered hoarsely, blinking away tears. Then Joe and the children stepped back, letting Terry have a moment alone with her friend. She spoke to Notchka between sobs. Joe couldn't hear what Terry said, watching her shoulders heave. He just shook his head as tears streamed down his face. Peter and Jackie held his hands. He heard them sniffle and saw Jackie rub her eyes.

After several minutes Notchka emitted a series of clicks and whistles, which the other two dolphins answered. They moved closer, as shallow as they dared. Terry saw them and cried, "No! Don't take her yet." Several seconds later Notchka splashed the surface with her fluke and the dolphins became agitated. Joe stepped closer and gently touched Terry's shoulder.

"Terry, it's time. You have to let her go."

She glanced at Joe, then turned, kissed Notchka and guided her into deeper water. The two dolphins swam along side, and then Gemini moved between Terry and Notchka, gently nudging Terry away. They slipped their pectoral fins under Notchka's fins and carried her out to deep water, toward the setting sun. Joe waded in next to Terry and held her while Jackie and Peter watched quietly from shore. Together they saw the three dorsal fins recede. Joe raised his binoculars and watched the dolphins swim away. A quarter-mile from shore, barely visible in the setting sun's golden reflection, the three dolphins stopped. Joe saw three fins sink deeper in the water and disappear. Terry heard Joe's breath catch in his throat. She grabbed the binoculars, snapping the lanyard around his neck. Seconds later, Terry saw only two dorsal fins emerge. The two dolphins waited, circled several times, and then continued on alone.

"Oh, Joe! Notchka's . . ." was all Terry could say, as she turned and buried herself in his embrace.

"Yes, she's gone. She was a gift," he said softly, thinking about how a dolphin had changed their lives. "But Gemini is still with us, Ter," Joe said, staring at the empty sea.

* * * * *

Epilogue
Arlington National Cemetery, Arlington Virginia

July 30th

Seven guns fired as one, three times; a 21-gun salute to Anthony Delgado's memory. From a lone bugler, the mournful notes of *Taps* drifted over his gravesite. Some mourners choked back tears. Many did not try. The gray, overcast weather reflected their somber mood.

Two U.S. servicemen wearing immaculate, fitted white gloves respectfully lifted the Stars and Stripes from Anthony's casket. Inside were the only human remains a Navy SEAL team could recover: A sun-bleached skull hanging from a rusted tent pole and a dozen animal-gnawed bones, some still covered in tattered battle fatigues, scattered in front of an empty cave in Pakistan.

The honor guard, dressed in crisp uniforms creased so sharply they could have sliced paper, began folding the flag. After making the initial fold the soldier holding the stars stood ramrod still. The other soldier walked toward him, making triangular folds until they met. One soldier held the folded flag until the other completed the final tuck. Then, he approached Betty Delgado with the flag. Tony's young widow sat next to Anthony Junior, who appeared brave for his mother. Betty wore Tony's Purple Heart, pinned to her black suit. Anthony Junior wore his father's Distinguished Service Cross, on a blue ribbon around his neck. Both medals had been awarded posthumously at an earlier ceremony. Tony's mother, Maria, wore a simple black dress. She held her granddaughter, Jennifer, who would only know her father through letters, photos and stories. The soldier leaned forward and whispered condolences, expressing the appreciation of the United States for Anthony's ultimate sacrifice. Then he extended his hands and presented the flag to Betty. She graciously accepted her country's banner and cradled it in her arms, pressing it against her heart. Tears fell from her cheek, spotting the blue field and white stars.

Hearing a distant rumble, the assembled mourners glanced upward. They watched six Navy F/A-18 Hornets approach. As the jets roared overhead, one peeled up toward heaven. The remaining five flew past in the missing-man formation, a military tribute to a fallen hero.

* * * * * * *

Afterword

Although **FIREWORKS** is fiction, many elements are true. Brave men and women from many nations serve on the front lines, battling international terror. U.S. Navy SEALS, U.S. Army Special Forces, and other U.S. and Coalition Special Forces teams perform heroic missions deep inside hostile territory, often without public recognition. They and their families make daily sacrifices for our security. Unfortunately, too many of America's Best have made the ultimate sacrifice.

The U.S. Navy does employ dolphins and other marine mammals to protect vessels and installations from attack beneath the sea.

The Verrazano Bridge's massive cables, when illuminated at night, do appear as a pearl necklace spanning the Narrows. However, the anchorages supporting the bridge are no longer unguarded. And security has been improved at all of New York City's bridges, tunnels and landmarks.

On a lighter note, Cozumel diving is as described, and *The Devil's Throat* is still one of Cozumel's most exciting dives, a true rite of passage for visiting scuba divers. Coco the crocodile really exists, and lives in the brackish lagoon behind the parking lot at Palancar Beach. And Jaime Rameriz is still selling beachfront condos in Cozumel to those searching for their slice of Caribbean paradise.

Paul J. Mila

July 4th 2008
Carle Place, Long Island, NY.
pjmila@hotmail.com

About The Author

Paul J. Mila retired after a successful corporate career, and now devotes his time to writing, scuba diving around the world, underwater photography, and speaking to groups about ocean conservation.

He has enjoyed the opportunity to photograph and dive with Caribbean reef sharks in the Bahamas, humpback whales in the Dominican Republic and in the South Pacific Tonga Islands, diverse sea life in the Cayman Islands, Cozumel, Bonaire, Hawaii, Antigua, and in his home waters off Long Island, NY.

Paul's underwater pictures have been featured in magazines, on web sites related to scuba diving, and shown at *the Mind, Body, Spirit Festival* in Australia.

Following the advice of writers who said to write about what you know and like, he has incorporated the ocean and diving as the core of his writing.
FIREWORKS is his third novel.

Diving in the same waters as the characters in his books has enabled him to write with realism, and to describe for non-diving readers the beauty and wonder of exploring our undersea world. He and his family reside in Carle Place, New York, a small town on Long Island.
You can contact Paul directly, via email: pjmila@hotmail.com and visit his website, www.cozumelisparadise.com

PREVIOUS BOOKS BY PAUL J. MILA

In DANGEROUS WATERS, Terry Hunter is determined to overcome any obstacles life throws her way. Diving with a research expedition off the California coast, a brutal shark attack changes her world. But Terry rebuilds her life in Cozumel, Mexico, where she becomes a successful businesswoman, running her own dive operation.

However, the waters turn dangerous for Terry once again, when she unwittingly uncovers a drug smuggling scheme and becomes entwined in an international investigation, risking her life to help a New York detective solve a baffling case.

"Reading DANGEROUS WATERS is almost as good as scuba diving. The book delivers adventure, suspense, thrills and romance, along with plenty of underwater action. The main characters, Terry Hunter and Joe Manetta, are appealing and attractive; totally modern yet with a touch of old fashioned values. This is an excellent novel for both divers and non-divers."

Bonnie J. Cardone, former editor of *Skin Diver Magazine*, author of *Shipwrecks of Southern California* and *Fireside Diver*.

WHALES'
ANGELS

A husband and wife battle whalers
in a seagoing adventure of
international intrigue and murder

Paul J. Mila

"In this sequel to DANGEROUS WATERS, Paul Mila has crafted another exciting adventure-mystery featuring Terry Hunter and Joe Manetta. Like Tony Hillerman, Mila skillfully combines an intricate mystery plot with engaging characters and insights from a different culture, allowing his readers to experience the world from a novel perspective: that of the whales and dolphins who inhabit three-quarters of our planet. Don't miss this one!" Judith Hemenway, author of *The Universe Next Door.*

"A solid plot, intriguing characters and a realistic depiction of scuba diving and marine creatures are the hallmarks of Paul Mila's second novel featuring Terry Hunter and Joe Manetta. This time out, Terry and Joe get involved with activists ("Angels") attempting to prevent a rogue sea captain from harpooning whales in the chilly waters off Iceland. Trying to save a whale, one of the Angels ends up dead — but was it really an accident? The resolution of the mystery will keep readers — divers and non-divers alike — on the edge of their seats."
Bonnie J. Cardone, former editor of *Skin Diver Magazine*, author of *Shipwrecks of Southern California* and *Fireside Diver*; Member of the Women Divers Hall of Fame.

Printed in the United States
205878BV00003B/1-45/P

9 781438 900681